In
Laguna

Kathy Sloan

For Jenn —
Follow your dreams!
With love,

Kathy Sloan

This book is dedicated to all the mothers who daydream about running away.

May this book be a reminder that *your* passion and happiness matters. Not that you have to runaway to be happy, but just make sure you don't lose yourself in motherhood.

PART I

1994

1

Sarah had thought about running away from the time she was nine years old, when her mother's depression became so bad that she spent all day in bed, forcing Sarah to play the part of mom for her little brothers. Now it was finally time for her to go.

She'd done everything her father had ever asked (or demanded) her to do her whole life—including getting a teaching degree she didn't even want. The one good thing about college was that it helped her realize there was more to life than her father's small-minded view of the world.

As she drove home from her college graduation—that no one in her family bothered to show up for—she practiced her words. She planned to tell her father that she was leaving in front of everyone at the party he insisted on having with relatives she hardly knew.

She turned onto her street and swallowed hard. She stopped the car. *What if he forbids me to leave?* Could he do that now? What if he took away her car? Technically it was his. She thought about turning around and leaving right then but she couldn't do that to her younger brother Billy. She had to say goodbye to him. Besides, her suitcase was packed in her closet, and she needed her cameras for the trip.

Sarah took a deep breath and grabbed the wheel.

"All I need to do is get through the afternoon," she said, and let the car roll towards her house.

She parked and let out a sigh. Compared to the pristine campus she'd just come from, her house looked dingy. All of the other ranch-style houses on her street had upgraded to vinyl siding, but hers had large chips of white paint blistering off it. Her neighbors had manicured lawns with colorful flowers surrounding their homes, while her yard was littered with dandelions, and the grass was ankle high. The rhododendron under the picture window was overgrown and completely covered the window as if it were trying to hide what went on inside from the rest of the world. The gutter on the far end of the house was still hanging off from last year's ice storm. Her father wasn't one to fix things.

She stepped inside, being careful not to slam the door behind her. The last thing she needed was her father yelling at her about that today. Rather than fix the door, her father yelled at everyone for letting it slam.

Her aunts, uncles, and cousins stood around the dining room table making small talk. Her father, George, sat at the table, one hand on his knee and the other holding his gin and tonic. He looked annoyed as usual. Her mother, withered and looking as if she might break if someone touched her, sat next to her father with a glass of water in front of her. Her Aunt Donna moved around the kitchen unwrapping deli trays and setting out plastic-ware—all the things that Sarah would normally be doing.

Donna was her mother's older sister. She'd moved back from Florida after her husband Tom died suddenly of a heart attack while jogging in Boca Raton where they lived. Donna and Tom had been living away from New Hampshire for twenty years, so Sarah hardly knew them. However, Sarah and Donna had bonded quickly. Not only were they both first-borns, but also they were dreamers who loved to read, were creative, and yet lonely. Donna was struggling to make friends in her new neighborhood. She was in her early fifties and living alone without any children, which made it hard to make connections with people in town. And Sarah, well, she was always lonely.

Having Donna around meant Sarah got a break from taking care of the house and the people in her life because Donna insisted on helping her—it gave her purpose, she said. Having a confidant, one who understood her family, lifted the burden that Sarah had lived with her whole life. She never had anyone who understood her life and therefore spent a lot of time alone. It was hard for Sarah to make friends because no one her age had the responsibilities that she did. Donna had insisted that Sarah live off-campus for her last semester.

"Everyone should experience living away from home at least once!" Donna had said to Sarah's father.

"I need her here to watch the boys, and to cook for us," her father had demanded.

Her aunt scoffed. "For God's sake, George. She's been your servant for how many years now? She needs to enjoy being twenty-one, not be your stand-in wife."

"She's not my servant! She's a good girl who knows where her responsibilities lie. Besides, do you know how much it costs to live on campus? I can't afford that!" he'd said.

"Well, it's time for her to not have any responsibilities for once. I'll help where I can. Sarah needs a life. She's taken care of everyone for far too long," Donna said.

Sarah had watched all of this unfold and was in shock when her father agreed to let her move out. The best part was that Donna paid for Sarah to live with some girls from one of her classes in an off-campus apartment, leaving Sarah's father little choice in the matter. Sarah could focus on her studies and experience college the way it was meant to be. She hardly ever came home, unless it was to give Donna a break.

Sarah stood in the middle of her own party unseen while fans blew hot air around the room. People fanned themselves with napkins that said 'Class of 1994' in colorful letters. She didn't see her two brothers anywhere. They were both in high school now: Frank, a senior, Billy, a junior. Frank's absence wasn't a shock. He'd always resented her even though she never asked to be the one in charge. However, not seeing Billy hurt.

Billy was only three when their mother's depression took hold and confined her to bed all day. He'd clung to Sarah, then nine, desperate for motherly attention. They were alike in so many ways, both sensitive and thoughtful and always eager to please, whether it was helping their mother, or just being quiet so Dad could hear his show on television. At night, they'd snuggle and read together and Billy would often fall asleep in her bed. As the years went by, their conversations became more introspective. However, when he reached adolescence, he and Frank became inseparable and Sarah's relationship with Billy became distant. It was hard to be someone's sister and stand-in mother.

"There's the graduate!" her father shouted.

Sarah cringed, the sound of his voice meant that he wasn't drinking his first gin and tonic of the day. All the eyes in the room turned toward her, making her face flush with embarrassment. Sarah preferred being invisible.

She took a deep breath and gave an exaggerated wave to the crowd as she said hello.

"Let's see that diploma! I want to make sure it's real," her father said laughing.

Others laughed too. Sarah wondered if they thought her father was actually funny or if it was just nervous laughter.

"Real?" she asked scathingly.

Her father glared at her. She didn't want to look away like she usually did. She wanted to stand up to him. She wanted to tell him she was done letting him boss her around. However, the courage she had in her car as she practiced those words was slipping, and she looked away.

"Don't be so sensitive. I'm just teasing," he said.

She had suffered a lifetime of his so-called 'teasing'; some would call it abuse. Whatever it was, it sucked, and she was no longer willing to tolerate it. Sarah reminded herself that freedom was only a day away as she handed him the diploma. Her father inspected it and then held it up for everyone to see.

"Look at that," he said. "It's real!"

Everyone clapped and offered their congratulations. Sarah stared at her feet. All of this—the party, the praise—felt awkward and phony. When Sarah graduated from high school, she was the only graduate there without a parent to greet them at the end of the ceremony. She had no one to hug or to take pictures of her in her cap and gown, and there were no celebratory flowers. When she got home, her father was watching golf on TV. Her mother was asleep in her darkened bedroom, and her brothers were outside playing. Now, for her college graduation, he insisted on a party. It was unnerving, although she wasn't exactly sure why.

"I'm going to change," Sarah said. Her floral knee-length dress with padded shoulders was damp from sweat. It was unseasonably humid for May in New Hampshire. Sitting out in the blazing sun wearing a black cap and gown at the graduation made her wish she'd gone naked. She couldn't wait to put on shorts and a tank top and pull her long, permed hair back with a scrunchie. Her hairdresser tried to talk her into getting the new Jennifer Aniston haircut that was all the rage, but she wasn't ready to give up her big hair yet. Sarah loved her curls.

"No, you're not. All these people are here for you. You're staying right here. Besides, I have an announcement," her father said wiping beads of sweat from his brow with his forearm.

Sarah cringed. Her father didn't make announcements he made demands. She instantly regretted not driving away when she had the chance. Sarah turned to her mother, hoping for some hint, or warning of what he was about to say, but as usual, her mother kept her eyes low as she picked at the imaginary lint on her skirt. Her depression had gotten worse recently and she was looking more frail than ever. She'd become more of a shell than a person which is why Sarah felt all right leaving her. Besides, Aunt Donna was around to help now.

"I just want to get out of this dress," Sarah said.

"I said no," he father said.

They stared at each other again. His nostrils flared, an indication he was about to blow. Why was standing up to him so fucking hard? She balled her hands into fists. Her fingernails dug into her palms. She forced a smile, nodded her head, and looked away.

"Great. Now someone bring me the champagne!" her father demanded.

Donna scurried to the kitchen and came back quickly. She handed him a bottle of cheap champagne. Her father popped the cork, and then poured the bubbly liquid into small plastic flutes. He summoned Sarah to his side with a wave of his hand. Sarah stood next to him. The energy between them felt like two opposing magnets. He began his toast by thanking everyone for coming. Then he turned to Sarah.

"I'm not sure how you pulled it off," he said. "I never thought I'd see you graduating from college. I thought you'd end up knocked up or something," he laughed.

How she pulled it off? Was he serious? She looked around the room. Everyone was smiling at her, as if they couldn't believe she'd done it either. Little did he know that having kids was the last thing in the world Sarah ever wanted. She'd played the role of mother long enough. It also wasn't worth telling everyone that she'd gotten straight A's since she was a little girl because studying was the only way to escape the hell that was her life. No one would care. They never had before.

He ended his speech and raised his glass. Everyone in the room raised their glass too.

"Cheers!" they all said in unison.

"Thanks," Sarah said.

Then, her father did something unprecedented. He hugged her. Sarah remained stiff as he put his arms around her and patted her back. Getting praise from her father should have made her happy, but the public show of affection only made her uncomfortable. It was like being in the grip of an animal that seemed tame yet at any minute, without warning, could turn violent.

Then, he dropped the bomb.

"I used my contacts and got you an interview at Smithfield Elementary School!" her father said beaming with pride. Her father had been the town manager in Lincoln for as long as Sarah could remember; he had a lot of connections.

Sarah pulled away from him as everyone in the room congratulated her. Smithfield was the elementary school that she and her brothers had attended. It was the last place on earth she wanted to work.

She regretted not putting her suitcase in the car before she left for graduation.

"Dad…"

"No need to thank me. You can work at Smithfield and live here."

The thought of living *here* for one more minute made her want to vomit. A hard lump formed in her throat. She wanted to scream, but what came out was barely a whisper.

"I don't want…"

"Don't be ungrateful, Sarah," her father said, his eyes pierced hers.

Her heart pounded and her inner voice screamed at her to speak up, to tell her father that she had other plans. She watched as everyone congratulated her and shook her father's hand as if he had just birthed the new king. Finally, her inner voice grew louder until she couldn't take it anymore.

"I want to travel across the country," she announced.

The room fell silent and her father stared at her. Even her mother looked up. Donna smiled and clapped her hands encouragingly. Sarah looked around the room and spotted Billy near the front door. He'd come after all. They exchanged a look. Billy pleaded with his eyes; Sarah knew what it meant.

"No daughter of mine is going to travel across the country," her father said.

"I saved money from working this semester, and I have a plan. I'm going to go to California. I'm going to take pictures of everything along the way. I won't even be gone long." She lied about that last part to soften the blow. Getting away was the first step, staying away would be the next.

"You will go to this interview."

"I've done everything you wanted me to do. I just want…"

"Don't be stupid. Your mother needs you," he said, grabbing her arm. The corners of his mouth pooled with white foamy spit. Then her father leaned in close to her ear. "Do not humiliate me," he hissed.

His fingers dug into her arm. She tried to pull away, but he held on tighter. He'd never hit her. Although, often he'd back her up against a wall while yelling. Spit flew from his mouth and his face got red as the arteries in his neck constricted. Sometimes he'd punch the wall behind her to make his point, narrowly missing her face. Other times he'd grab or poke her really hard. As a little girl, she learned to duck to avoid the full beer cans that were hurled at her. When she got older, she learned how to cover up or justify the bruises by saying, 'I bumped into the corner of my desk.', or, 'My car door hit me.'

Sarah shook her head. It wasn't worth fighting with him now in front of everyone.

"I'm sorry. I'll go to the interview," she said, forcing a smile.

Her father beamed, and everyone in the room let out a collective breath. Sarah fought back tears, swallowing several times to release the lump in her throat. She was terrified of being trapped in this hell forever.

She dared a glance at her mother, and found her weeping. Sarah tilted her head. Something wasn't right, but she couldn't put her finger on it. Her mother always looked frail, but now she was pale and her eyes were sunken. She seemed to be wincing in pain. Why hadn't Sarah noticed that this morning before she left for the ceremony?

2

The next morning, Sarah was woken up by the sounds of yelling in the basement. Her brothers slept down there. They had shared a bedroom upstairs until Frank was in middle school. That's when he decided he needed his own space. He began sleeping downstairs in the damp, unfinished space on a couch that he and Billy had found on the side of the road. Sarah knew Frank just wanted to be down there so he could sneak out at night undetected. She tried to stop him at first, but he didn't care what she said. She never told her father that Frank snuck out because she knew her father would hit him.

Her father had once said that he needed to toughen them up, to turn them into men, and that's why he hit them. Apparently, that meant punching them over things like getting a bad grade. Part of Sarah was grateful that he didn't hit her, but every time she saw her father hit the boys, especially Billy, she couldn't help but feel guilty that she had always been spared. Now that the boys were older they fought back. The last time her father threw a punch at her brother, Frank fought back, leaving George with a broken wrist.

The yelling escalated and suddenly she heard something crash. Sarah flew out of bed and ran down the stairs. She saw Billy splayed on the floor. Their father stood over him.

"You fucking little shit! When I ask you a goddamn question, you fucking answer it!" He shouted.

Sarah ran to Billy's side. Her father had backhanded him. His cheek was red from where their father's hand made contact with his skin. She reached out to touch him, but Billy pushed her away.

"I don't fucking know where he is!" Billy yelled. His voice was deeper and angrier than Sarah had ever heard it. She knew he was talking about Frank. He hardly ever came home anymore.

"What's the problem?" Sarah yelled.

"The fucking *problem* is that your brother Frank didn't come home last night and he has my goddamn car! And this little shit won't tell me where the fuck he is!"

She turned to Billy. "Where is he?"

"I said I don't fucking know! For fucks-sake…"

"I swear to God!" her father roared and lunged toward Billy.

Sarah stood between them.

"Dad! He said he doesn't know where Frank is. Take my car to work."

"There she goes again, sticking up for the little pansy ass Billy. Where are your fucking keys?"

"Upstairs on the table by the front door."

Her father took the stairs two at a time. Billy punched the wall before he flung himself on the couch.

"You OK?" she asked.

"Leave me alone."

She shook her head and let out a sigh. "I was just trying to help," she said.

Sticking up for him came natural but she knew it only caused her father to treat him as if he was less than. Ever since she'd moved out, Sarah and Billy's relationship became different. She sensed it was because he was angry with her for leaving him behind, and she felt guilty about that. Donna told her it was normal for the younger siblings to feel that way and that Sarah should just give Billy some time, but things only seemed to get worse between them. Now, he felt like a stranger. She went back to her room.

Sarah looked in the mirror. "I have to leave this shit hole before it swallows me," she said to her reflection. She went to her closet and pulled out the bag she had packed. She opened it and stared at its contents. She turned on her Walkman and pressed play. With the headphones on, Sarah rearranged the items in the suitcase. The cassette she was listening to was a mix tape that her college friend—with benefits—Todd had made for her with all of his favorite music. It was a good-bye present. Sarah had always liked pop music, but Todd introduced her to grunge. It was growing on her. Stone Temple Pilots and Nirvana were becoming a few of her favorite bands.

She met Todd in her biology class sophomore year. They were lab partners. They studied together, and one night as they were doing a lab report in his room, he kissed her. Then they had sex. It was her first time. Todd taught her everything about the giving and receiving of sex. He was funny and sexy, but to call him a boyfriend would have been a lie. Sometimes they'd go to the pizza shop to get food after a night together, but for the most part, they spent all of their time in his room. She had fallen in love with him, even though she never told Todd that.

Todd gave her the mix tape before he went home to Virginia. He promised to keep in touch, but Sarah knew he wouldn't.

She heard a soft knock at her bedroom door.

"Come in."

Billy entered, looking as if he hadn't slept at all. He was dressed in jeans and a t-shirt. His eyes were red and puffy. His hair was a mess. He sat on the edge of her bed and let out a deep sigh.

"You aren't really leaving are you?" Billy said.

"Billy…," she said. They'd talked about this for months. He understood why she wanted to leave, but he begged her not to go.

"I can't be here without you. I just can't," Billy said, his lip quivering.

Sarah sighed and sat down next to him, putting her arm around him. He rested his head on her shoulder. The thought of leaving him behind made her feel guilty. Hell, she always felt guilty. Guilty that she lived away. Guilty that she didn't want to take care of her mother anymore. Guilty for wanting something more for herself. Guilty knowing that Billy would be lost without her. She *hated* guilt.

"I'll be back. I just need some time on my own. We've talked about this like a hundred times already," she said.

"Yeah, but I never thought you'd actually do it. I mean, planning it's one thing but when you said it yesterday in front of everyone, to *Dad*, it was all so…real."

She let her brother go and rubbed her eyes. "I can't keep going through this Billy. I need to leave at some point. You gotta understand that, don't you?"

He shrugged.

"I just have to get the courage up to actually go through with it," Sarah said.

"Dad was pissed when you told him, huh?"

"How could ya tell?" Sarah asked sarcastically.

They both laughed. Sarah checked Billy's cheek, then his hand. His knuckles were red and he'd broken the skin when his hand made contact with the wall. She grabbed a tissue from her nightstand and wiped the blood away. When she was done, she ran her hand over his head.

"You'll live," she laughed. "I gotta make Ma's breakfast. Can we talk about this later?"

"Yeah," Billy said, as he stood.

She hugged her not-so-little brother. He'd just had the biggest growth spurt of his life and now, at sixteen, he was eight inches taller than she was.

"Love you, little bro."

"Love you too, big sister," Billy said.

Sarah helped her mom get dressed, and then brought her to the kitchen. She made a soft-boiled egg and toast for her mother and made herself an English muffin with peanut butter and bananas on top.

The night before, as Sarah helped her mother get ready for bed, her mother had insisted that she was fine and that nothing was wrong, even though she winced as she moved. Sarah couldn't shake the feeling that something was wrong, but her mother waved her off. "I'm tired. It's been a long day for me," she had said.

Sarah set the plate down in front of her mother with a cup of tea. Sarah sat down across from her with a steaming cup of coffee. She took a bite of her English muffin while her mother stared at her food apathetically. It was hard to imagine her mother as Donna had once described.

"Your mother was the life of the party! Always smiling and talking to everyone. She loved to strike up conversations with total strangers," Donna had said.

Sarah didn't have any memories of her mother being full of life. All she ever knew of her mother was a sad shell of a person who didn't seem to care about anything at all. Sarah often wondered if she would end up like that someday. She figured if she never had kids (the catalyst for her mother's own depression) that she wouldn't.

"Mom?"

Her mother raised her head slowly, expressionless.

"Yes?"

"I need to talk to you about something."

The corners of her mother's mouth lifted slightly. Sarah looked at her closely. Her mother was in her mid-forties, but she looked sixty. Strands of gray peppered her dark brown hair that was cut short and permed every couple of months—mostly because her father insisted on it. Her mother never wore make-up, and so her face was dull and there was sadness in her eyes. Sarah wondered if her mother wished she'd done things differently in her life. Maybe then she would understand why Sarah needed to get away.

Sarah took her mom's effort to smile as an invitation to speak, and she told her mother about her plan to drive to California. She described all of the places that she wanted to see, like New York City, Niagara Falls, and the Grand Canyon. She told her mother about the new camera she got as a graduation gift from Jim, her mentor at the photography studio. Sarah talked about her dream of traveling the world to take photos for magazines. If that didn't work out, she had a back-up plan of owning her own studio someday.

Her mom lit up as she spoke, and Sarah felt encouraged. Maybe, just maybe, she had reached her mother. She waited for her mom to say something, anything, but her mom turned her vacant gaze back into her teacup.

With each passing second, the smile on Sarah's face slowly vanished. The clock in the kitchen ticked loudly, cutting the silence in the room. Her mother stared out the window with tears in her eyes. Sarah wondered why her mother wasn't telling her to go. To run. To get the hell out of this godforsaken town and away from her controlling father. Something!

Then, her mother began to speak slowly.

"Sarah," her mother whispered.

"What is it Ma?" Sarah asked, sensing once again that something wasn't right.

Her mother let out a deep sigh. "I have bone cancer," she said.

Sarah blinked as she let that sink in. "What do you mean you have bone cancer?"

Her mother looked at her and shrugged.

"When did you find this out?" Sarah asked.

"About a month ago," her mother said meekly.

"A *month*? Why am I just hearing about this now?" Sarah shrieked.

"I didn't want you to worry."

In that case, Sarah would have preferred her mom kept it to herself forever. It was ironic that her mother was trying to save her from worry after a lifetime of Sarah having to be the responsible one.

Now everything she wanted was ruined. Cancer! That, coupled with her mom's depression, meant only one thing— Sarah would need to take care of her mother now more than ever. Her father would need Sarah to continue to do all of the things her mother could not, and of course, Sarah would have to help with the boys.

Frank and Billy, who were more like twins because of their thirteen-month age difference, got all the attention and freedom, while Sarah got all the responsibility. "Sarah help with this." "Sarah bring this to your mother." "Sarah watch the boys!" When the boys were little, Sarah helped get them their breakfast, helped them get dressed, helped to get them on the bus, helped them with homework, helped bathe them, help, help, help. She was expected to help with everything because she was the oldest, and Sarah did it all, reluctantly, but well. Before she went to live at school, the house was always clean, the laundry never piled high, and she became a great cook by watching cooking shows on PBS on Saturdays. And she never complained. Who would listen anyway?

"You didn't want me to worry? I can't believe this!"

"Donna thought you had enough to worry about with graduation and all."

Sarah's mouth dropped. She thought she had an open, honest relationship with her aunt. Why would Donna keep this from her? She knew how much Sarah wanted to get away. Donna had even encouraged her to go. Yet, Donna knew her mother was dying and didn't tell her.

The clock ticked loudly in the background as Sarah rubbed her eyes, trying to gather her composure. She understood now why her father got her the interview, and why he'd hit Billy earlier. It had been a while since her father had struck either of her brothers, at least that she knew of. Her father never handled stress well, if he handled it at all. After couple of minutes, she took a deep breath, and let it out with a heavy sigh.

"Do the boys know?"

"We thought you could help us tell them," her mother said.

Sarah rolled her eyes. Of course, she would have to be the one to tell them. Although, part of her was relieved they didn't know yet. If everyone had known except for her, she'd be even more upset.

"What did the doctor say?" Sarah asked.

"I could try an experimental treatment, but I don't know…"

Sarah flung back in her chair, holding her forehead.

"How long, Ma? How long does he think you have?"

Her mother didn't look up; she simply shrugged.

"Ma! I need to know! One month, two, three? Six? What?"

Her mother's shoulders shook up and down as she wept. She held a napkin over her mouth. Sarah waited for her mom to speak. Finally, her mother collected herself.

"Three to six months," her mother whispered.

Sarah stood up, pushing the chair back forcefully. *Three to six months?* Her aunt didn't think it was necessary to let Sarah know this? Was she going to let Sarah leave without telling her that her mother was dying? Sarah wanted to call Donna to hear her explanation, but then she realized her mother was sobbing.

"Oh Ma, I'm sorry," Sarah said, bending down to put her arms around her mother. "We'll fight this, OK? You're going to get better," Sarah said, cringing at the lie. Tears streamed down her face.

Even though Sarah resented having to take care of her mother and brothers all those years, sacrificing her own hopes and dreams, she understood that sometimes life wasn't fair. This was the deck of cards she was dealt. She knew there would be plenty of time to live *her* life. She had her whole life ahead of her. Her mother did not.

3

Sarah arrived at the interview early and waited outside the principal's office. The secretary offered her coffee but Sarah didn't need the caffeine. She was nervous enough.

Seamus O'Leary, the principal at Smithfield Elementary, called her into his office. She shook his hand.

"Your dad and I go way back!" Seamus said.

"Yes, he told me that. Thanks for meeting with me," Sarah said, even though she couldn't have cared less.

"Well, your father said you graduated with high honors, and I'm always looking for great teachers. Tell me about yourself," Seamus said, smiling. He was the same age as her father, mid-forties, but in much better shape. He had a full beard that was peppered with gray. His hair had slightly more gray around the temples making him look distinguished. His energy was infectious, and Sarah liked him immediately. The principal where Sarah had done her student teaching was a reserved woman who was completely unapproachable. She hardly ever smiled and spoke so softly that you had to lean in to hear what she was saying.

Sarah told Seamus about her student teaching and showed him some of the lesson plans and projects she'd done with the children. She tried to sound enthusiastic, and he seemed impressed.

She left the interview praying she didn't get the job, but Sarah had a feeling she would. Working full-time wasn't part of her plan right now. It'd been almost a month since Sarah found out about the cancer, and her days were spent caring for her mother. When she wasn't doing that, she spent time in her room staring at a map of California.

She drove to the one place that felt like home, the studio. Jim pulled in next to her.

"Hey there, Sarah!" Jim called out cheerily as they got out of their cars. He'd been the town's photographer for over twenty years. Sarah met him when she was a junior in high school. Jim helped run the photography club at school. She took one of his classes at the studio, and then she began working there. She loved going with him on the wedding gigs and helping with equipment. Sometimes he'd hand her a camera to take the candid shots—the brides always loved those, and Sarah loved taking them.

"Hi, Jim," Sarah said.

"Surprised to see you here so early," he said.

"I just had my interview. I don't want to go home yet."

"Ah, the interview. The one your dad arranged. How'd it go?"

Sarah rolled her eyes. "Fine."

"Ah. Well, I've been married for a long time, and when a woman says 'fine' there is a whole lot more to the story."

Jim unlocked the studio and they went inside.

As soon as Sarah entered, her entire body relaxed. She took a deep breath, allowing the air to cleanse her soul. In the front of the studio was a small retail area with cameras and accessories for sale. One back corner had props, lights, and scenes for every occasion. This was where the majority of the portraits were taken. Outside, in the back, there was an area where Jim took subjects for more intimate portraits. New Hampshire's changing seasons made a perfect backdrop for photos. The other back corner was Sarah's favorite space, the photo lab where she developed film. It was where she'd come at night on the weekends to escape while everyone else her age was out partying or spending time with friends. It was hard to relate to kids her age who only had to worry about themselves.

"So," Jim said as he put down his bag behind the counter. "Tell me about the interview."

Instinctively, Sarah turned on the computer and opened the appointment book. "It went OK, I guess. It's just not what I want to do. No. It's the last thing in the world that I want to do."

Jim sighed and shook his head. "You don't have to take the job, you know? I mean, he got you the interview, you went, and now the rest is up to you, my friend. You have free will."

Sarah laughed. "I'm not so sure about that. My mother is *dying*. And who knows when that will be. I'm in a holding pattern, and I hate it!" She knew she sounded like a bratty teenager, but she couldn't help it. Besides, Jim understood where she was coming from.

"You could work here full-time."

"I wish. My father would never let me do that."

Jim shook his head.

"He thinks photography is a stupid hobby," Sarah said. "Besides, he would never approve because it's not what I got my degree in. He's all about the *degree*."

"Maybe it's time to stand up to him and tell him you want to be a photographer."

Sarah shrugged. "I've tried. It's not as easy to convince him as you make it sound."

Whenever she tried to tell her father about her passion for photography, he'd shut her down. "That's not a real job!" he'd say. Her father never liked the fact that she spent so much time at the studio. He didn't see the value in art, and he felt the time she spent there was time away from taking care of him and the home.

"Well, the offer stands if you ever change your mind. I have three one-year olds coming in twenty minutes. Why don't you stay and help me for a little bit?"

***

Sarah arrived home before her father, thankfully. If dinner was late, she'd hear about it.

When she walked in the front door, her aunt was putting on her shoes. Donna acknowledged Sarah with a wave and held up a finger to say, one minute. Her aunt's favorite soap opera was on and was almost over. Sarah sat down to watch the last few minutes.

Right after Sarah's mother told her about the cancer diagnosis Sarah confronted her aunt to find out why she hadn't told her about her mom.

"You needed to focus on finals," Donna had said.

"Yeah, but I could've come to the doctor with you."

"You need to be a kid, Sarah. You should be going out with friends or traveling the world, not taking care of your family."

"You're a little too late, I've taken care of them my whole life. Now I can't travel. I'm stuck here! So what did you save me from exactly?"

"Well, I tried Sarah. I did," her aunt sighed.

"You tried what?" Sarah asked.

"I tried to do what was best for you. I wanted you to be happy and not worry about everyone else, for once."

"So when were you planning to tell me?" Sarah asked.

"I don't know. When you called home, I guess. I just wanted you to be able to get away for a little bit, that's all," Donna said.

Sarah shook her head. Get away for a little bit? Sarah didn't know which was worse, the fact that her aunt had allowed Sarah to dream about traveling, knowing all along that Sarah would never really get to live her dream, or that Donna didn't realize Sarah would never leave her mother at time when she needed her the most.

Even though a few weeks had gone by, Sarah still couldn't shake the feeling of betrayal. She went on appointments with her mother so she could hear information for herself, rather than rely on her aunt or father to tell her the truth.

When the commercial came on, Donna turned to Sarah.

"Hi, honey!"

"Hi."

"Your mom is sleeping. Walk me to my car. I have something for you."

Sarah held the door open and waited for her aunt to pass. They talked about her mom's day.

"She's feeling a little better today," Donna said.

Sarah's mother had a chemo treatment three days ago. The first few days were always the worst. Her mother had a strong gag reflex and refused to drink the water she needed to drink after treatment, which made it hard to get her to take the anti-nausea medicine, so she spent the first few days getting sick. Recently, they'd discovered that her mother could take her medication with Kool-Aid without gagging, so that's how they got fluids in her now.

They got to her aunt's car and Sarah opened the door.

"Oh, I almost forgot!" Donna said. "You got a call from Seamus. Did you know that I dated him in high school?"

Sarah shook her head. She knew the fact that he'd called could only mean one thing.

"What a riot it was to hear his voice!" Donna laughed. "Anyway, after we caught up he said he was calling to offer you the job. He wants you to call him back."

"Wait, he told you I got the job?"

"Well, he wasn't going to, but I pulled it out of him."

Sarah's heart sank. *Shit.* She looked up at the sky, willing the tears away.

"OK, thanks," Sarah said. "I'll call him back."

Donna touched Sarah's arm. "Honey, you can go on that adventure you have planned before you start the job. Go away for a couple weeks. I'll take care of your mom."

Sarah sighed heavily. A couple of weeks wouldn't be

enough. The point was to leave and never come back.

"No Auntie, I can't leave her now. I'll go on that adventure someday."

"You can't be a teacher if that's not what you want, sweetie. Life is too short to be unhappy. Stand your ground," Donna said.

Sarah hugged her. "Thanks. Actually, I have some news. Jim offered me a full-time job today."

Donna squealed and hugged Sarah tightly. "That's wonderful! Thank God for Jim!"

"Well, I told him no. My father would never let me work there full-time."

"Oh, honey…," Donna said, looking defeated.

Sarah wasn't in the mood to go through all of this again. She shrugged. "It's fine," Sarah said, and then changed the subject. "Can I ask you something?"

"Of course," said Donna.

"Why did my mom marry him?"

Donna sighed. "Oh, well. Love, I suppose."

Sarah let out a laugh. "I can't even imagine my father being loving."

"It was her depression that changed everything. Before that, they were happy. When you were born, your parents were in love. Jane always talked about how George made her laugh and how well he took care of her."

Sarah tried to imagine her parents happy and in love, but it wasn't easy.

"You know my mother had the depression too, right?" Donna asked.

"I think I remember hearing that," Sarah said.

"Back then, my father sent her to live in a hospital when she got too depressed and couldn't care for us anymore," Donna said. "That was hard on your mother, being the youngest. The six of us tried to help take care of her, but then us girls left to get married, my brothers enlisted, and Jane got left behind. Then our father died, and she was bounced from sibling to sibling until George came along. Jane was desperate for someone to love her, to make her feel secure. George did that. He took care of her and provided for her. As much as I hate to admit it, I think he still loves her, deeply."

Sarah shook her head. He had a funny way of showing it, she thought.

"Oh! I have something for you!" Donna said.

She went to her car and rummaged through a bag in the trunk, mumbling that it was in there somewhere. Her aunt was always giving her small token gifts. Things that she'd picked up at flea markets or yard sales.

Suddenly, Donna pulled up a box and smiled. "Here it is!" she said proudly, then handed the box to Sarah. "Open it."

"What is it?"

"A present, honey. Open it."

Sarah broke the seal on the box with her fingernail, lifted the lid, and pushed aside the tissue paper to reveal a hummingbird.

"It's a Christmas ornament," Donna said.

"It's so pretty!" Sarah said, turning the ornament around to get a good look at it. The tiny colorful body had iridescent feathers and a long tapered beak.

Donna took it from her and wound the dial on its back. As she let the dial go, the wings on the bird fluttered, making a soft humming noise.

"I've never seen a real hummingbird before," Sarah said.

"When you see one, it's a reminder from the spirit world to enjoy life. Hummingbirds also symbolize freedom, independence, and resilience. Those little birds may only weigh a few ounces, but they have the courage of a lion. I saw this and thought of you," Donna said.

"Yeah well, I don't have courage."

"Of course you do. You just don't realize it. Do you know these little birds can fly great distances? They've been known to migrate from Canada to Central America! My friend Gail says that hummingbirds remind us that even though we may have a difficult journey and obstacles ahead, we must persevere with our dreams to fulfill our destinies."

Sarah's eyes filled with tears. It all sounded so easy when she said it.

"It's so pretty. Thank you."

"Keep an eye out for these little birds. They're always around. You just have to look for them. If you do see one, take notice because it's a symbol that anything is possible. Life is meant to be enjoyed. You're allowed to be happy, Sarah."

Donna and Jim were the only ones who seemed to think so. She hugged Donna and thanked her again. Just then, her father pulled into the driveway.

He shouted through his open window. "My daughter is a teacher! Can you believe it?"

Donna rolled her eyes and gave Sarah a look. They both knew that Seamus had already told her father she got the job. Oh, the joys of living in a small town in rural New Hampshire—everyone knew everyone else's business.

"What if she doesn't want the job?" Donna said.

Sarah cringed.

"Why wouldn't she want the job? Of course she wants this! This is what she's worked for. It's is the education I paid for. She's taking the job for Christ's sake," he said as he slammed his car door and walked towards them.

He looked disheveled as usual. His pants were baggy and hung low. They had to buy his pants two sizes too big for his legs to make room for his fat belly. His shirt was half-untucked, and his tie was loose around his neck. He was forty-six but looked almost twice his age. Sarah attributed that to the fact that he didn't exercise or eat right. His thick hair, which he kept on the longer side, turned white in his twenties, which made him seem much older. That and his lumbered gait due to the early onset arthritis he had in his hips.

"I just think it should be up to her, George. It's her life," Donna said.

Sarah felt uncomfortable. She didn't want her aunt to get into a fight with her father. Besides, it would only make things worse for her later.

"Thanks Auntie. I'll see you tomorrow, OK?" Sarah said, pleading with her eyes for her aunt to get the hint.

"Tell him your news," Donna said, urging Sarah with her eyes to tell her father about the job at the studio.

"What news?" her father said.

"Nothing, Dad. Just the news about the job."

Sarah and her aunt exchanged a look. Donna curled her lip and made a sound indicating she disapproved. As she went to her car, she called out to Sarah.

"I'll see you tomorrow, my love. We can talk more then."

Sarah waved, and then turned to go inside. She knew her father would be upset that dinner wasn't started yet. He followed closely behind.

"You're taking the job I got you, Sarah Jane."

"Dad...," Sarah said, waving him off.

She didn't want to say anything else; she wasn't in the mood for a fight. Thankfully, Frank and Billy arrived home and distracted her father while she went to the kitchen to start dinner.

At dinner, as they all sat around the small dining room table, her father announced that she had gotten the job. Her mother stopped pushing the food on her plate with her fork and looked up with the faintest of smiles. She'd gotten so thin and was now an upsetting shade of gray.

"About that," Sarah started. "I got another job today too."

"Where?" her father demanded with a mouth full of mashed potatoes.

"At the studio. Jim offered me a full-time job."

"No way! You went to school to be a teacher; you're going to be a teacher."

"I don't want to be a teacher!" Sarah said, slamming her hand on the table and standing up. Her brothers jumped, and her mom winced. She felt powerful standing over her father, until he stood too. His six-foot frame towered over her five-foot three-inch body, making her suddenly feel weak.

"Don't. You. Shout. At. Me," her father said emphasizing

each word through gritted teeth.

"I don't want to be a teacher!" she yelled desperately.

"You ungrateful bitch! I paid for that diploma you have. I get to say what you do with it!"

"This is 1994. You don't own me!"

"Wanna make a bet? Who pays for the clothes you have on your back? Me! Who pays for the roof over your head? Me! Who pays for the food you eat? Me! And I paid for your education. So yes, I own you. You *will* take this job!" he yelled, slamming his fist on the table.

Her brothers left the room with their plates and went down to the basement. Her mother wept. Sarah started to cry too. He was right. She only had a little bit of money, not enough to be on her own completely. The car she was planning to use to escape with was his too. She fell back into her chair.

"I hate being a teacher, Dad! I hate it!" she shrieked.

"You're taking the job!" her father stubbornly insisted.

Sarah put her head in her hands, feeling trapped and frustrated.

"Sarah," her mother said.

Shocked by the sound of her mother's voice, Sarah looked across the table. Her mom leaned forward, mustering the strength she needed to speak.

"You can work at the studio if that makes you happy."

Sarah's mouth hung open. Her mother had never stuck up for her before. She looked at her father. His mouth hung open too.

"Jane!" her father shouted.

"George, just let the girl be happy, will you? I'm dying. Let her be happy, for once."

Sarah looked from her mother to her father. They didn't talk about her mother dying. They discussed her treatments, but never the fact that she was dying. Her father fell down into his chair, defeated.

"Jane..."

"I'm too tired to fight, George."

Sarah waited, barely breathing. Was this really happening? Was her mother sticking up for her? Time stood still as she waited for her father to speak again. She didn't dare move a muscle. After what felt like an eternity, her father turned to her, his eyes cast down at the floor.

"Fine. You can work for Jim," her father said. Then he stood and walked to the front door. "I'm going out."

Tears streamed down Sarah's face as she walked over to her mother and hugged her.

"Thank you, Mom. You don't know what this means to me."

"When I'm gone, you need to leave. Go on that adventure you have planned. Your father will never change."

Sarah sobbed. Billy appeared and stood behind Sarah. He put a hand on her shoulder. She could hear him crying too.

4

Two months had passed since her mom started the experimental treatment. It was working, even though the chemo made her sick most of the time. Nevertheless, the tumors were shrinking and she was hanging on, barely. Sarah didn't understand why her mother's soul didn't let go and leave this life.

Her father had become even more unbearable to live with, if that was even possible. He just couldn't handle the stress and wasn't able to face the fact that his wife was dying. He kept saying she'd get better, which drove Sarah crazy that he couldn't just admit she was dying. And her brothers were never home. She and Billy were drifting further and further apart. He was becoming more like Frank—elusive and distant. Billy was failing school now too. Frank they knew would barely graduate, but Billy was always different. He was smart, like Sarah, and cared about getting good grades. Not anymore though. Sarah worried about him the most. He just didn't care about anything anymore.

Living at home, taking care of her mother, and working full-time at the studio left zero room for Sarah to have a social life. So when a coworker invited her to a Fourth of July party, she went.

Sarah arrived at Julia's parents' house with a veggie and dip tray she bought at the grocery store. There were people everywhere but no one she recognized. She made her way through the house to the back deck where people were talking and eating food. Julia's mother took the veggie tray from Sarah.

"The other kids are down by the pool," said Mrs. Lane. Then she called down to Julia, who waved. Sarah wondered when she would stop being considered a "kid." She certainly never felt like one, but now she was an actual adult and resented the implication that she was young and immature. Even though Mrs. Lane was twenty years older than Sarah, she looked young, dressed young, and always wanted to hang out with Julia and her friends. Sarah thought she dressed inappropriately for her age too.

"Grab a beer from the cooler!" Julia said, as Sarah approached.

Julia had started working at the studio last summer. She and Sarah were opposites in many ways. Julia was blonde, petite, and popular. Sarah had dark hair, a fuller frame, and was unpopular by virtue of being invisible to her peers. Julia was always trying to get Sarah to go out with her. Sometimes Sarah would meet her at a party, but she only went to appease Julia and usually snuck out early. Other times they went to the movies or to the bar in town to play darts. They both had a passion for photography, and Sarah liked being with Julia because she was fun and adventurous.

She looked through the cooler and picked a light beer before she joined the others. They swam and played volleyball all afternoon. Then, a group of guys arrived. They were loud, obviously drunk, and seemed to know everyone. One of the guys made his way around the crowd, hugging and kissing women on the cheek and shaking men's hands. Sarah kept an eye on him as he made his way down to the pool. He wasn't her type, but there was something about him that made her curious. She was attracted to guys who were tall and funny, and this guy was short and loud. Nevertheless, he had flirty eyes and an irresistible smile. Julia introduced the guys to everyone.

"These pricks are my neighbors. They came for the free food and the fireworks," Julia said.

"What's wrong with that?" said the guy Sarah had been watching.

"Shut up Joe," said Julia, punching his arm. She turned to Sarah. "He's an asshole. Don't talk to him."

"Aw, now don't tell her that. I'm not an asshole. She's just bitter because I didn't date her in high school."

"Ew! No," Julia said, rolling her eyes.

Joe pulled out a bottle of tequila from his back pocket.

"Everyone has to do a shot," he said, smiling at Sarah.

"Oh, thanks, but I don't really drink."

"You have to do the shot. Just one, come on?" he smiled at her.

She couldn't help but blush. "OK. Maybe one," she giggled.

They all did shots and then played some more volleyball. Sarah watched Joe all day. When he played in the pool with the little kids, she noticed how great he was with all of them, even the dainty little girls who complained when water was splashed in their eyes. He was protective over them, telling the tween boys to be careful of the little ones in the pool. The boys seemed to love Joe too. Probably because he was in the pool for what seemed like hours, throwing them in and having a cannonball contest. Of course, Joe won.

"You've been looking at him all day," Julia said coming up behind Sarah.

"No I haven't."

"Mmmk," Julia said, rolling her eyes.

"Is he the Rossi that owns the restaurants?" Sarah asked.

Julia laughed. "He's not. But his dad, yes. Joe worked at the one on Pleasant Street when we were younger until he got fired."

Sarah's eyes widened.

"Oh yeah, he was constantly giving his friends free food and drinks. His father got pissed and fired him."

Sarah laughed.

"The Rossi's have a lot of money," Julia said. "Like a lot. I mean, yeah, they own three restaurants, but my dad thinks Mr. Rossi is in the mob. Can you believe that?"

"Does the mob really exist in New Hampshire?" Sarah scoffed.

"Who knows? Anyway, stay away from Joe. He's a player. He'll use you and dump you before you know what happened."

Sarah sighed. She looked around to find Joe. He was very charming. *How could he be as bad as Julia says?*

As it got dark, they all gathered on the front lawn where Julia's dad would be setting off fireworks. They laid blankets down and huddled together. Sarah felt dizzy. She'd had too many shots of tequila. She hated the feeling of being out of control and knew that the next morning would be hell. Joe remained by her side the rest of the night, flirting with her. It felt so good to have a guy pay attention to her like that again. Todd still hadn't been in touch even though she'd left him messages.

Now Joe was giving her attention, and she felt turned on by it. She pictured kissing him and touching him. She kept telling herself she needed to stay near the crowd of people so she wouldn't do anything irrational. Then, as they waited for the fireworks, Joe sat next to her, rubbing her leg. He looked into her eyes and kissed her and she instantly melted. His warm tongue teased hers, and suddenly her body longed to be touched. As if he read her mind, his hand slid up inside her sweatshirt. She let out a soft moan in anticipation.

"Yeah, that's it," Joe said, cupping her breast.

The fireworks blasted above them as they kissed. Then, he pulled her up and led her inside.

He took her to the basement. "No one will come down here," he said.

She knew he wanted to have sex. She didn't have a

condom. She hoped he did.

As they reached the bottom step, he pulled her to him and began kissing her passionately. He was a great kisser, she thought. His stubble scratched her face, but it wasn't painful. She ran her hands through his dark curly hair as she kissed him. After a while, he lifted her sweatshirt and pulled her bikini top aside so he could kiss her hardened nipples. Then he made his way up to her mouth, kissing her chest and neck along the way, sending chills up her spine. She slid her hand down his swim trunks and grabbed his bulge. He slid his hand inside her bikini bottom. She moaned again.

"Yeah baby," he said. "Keep moaning like that."

She complied. Then, without warning, he pushed her head down to his groin as he wriggled his swim trunks down, exposing himself. She tried to resist him, but he put both hands on her head and drew her to him. Her mind was foggy from the tequila. What was happening?

"Come on baby," he said, enticingly.

She wasn't sure if this was normal, to have her head forced down there like that. Todd never did that. She'd always gone down there willingly. This didn't feel right, but she didn't want to seem inexperienced. She took him in her mouth. After several minutes, he pulled her up and turned her to face the wall. He was rushing things and being rough, so unlike her encounters with Todd. She wanted to stop, but didn't know what to say. He entered her from behind. She moved her hips, feeling him deeply. Then…

"Oh god…," he called out.

She turned her head and caught a glimpse of his face. She realized what was happening and panicked.

"Not inside!" Sarah yelled back, but it was too late. He had finished.

"Sorry about that. Couldn't help it," he panted. He held her hips so he could stay inside for a minute before he pulled away. He quickly pulled up his swim trunks.

The realization of what had just happened began to sink in. The stickiness between her legs felt strange. She'd never had sex without protection. Todd always wore condoms. She zipped up her sweatshirt and pulled up her bikini bottom, unsure of what to do or say next.

"Ready?" Joe asked.

Sarah looked at him confused. "Ready for what?"

"To go upstairs?"

Her stomach dropped. Todd had always stuck around after to cuddle or talk. Joe was about to walk away, as if she were a hooker.

"Oh, right. Sure," she said. A wave of nausea came over her. "I'm just going to use the bathroom first," she said, fighting back the lump that was in her throat.

"OK. See you up there," Joe said. Then he was gone.

Sarah went to the bathroom and stared into the mirror. "What did you just do?"

Suddenly, she felt very sober, and ashamed. She fixed her hair and wiped the eyeliner from under her eyes. She needed to get home and take a shower.

Sarah went outside and sat down on the blanket near her friends. Julia straddled her boyfriend; they were kissing and completely ignoring the fireworks that were still going off. She didn't see Joe. The nausea was getting worse so she went inside to get her bag so she could go home.

She stopped at the sliding glass door that lead to the deck. Joe was smoking pot with some people Sarah didn't know. Was she supposed to go out there and stand by his side like some claimed prize? Was she supposed to pretend they hadn't just had sex? She wondered if he was out there bragging about it. Would everyone think she was a slut? He didn't notice her, so she backed away and went back to the front. She'd get her bag tomorrow.

Sarah slipped out of the party without saying goodbye to anyone and went straight home.

5

Over the next few weeks, Sarah did her best to forget about what happened with Joe. She never told Julia about it because every time she thought about that night, she felt embarrassed that she let him use her like that. Julia was right and Sarah didn't want to hear, 'I told you so.' Sarah kept to herself, declining the constant invitations from Julia to party with her. She didn't want to risk seeing Joe.

As she booked a photo shoot for a customer, Sarah realized it was mid-August. She counted the days on the calendar—she hadn't had her period since before the Fourth of July.

Shit!

She went to the drug store after work and bought a test. She prayed she wouldn't see one of her father's friends in the store; thankfully, she didn't. At home, she ran to the bathroom without checking in on her mother. She heard Donna calling out for her.

"I have to pee! I'll be out in a minute!"

She tore open the package, sat down on the toilet, and stuck the stick between her legs. As she put the cap on the stick, she could already see the positive lines taking shape.

Fuck. Fuck. Fuck. It's supposed to take three minutes. It can't possibly be positive already, she thought.

She looked at her watch and told herself she'd wait the full three minutes before getting upset. She set the stick upside down and waited. After three minutes, she turned the stick over—the positive sign was bright pink now.

Fuck.

She heard a soft knock at the door.

"Hun, I need to leave. Are you all right in there?"

Sarah stared at herself in the mirror. *A baby...* With a guy she had a one-night stand with. She put her hands over her face and sobbed as silently as she could, knowing that her aunt was on the other side of the door. *What am I going to do?* A baby would ruin any chance she had of escaping her miserable life.

Her aunt knocked again.

"I'll be out in a minute," Sarah said, trying not to sound annoyed.

"Sarah..."

Sarah sighed then wiped her face and fixed her hair. She looked hard at herself in the mirror and wondered why God stuck her with such a shitty life. Maybe she'd been a horrible person in another lifetime and this was her punishment.

"I'm coming out."

***

The next day Sarah asked Julia for Joe's number while they ate lunch in the break room.

"You like Joe?" Julia asked, incredulously.

"He was nice," Sarah said. She couldn't actually remember if he was nice or not. She just remembered that he was loud.

"He's an asshole. You don't want to get involved with Joe Rossi, Sarah."

Too late, Sarah wanted to say.

"I just need to ask him a question about something we talked about that night at the party," Sarah lied.

"A question? What is it? Maybe I can answer it for you."

"No. It was about his work."

"He doesn't have a job, Sarah. What is this *really* about?"

Sarah's face grew hot as blood rushed to it. She couldn't think of anything to say as Julia stared at her. Sarah shifted in her chair suddenly feeling queasy. She looked for the nearest trash can to vomit in.

Julia's eyes widened. "You slept with him, didn't you?"

Sarah shook her head. Words were stuck in her throat, but her tears gave away the secret she desperately wanted to hide.

"Oh my god, Sarah! Listen to me. Joe Rossi is a prick. I've known him my whole life. You don't want to get involved with him. He's nothing but trouble. He doesn't have job, he drinks all the time, does coke and smokes pot every day. He's a loser. He has no future. Seriously. Stay away from him. You can do so much better than him."

Sarah wanted to tell Julia her advice was too late.

"You're turning white. Are you OK?" Julia asked.

Sarah nodded.

"I'm fine, Jules. Can I just have his number? Please," Sarah pleaded, her eyes filling with tears.

Julia's mouth hung open, and Sarah could tell her wheels were turning.

"You're pregnant!" Julia yelled.

Sarah pushed away from the table knocking over her bottle of iced tea. She ran to the bathroom with Julia running after her. Sarah heaved over the toilet while Julia stood behind her in silence.

Sarah's stomach emptied but she felt worse than she had before. She was dizzy and sweating. She knew Julia was standing there, waiting for her to confirm that she was in fact pregnant. At this point, there was no use trying to hide it.

"Yes. I'm pregnant. I just want to talk to him," Sarah said after several minutes.

"And then what? Raise the baby together as a happy family?"

Sarah was getting annoyed with Julia. She was being judgmental and rude. So what if she wanted to raise the baby?

Why did Julia care anyway?

"I just want to let him know."

"Are you keeping it?" Julia asked.

Sarah stared at Julia unsure of what to say. She knew if she kept the baby, it would mean Sarah would never leave New Hampshire, and never see the world she'd always thought was out there waiting for her. She feared ending up like her mother, depressed and non-existent. Then again, a baby might be a ticket out of her father's house away from her own stupid personal hell at home.

"I don't know...," Sarah said.

"You can't keep it," Julia said. "You do *not* want to be connected to Joe for the rest of your life. If you keep it, how will you raise it? I mean, you live with your parents."

Sarah didn't answer. Her mother's chemo and radiation seemed to work for the first few months, but now tumors were growing in other places. The doctor said her body was full of cancer and treatment was no longer going to make a difference. They ordered a hospital bed and put it in the living room. Her father wasn't happy about it, but they had no choice. Hospice now came every day, and her mother was on a heavy dose of morphine. They predicted she'd be gone within a few weeks.

During the moments when her mom came in and out of lucidity, she would tell Sarah about life back when Sarah was born. It was as if her brain was reliving all of the good times in her life before she passed. Sometimes Sarah told her mom about all of the places she wanted to travel. Her mom would smile and gaze off into space as if she was picturing what Sarah was describing. On rare occasions, Frank and Billy would sit with them but they didn't say much.

One day, Frank told Sarah that he wished their mom would die so they could have a normal life. On some level, she knew what he meant, but he was naïve. Life would never be normal in the Kush household, not as long as George Kush was alive. Billy struggled, as he always did, with the guilt he felt that he'd caused their mother's depression because their father had always said that their mother took a turn for the worse after Billy was born. Sarah tried to tell him that it wasn't his fault but he still carried the burden. Now Billy took on the burden of the cancer too even though everyone tried to tell him that none of that was his fault.

Julia kept talking. "Besides, I thought you had plans to travel the country to take pictures. I thought you had dreams of being a photographer. Are you willing to give up all of that?"

"I don't know!" Sarah yelled. "I never saw this coming! It's fucked up I get it. I don't want this! I was planning going to California in the spring. I've just always felt like I need to go there, you know? But now I'm pregnant from a guy I hardly know! So, yeah, Julia, my life is over if I keep this baby. But, I just want to talk to Joe to see if he wants to have a say in this. I mean it's his baby too."

Julia rolled her eyes. "Joe isn't gonna care."

"Will you just give me his number?" Sarah pled.

Julia leaned against the wall, her arms folded across her body. Julia was looking at her with so much disappointment, Sarah turned away. She felt like she'd somehow let Julia down by getting pregnant.

"I'll give you Joe's number, but don't expect him to be all happy for you. If you want to get an abortion, don't expect money from him either. He doesn't have a job remember? Did you know that he got kicked out college for running a gambling ring out of his dorm?"

"No."

"Yeah, well...," Julia said. She pulled a paper towel from the dispenser and took a pen from her pocket. "Here's his number. Just don't expect anything from him."

Sarah took the paper towel and thanked Julia, who stared at her sympathetically.

"I'm not trying to be a bitch. I just know Joe very well, and I've gotten to know you pretty well too. You're too good for him."

Sarah shrugged. "I know."

"Do you? I mean, baby or not, you should take that trip to California. Otherwise, you'll regret it for the rest of your life."

Sarah nodded. "Yeah, maybe."

***

Later, when she was alone in her room, Sarah pulled out the paper towel with Joe's number on it. She stared at the numbers for several minutes thinking about the baby growing inside of her. His baby. A guy she didn't even know. If Julia was right and Joe was such an asshole, maybe calling him was a mistake. She wasn't expecting him to marry her. Hell that was the last thing Sarah wanted. She just needed someone to talk to about her situation and besides, she felt he should at least know that he'd gotten her pregnant.

She dialed Joe's number and when he answered, she hung up and starting pacing around her room. Why did she just hang up?

Dammit.

She pushed the buttons on the phone again and told herself to be brave. After several uncomfortable minutes of explaining who she was and where they'd met she finally asked if they could get together.

"Look, I'm busy," Joe said.

"I'm pregnant!" Sarah blurted.

"What the fuck? You call me out of the blue to tell me you're pregnant? I don't even remember sleeping with you. I don't even remember what you look like."

"Oh," she said. It was as if she'd been punched in the gut. Julia was right she shouldn't have called. She hung up the phone. As she sat on her bed her whole body went numb. What the hell was she going to do? She wasn't even sure she could have an abortion. The thought of it made her uncomfortable. She knew that if her father found out she was pregnant from some random guy he would never let her forget it. He would call her a whore, and her child a bastard.

The phone rang, startling her.

It was Joe.

***

They met in a McDonald's parking lot. She saw the beat-up red truck that Joe had told her to look for and parked next to it. She looked over at him and waved. He raised his hand to acknowledge her but he didn't smile. Sarah's stomach churned as they each got out and met at the back of his truck.

"Hey," he said, avoiding eye contact. His hands were stuffed in his pants pockets. He looked different than she'd remembered. His hair was longer and his tan had deepened over the last few weeks. He also had a beard now that made him look older.

"Hey," Sarah said.

Joe nodded.

After a minute of awkward silence, he cleared his throat. "Are you sure the kid is mine?"

"Yes," Sarah said, trying not to sound annoyed.

"You haven't been with anyone else?"

"No, I haven't," Sarah said.

"Really?" he asked.

Sarah stared at him in shock. "Ah, yeah, really. I'm not a slut."

"But that was like weeks ago. I've been with a few other girls since then."

"Good for you. I've only been with one other guy *ever* and that was in college. So, you are the father!"

Joe pulled a pack of cigarettes out of his pocket. He tapped the package against his palm, pulled one out, and lit it, taking a long drag. "At least I wasn't your first," he said, turning away from Sarah to blow out the smoke.

Sarah thought of what Julia had said—he really *was* a prick. Calling him was a huge mistake, Sarah determined.

"You know what? I'm gonna go. I just thought you should know," Sarah said turning to walk back to her car.

"No, wait," Joe said.

He apologized for not using a condom and blamed the tequila, which he said he would never drink again. He kept his eyes downcast as he told Sarah he didn't want to raise a baby.

"I'm not sure *I* want to raise it. I've spent my entire life taking care of people. It's just…the thought of abortion…I just can't," Sarah said.

"Adoption then?"

Sarah shrugged. "This is all so confusing," she said.

"What do you want from me?"

"I dunno. I guess I just thought you should know."

"I'm not interested in a kid," he said taking another drag of his cigarette.

Her throat tightened. She looked away because she didn't want him to see her cry. She wasn't even sure why she was crying. It wasn't as though she was in love with this guy. How could she abort an innocent baby because of her stupid mistake? Because she was too drunk to ask some stranger if he had a condom. It wasn't the baby's fault, so why should it pay for her stupidity? Unsure of what else to say she told him she'd call to let him know what she decided.

"I don't want to raise a kid, and I don't want to pay child support for the next eighteen years. I'm almost twenty-three and about to get my first real job. My entire life is ahead of me," he said. He raised his voice loud enough that a couple of people turned around as they made their way through the parking lot.

Sarah wondered if the part about the job was a lie based on what Julia had said about him.

"I don't need your help," she said.

"God! Then what do you want from me? I can't handle this pressure."

Pressure. He felt pressure?

"I'm not asking you to marry me. I'll figure it out. I haven't told anyone about this baby yet. I thought you should know since it's yours. You should be careful though; the next girl might not be so nice," Sarah said. Then she got in her car and drove away.

***

Sarah managed to keep her secret from her father and aunt even though she threw up quite frequently and wasn't able to eat much. Her father didn't seem think any of that was strange, but her aunt questioned Sarah a couple times. Sarah told her she'd gone out drinking and that's why she wasn't feeling well. That seemed to appease her aunt.

Sarah still wasn't sure what she was going to do about the baby. As the weeks passed though, she knew she had to make a decision soon. Then at her three-month appointment with the obstetrician, the nurse checked for a heartbeat and everything changed. A few days later, Sarah went back for an ultrasound to confirm what the nurse had discovered.

She rushed home from the doctor and dialed Joe's number. She had expected to leave a message, but he picked up after two rings.

"Twins," she blurted.

"What the fuck?" Joe shouted. Then she could hear him screaming obscenities from far away as if he'd put the phone down and left the room. Sarah bit the skin on the side of her fingers as she waited.

"Seriously, what the fuck?" Joe asked when he came back to the phone.

"I can't keep twins. I'll give them up. Don't worry," she said.

The silence between them lasted several minutes. She could hear the *Price is Right* on the television in the background.

"No. I think we should keep them," Joe said.

Sarah stood up and began pacing around her bedroom. A flutter of excitement, a twinge of anxiety, and a lot of confusion overcame her. "What are you saying?"

"Can I pick you up?" Joe asked.

6

Sarah brushed her teeth and fluffed her permed curls with a pick. She put on lip-gloss and then waited by the front door for Joe to arrive. Her mother was out with Donna at a chemo treatment and her father was at work. She still hadn't told anyone about the babies. She just couldn't deal with that yet.

Joe pulled up exactly twenty minutes after they'd hung up. She ran out to his truck and got in.

"Hi," she said as she climbed up into the cab of the truck.

"Hey," he said without looking at her.

The hole in the floor by her feet, about the size of volleyball, made her nervous. She could see the asphalt below and feel the warmth of the engine on her feet. She tried to act as if it was no big deal, but she couldn't take her eyes off it. She put her purse on her lap and shifted her feet as close to the door as possible.

He was wearing hunting gear—camouflage pants and shirt and a bright orange hat. His face was dirty. Practically everyone in New Hampshire hunted. Her dad even took her hunting as a kid but she never liked all the waiting and being quiet.

The radio blasted a Green Day song as they drove to the

state park. The beach was loaded with families despite the fact it was a cloudy day. They got out of the car and walked towards the lake. Joe led her to the far end away from the people. He picked up some rocks and threw them into the water. Then he skimmed one so far that they both laughed, breaking the ice, as it bounced on top of the water.

"All of this really sucks," Joe said.

"I know," Sarah said.

"I didn't get that job in Boston. My friend told me I had it but I guess the company changed their mind. Anyway, I took a job at a furniture store."

"Congratulations," Sarah said, meaning it but wondering what this had to do with her.

"Thanks. The thing is that this company is very *family-*oriented. The guy I interviewed with said the company liked to hire guys with families. He said I'd have a better chance of getting promoted if I had a one."

"Can they say that?"

"Who the fuck knows. Anyway, my mom always says that accidents don't happen, that everything happens for a reason. I'm beginning to think that maybe you and I are meant to be."

Sarah didn't hide her stunned expression. Was he kidding? They had no connection other than this pregnancy. She wasn't even attracted to him. It wasn't that he was unattractive he just wasn't her type. He was five-ten and had a stocky build. His hair was long in the back and short on the sides and had a natural wave to it. He had olive skin that was golden brown from the summer sun. His eyes were his best feature. They were green and had a certain spark in them that intrigued Sarah. But...he was a furniture salesman; well he was going to be one.

She had always pictured herself with someone tall and blonde. He'd be a doctor or a scientist, someone smart, thoughtful, and well traveled. Someone who would change the world. She imagined her future husband being the guy who took her away from her family, far away. Could she just settle for someone like Joe? Joe the furniture guy. Then again, she was having his babies.

Joe picked up another handful of rocks and began throwing them into the water. She knew he was waiting for her to say something, but what could she say? See this thing through? Meant to be? She wasn't sure how to respond.

Joe turned and walked away from her. She knew she should call out to him, but the words didn't come. She looked for the nearest bench and sat down.

Sarah pulled out the ultrasound images from her pocket and stared at them. Tears filled her eyes as she traced each baby with her finger. She looked up a few minutes later. Joe walked towards her. She stared at him, really looked at him this time. His hands were stuffed in his pockets, his head hung low, and he kicked the sand with his feet. He looked vulnerable and scared. And, well, kinda cute.

Sarah stood up and went to him. When he looked up at her, she saw that his eyes were red. Had he been crying? She melted and threw her arms around his neck. He held her tight.

Sarah showed Joe the ultrasound pictures.

"These are ours?" he asked in awe.

"Yup," Sarah said, putting her arm around him.

They both stared at the pictures of the babies marveling at the detail they could see—their heads, button noses, each spine, their little hands and feet. Sarah told Joe how she could see their hearts beating on the screen.

"It was so cool. They're *alive* in there," Sarah said.

"When you put it like that...how do you...," Joe said trailing off.

Sarah sighed. She'd known too, as soon as she saw the babies, that she couldn't abort them.

They stayed at the park until five, talking and getting to know each other. He didn't seem as bad as Julia had made him out to be. They had some things in common. They both watched the *X-Files* and loved the movie *Rudy*. They also both liked pop music, like Madonna and Boyz to Men, and grunge music. A strange combination to say the least. Stone Temple Pilots was one of his favorite bands too. And they both had a controlling father. Joe was sensitive, and maybe a little immature, but he was nice.

"My father will kill me when he finds out I got a girl pregnant," he said.

"Mine will kill me too," Sarah said, shuddering at the thought of his reaction.

"Maybe if we got married, or at least engaged, it would make them less pissed," he said.

She looked at him. She could tell he wasn't kidding. "It's not the 1950s. We don't have to be married to have a kid," she said.

"You don't know Mario Rossi. He's a religious freak. Trust me—we need to be engaged."

She looked at the families at the lake. Some of the dads swam with their kids, others fished. Her father never did any of that. She looked at Joe and wondered what life would be like with him. Would he be like those dads? She imagined them with the twins at the lake, laughing, swimming, having a picnic. Then, she imagined her father's reaction to the babies and shuddered at the thought.

She thought about California and felt a pang in her heart at the thought of that dream drifting further and further away. Her soul grieved for the life it would never know. She knew her chances of traveling now were slim to none. Why hadn't she left when she had the chance? However, even if she had left, she would have been back by now given her mother's declining health.

Now *she* would be a mother. Not just a pretend one to her brothers who resented her for it. She vowed to make her boys' life better than hers. She would love them and make sure they had birthday parties with lots of friends. She'd make sure they followed their passions. She would never let them go through what she had to taking care of everyone in their life, sacrificing their own hopes and dreams. She'd let them be kids.

"I guess we could get engaged," she said. "I mean, if it doesn't work out, no biggie. But being engaged will help my dad not flip out as much too," Sarah said.

"Cool," he said. "Should we go get a bite to eat?"

"I can't. I have to get home and make dinner for my family. My dad likes his dinner on the table when he walks through the door."

"Maybe I could come with you, and we could tell your folks about us?"

Sarah sighed heavily. She knew that she would have to tell them soon about the babies and now an engagement. She dreaded it. She hated that she had been 'knocked up', just like he had predicted. He would never let her live that down.

Getting married was something she thought she would do when she was thirty, not twenty-two, and definitely not to someone she had a one-night stand with and hardly knew at all. She had pictured romance, love, and passion, not settling for someone and hoping that she'd fall in love later. Nonetheless, the babies were coming whether anyone liked it or not, and now she and Joe would be getting married. *Married.*

Sarah would be *Mrs. Joseph Rossi.*

PART II

2012

7

The dogs greeted her at the bottom of the stairs, whining and wagging their tails. As Sarah patted them, the empty couch came into focus. Joe wasn't there. She and Joe hadn't slept in the same bed for years, but when he came home at night—which was rare lately—he slept on the couch. Her eyes welled.

"He didn't come home on Christmas. That's just awesome," she said to the dogs.

She hated what she was doing to herself, trying so hard when everyone else wasn't, but then again old habits were just that. After she turned forty, she'd begun to see her life differently. Everything that she had dreamed about when she was twenty seemed so distant and childish now. Yet she couldn't stop thinking about the what-ifs. What if she'd run away the day of her graduation and never came back? What would her life be like now? Imagine traveling across the country or maybe the world! Being alone and not having to take care of anyone but herself. Whenever she started to think like that, she stopped herself. If she'd done anything different, she wouldn't have her boys and that was unimaginable.

Lately though, she couldn't stop thinking that soon she'd be the age her mom was when she died. Even though Sarah wasn't depressed like her mother, she could possibly develop cancer and die young like her mother did. Every time Sarah got even a little bit sick, she'd call the doctor and demand blood tests convinced that *this* was the time she'd be diagnosed with cancer but the tests always came back negative.

She also couldn't stop thinking about all of the things she hadn't done or was too afraid to do. She thought of the boys who no longer needed her, her father who was getting more frail, and her marriage that was over the minute it began, so toxic now that if she didn't get out soon it might actually kill her.

For weeks she had tried to remain hopeful that this Christmas was going to be different. Christmas, after all, is a time for forgiveness, a time for cherishing the important people in your life. Life hadn't been easy the last few years, but everyone had bumps in the road every now and then, didn't they?

When they were first married, Sarah and Joe were determined to make things work, if anything to prove to their parents that they could. Joe was romantic and thoughtful—always bringing home flowers or leaving her notes before he left for work. At Christmas, Joe always went all out buying the kids loads of presents. He'd shop after work and sneak whatever he bought in the house when the boys were in bed. He'd proudly show Sarah everything he bought: foam dart blasters, team shirts, and toys that he would stay up for hours to put together. She loved him for it.

However, over the years, all that changed. Life got hard as the bills began to pile up and the boys became harder to manage. Not to mention that sex, which had been wonderful during and after her pregnancy, had become routine, a chore. The mystery was gone.

But all that was normal married stuff. Sarah loved Joe, despite his flaws, because he was attentive, and he took care of her and the boys to the best of his ability. They had their ups and downs but she had always been committed to making the marriage work for the sake of her boys, until recently. She was realizing how short life could be and wasn't sure staying with Joe for the boys was the right thing to do anymore.

Sarah let the dogs out, and then turned on the lights on the Christmas tree and the mantle. A photo on the mantle caught her eyes. The boys were six and sitting on Santa's lap. She took down the frame and ran her fingers over the photo. Zach was crying and Cam had his arms stretched out, desperate for Sarah to get him out of there. Her eyes filled. She tilted her head back and blinked the tears away. She would give anything to go back to a time when her boys needed her and her life had purpose. She set the frame down and looked at the picture next to it. They'd taken the twins to Fenway Park for a game for their thirteenth birthday. In the photo, they all wore Red Sox jerseys and hats that Joe had bought for them with money they didn't have. She and Joe had argued all day over just about everything from the best way to get to Fenway, where to park, how much money they were spending; it went on and on. The boys kept their distance mostly because they were teenagers and everything their parents did embarrassed them but Sarah couldn't blame them on that day. When someone had offered to take their picture, they all smiled as if they were a happy family. Looking at the photo now, you'd never know it had been a disaster of a day.

Sarah had tried so hard all those years to give the boys the childhood she didn't have. She did everything for them because she wanted them to be kids, not mini-adults. She wanted them to have fun, and to remember their childhood as carefree. There would be plenty of time for responsibility and work when they were older. They didn't have to do chores or even bring their plate to the sink when they were done eating. She signed them up for every sport and spent hours in the car driving to this practice or that game or tournament. She volunteered at the school as the room mother in their classes. She served on the PTA and volunteered as the team mom for sports. She helped them with homework and projects for school. When they were older, and all the kids their age were getting jobs, she told the boys they didn't have to work. However, all of that had consequences. Her boys were entitled and disrespectful, and she had let all that happen.

She looked at the tree. All of the ornaments that the boys had made at school over the years peppered it. The boys made fun of her for putting them on each year but those ornaments made her happy because they reminded her of the good times because the good times were now few and far between.

She touched the gingerbread ornament with Zach's photo in the center as the face. Cam's was on the other side of the tree. They were three at the time. That was the year that Joe began staying at work later and later and making frequent trips to Boston for work, or so he claimed. Whenever Sarah questioned him about it, he'd get defensive. She knew he was having an affair but she didn't make a big deal about it because then what, she'd have to leave him? Then where would she go? The thought of going back to live at her father's house was worse than living with a man who cheated so she ignored the fact that Joe smelled like perfume or that he left hotel receipts in his pants pockets. After a year, he started coming home more often and she knew that the affair was over.

She reached for the snowman made out of marshmallows that the twins made in kindergarten. Cam's had black and white googly eyes glued on askew while Zach had drawn the eyes on his. As the twins reached kindergarten, Sarah and Joe had felt like victims of war. They had gotten married, raised two babies, dealt with her mother's illness and death, all before any of their friends had gotten married, let alone had children. Sarah was a stay-at-home mom while Joe worked, but life wasn't easy because money was tight. They were both angry all the time, full of resentment, and exhausted by life. When the twins reached first grade, Sarah decided to put her teaching degree to use and got a job in town as a substitute teacher. Eventually, she got a full-time teaching position in one of the fifth-grade classrooms, and she'd been there ever since. She hated it, but it helped to pay the bills.

Just as she turned to let the dogs in, Sarah spotted something. The hummingbird ornament her aunt had given her was in the middle of the tree, tucked behind a shiny glass ball ornament. She definitely hadn't put the hummingbird there. In fact, she couldn't find it when she had decorated the tree alone one night. She'd searched all of the boxes for it and couldn't imagine where it had gone. Now it was there, staring back at her.

She reached in and pulled it out, remembering her late aunt's words, "Life is meant to be enjoyed." Sarah sighed. If only her aunt was still alive. She turned the white dial on its back and watched the wings flutter. She missed her aunt more than words could describe.

Donna had developed ALS and passed away just two years after her diagnosis. Sarah had cared for her and tried to make her final days as full as she could while she worked and took care of her own family, including her father. When Donna passed, it sent Sarah reeling. Sarah began drinking to numb the pain and taking anti-depressants to help with the grief. If Joe saw her crying, he'd roll his eyes and tell her to "get over it." As if you can simply decide to get over the pain felt from loss. If only it were that easy.

Sarah began seeing a therapist at her doctor's insistence once Sarah began asking for sleeping pills. Now, she was taking so many different medications just to get through the day that she hardly recognized herself in the mirror anymore. Brown bags had settled under her eyes that drooped. She'd gained twenty-five pounds since Donna's death, but the doctor's insisted it wasn't the medication but because Sarah was now "over forty."

Donna had been the one person who truly saw Sarah. She

understood Sarah's plight and the choices that Sarah made, especially the one to stay with Joe.

Sarah knew that seeing the ornament now wasn't a coincidence. Hummingbirds always seemed to show up in her life when she needed the reminder that happiness was there for her if she wanted it. Her boys would be moving out soon, if they made it to college. Then she'd be left with her father and Joe. Her eyes filled with tears just thinking about it.

"Sarah!" Her father called from his room.

"Duty calls," she said as she went to help him out of bed.

After her mother died, Sarah continued to take care of her father. She did his laundry, made his meals, shopped for him, and paid his bills. George couldn't do anything for himself and he refused to learn.

After the stroke, he insisted on living alone rather than go to a facility. He had nurses to care for him but Sarah still had to be over at his house three times a day to check on him, feed him, bathe him, and so on. It was a mild stroke but it caused the left side of his body to be weak and he had trouble with balance. The left side of his face drooped and he needed therapy to help him with everyday tasks like eating. He hadn't lost function of his body but he lacked control, which drove him mad.

When he started a fire on the stove, the doctors told him that it wasn't safe for him to live alone. Of course, her stubborn father fought them. He refused to go to an assisted-living facility or let a nurse live with him full-time. The doctors finally took Sarah aside and suggested she take him in. It was just too dangerous for him to be alone anymore. His physical therapist told Sarah that her father wasn't making progress and that he was getting weaker. Soon he wouldn't be able to get out of bed on his own. Taking him in wasn't something Sarah wanted to do at all but her father's doctors kept insisting he couldn't live alone.

Joe and the twins were mad at her for agreeing to let George move in that they stopped talking to her for weeks. She promised them it would only be temporary—that was six years ago.

Sarah helped her father dress then helped him to the bathroom. When he was done, she brought him to his chair in the living room and turned on the television to his favorite news channel. She went to the kitchen and made coffee before she went up to wake the boys so they could open presents.

The stench of her sons' room filled her nose—a mix of sweat, dirty laundry and something else she couldn't quite place. The room was too small for such grown men. They had given her father the master bedroom downstairs and she and Joe moved upstairs forcing the boys to share a room. She tiptoed carefully around the piles of clothes and shoes that covered the floor. Her heart sank when she saw that Zach's bed was empty.

"Cam, wake up," Sarah said, shaking his leg gently. "Where's Zach?"

Cam mumbled something she didn't understand.

She shook his leg again. "Cam, where's your brother?"

"Ma! I don't freaking know!" he yelled without opening his eyes.

She took a steadying breath. His attitude was at its worst these days; there was no reasoning with him anymore.

"Who had Grandpa's car last night?"

"I did. I dropped Zach off at Mike's," he said from under his pillow.

"Was your father's car home when you got home?"

"Ma! What's with the third degree! *God*…Leave me alone!"

Sarah sighed. "Come down and open your presents. It's Christmas."

"I'll be down in a while."

"I want you downstairs," she said, but Cam's head was buried under his pillow again. Sarah stood over her son, looking around at the messy room. Cups and plates were scattered about; clothes covered the floor so she could no longer see the carpet. She sighed.

"Come on, Cam, please. It's Christmas."

"Mom, chill!"

She left his room hoping that Zach was all right. She told herself that if he'd been in an accident that she would have heard by now. He was like Joe; he hardly ever came home anymore. If he did come home, Zach snuck out in the middle of the night (just as her brother Frank had done at his age) to do God knows what.

Halfway down the stairs she sat down and burst into tears. She had spent weeks shopping, decorating, and praying they could have a civilized Christmas. Now Joe and Zach weren't even home, and Cam wasn't interested either. The last person she wanted to spend Christmas with was in her living room, and yet he was the only one she had.

The dogs must have heard her sobbing because they came up to meet her. Sadie, the Golden Retriever, nudged Sarah's arm for some rubs. Shep, the German Shepherd, panted in her face. She turned her head away from his stinky warm breath.

"OK, OK," she exhaled and stood up to go the rest of the way down the stairs.

In the kitchen, she poured herself a half-cup of coffee and then topped it off with some Irish cream liqueur. She took a long sip before she brought her father his coffee. When she entered the room, she saw Cam sitting cross-legged on the floor looking pissed off. She couldn't help but smile at the fact that he'd come down. She saw remnants of her little boy with his hair sticking up in all different directions; it made her heart tug. Sarah did her best to forget that Joe and Zach weren't there as she pulled out Cam's presents and piled them in front of him.

"God Mom, did you go a little overboard this year or what?"

"I had fun shopping this year."

Cam opened his presents but his enthusiasm was non-existent. Sarah anticipated a reaction to each gift but he'd look at it and then put it to the side, moving on to the next one.

"Can I get some reaction?" Sarah asked after Cam opened Bruins tickets.

"Mom, chill. I like everything, OK?"

If she heard chill one more time, she'd scream.

Cam had always been the one who was up first on Christmas morning making sure that everyone came downstairs at the same time because he didn't want anyone to see their presents first. He wanted everyone to be surprised together. Cam loved to help her make the frosted cutout cookies each year while Zach just liked to lick the frosting off the spoon. She always knew the day would come that the boys would be grown and Christmas would be different but lately the boys were like strangers living with her. Adjusting to that was harder than she thought it'd be.

Her father seemed happy with the presents she gave him—a new pair of slippers, a new robe, books and crossword puzzles, and two flannel shirts. Shep and Sadie sat by Sarah's side, chewing on their new bones as she stared at the tree. She was worried about Zach but the anger grew with each passing minute overshadowing the worry. She wasn't the least bit worried about Joe. She knew he'd probably picked up some slut at a bar and was sleeping off the alcohol he'd drank the night before.

Then the door slammed and like a flash, Zach rushed passed her taking the stairs two at a time.

"Zach!"

"I'm in the bathroom!"

"I need to see you. Now!" Sarah yelled from her spot near the tree.

Her father struggled to stand. He was so stubborn he would never ask for help. He refused to give up the little control he still had. He mumbled something as he hobbled to the kitchen, which Sarah ignored.

Zach came halfway down the stairs and looked over the banister. His eyes were puffy and red. She knew he was hung over.

"It's Christmas. Where the hell have you been?"

"I stayed at Mike's. What's the big deal?"

"The big deal? The big deal is that it's Christmas morning. You *and* your father didn't come home last night."

Zach shrugged. "Whatever."

"It's disrespectful, Zachary. You know how much this day means to me. You could've texted me."

"Mom, I'm seventeen. I don't have to tell you where I am at every second of the day. In like four months I can go to war so I don't need to tell my *mommy* where I am."

Sarah seethed. "Well, you aren't in the Army. You live here, and I have every right to know where you are."

"Mom, chill!"

"Christmas is important to me! Doesn't that matter to you?" Sarah asked. None of the other holidays mattered to her. Christmas made her happy, truly happy. The specials on TV, the decorations, the twinkling lights on everyone's houses, and the fact that everyone seemed a little nicer even if they were faking it.

"Whatever," Zach said shrugging. Then he ran up the stairs and slammed the bathroom door. The shower turned on a few minutes later.

Zach reminded her so much of her brother Frank. He was strong-willed and opinionated and she could never seem to reason with him. Cam, on the other hand, was more passive, like her, until recently.

"They're men now for God's sake. Stop treating them like babies," her father said as he settled back into his chair.

"Dad, not now," Sarah said, holding up her hand.

"You treat them like pansies. Especially him," he said, gesturing towards Cam.

"Fuck you," Cam said to his grandfather as he ran up the stairs to go back to bed.

"Cam!" Sarah yelled, but it was no use. She turned to address her father and saw Joe standing in the doorway. The sight of him made her stomach roll.

"Hey," he said. "Merry Christmas."

"Merry Christmas," her father said.

"I went out with the guys last night and drank too many beers so I stayed at Brian's."

Sarah knew he was talking to her but she couldn't bring herself to look at him. Her father continued the conversation.

"You didn't miss much. Zach just got home too."

Her father had said that all too casually. *You didn't miss much.*

"Um…You didn't miss much? Really? I'd say he missed quite a bit, Dad. It's Christmas morning."

Joe rolled his eyes.

"I spent all day yesterday cooking and cleaning for *your* family today. All so that Joe looks like he has the *perfect* life."

"Oh *whatever,*" Joe said. "You make a big deal out of everything. Just be happy we're home now."

Sarah looked at the tree. She was tired of pretending to be happy everywhere in her life. The pills she took to help with her anxiety were no longer working and neither was the alcohol. She couldn't start her day without some liquor in her coffee, and as soon as she got home from work, she poured herself a large glass of wine. One glass was never enough. She finished a bottle every night. At work, Sarah was short with the children and her co-workers. Teaching was never something she enjoyed doing, but now it felt more like a lifetime sentence than a job.

Joe went to the kitchen. She could hear him fixing his coffee. Life would go on. No one cared that she was upset. His family would come over later and she would have to pretend that everything was fine.

She reached under the tree and picked up the present she had bought and wrapped for herself. It was a new lens for her camera. She wanted to take a photo of the lake on the way to the studio.

"I'm going to the studio. I'll be back later," she called out as she put on her coat.

"Are you fucking kidding me?" Joe asked. "You just bitched at me for not being home, and now you're leaving? *It's Christmas,*" he mocked.

"I'll be home before your parents get here, don't worry about it."

"Why do you get to leave? When I go out, it's the end of the world but you can do whatever you want? I thought this day was *important* to you?" he said, sarcastically.

"The difference is that I'm telling you I'm leaving and when I'll be back. Besides, your family isn't coming over until three. I'm not sitting here all day while you all sleep off your hangovers."

"I'm not taking care of your father."

"He'll be fine for a couple of hours."

"You don't even see how selfish you are," Joe said, as he pointed his finger into her chest.

She could sense the familiar feelings begin to rise of wanting to yell back, or retaliate his poke with a slap, but she didn't do that anymore.

"I'll be home before anyone arrives," she said, then walked out the door as Joe yelled at her.

8

Sarah drove with the radio off so she could concentrate on driving. The roads were slippery from the recent snow and her window kept fogging up. She fought back tears whenever she thought about the fact that Joe hadn't come home last night. She knew it only meant one thing—he was cheating again. She couldn't, no she wouldn't, handle that anymore. It was time to make a change, she knew that, but she also knew taking the next step would be the hardest.

She stopped at the lake and attached the new lens for her camera. She got out and walked around a little bit snapping pictures staying only a few brief minutes before continuing to the studio.

She unlocked the door to the studio and turned on the lights. Sarah could see her breath inside, which meant Jim had turned the heat down since no one would be in there for a few days. She kept her coat on while she turned on the equipment. Within a few minutes, she began to smell the heat.

Whenever she was at the studio, she never thought about the drama at home or at school, and today was no different. She turned on her iPod, put on the Jennifer Lopez station on

Pandora, and spent a couple hours developing the pictures from her last trip to the lake.

"You're still here?" Jim said, as he walked in.

Sarah was packing up to leave. It was just before one in the afternoon. She had texted Jim to let him know she'd be there. The fact that he showed up meant that he'd come to check on her.

"Just packing up," she said. "Merry Christmas."

"Same to you, but I have the feeling it wasn't so merry for you."

She shook her head and turned away. She knew that if she looked at him she would start to cry.

"Wanna talk about it?" he asked.

"Not really, but thanks. It's just the same stuff over and over, that's all."

"You know how I feel."

"Yes, I know," Sarah said.

Jim had never liked Joe and for years had tried to get Sarah to leave him.

"Life's too short. You should be enjoying it not just getting through it," Jim said.

Jim and her father had grown up together although her father never mentioned it. Jim said that they played basketball together for the high school team. "I remember when he started dating your mother," Jim once said. "She was a pretty girl, very nice too. Always smiling."

Sarah couldn't remember her mother *ever* smiling.

"Someday I will get to live my life," she said laughing at the thought. Her life…what was that?

Jim sighed. "You keep saying that but you never do anything about it."

She wasn't in the mood to go through all of this again. Jim meant well but he didn't live her hell or know the real reason she stayed. She said goodbye to him and kissed him on the cheek.

"Thank you for caring," she said.

Jim patted her shoulder and then squeezed it. "I mean it,

kid. Life's too short."

Jim came out of the studio as she got into her car. He was waving a piece of paper and saying something. Sarah hurried over to him so he wouldn't slip on the ice. He was in his sixties now and recently had bypass surgery.

"I almost forgot," he said, as Sarah approached. "This came the other day, and I think you should go. I'd be willing to help you pay for it if money's an issue."

He handed her a pamphlet for a photography conference in Las Vegas in January. She read the details of the conference. She could learn technical skills, new shooting styles, meet some of the most famous photographers, and learn how to start or grow her own photography business. The last one made her insides flutter. She would give anything to quit teaching and focus on photography full time.

"I have school. And my dad…"

"Take some time off. You hate that job anyway. Besides, it's only four days and two of them are on the weekend. As for your father, Linda's there."

Linda was the visiting nurse who'd been taking care of Sarah's father for years. She spent eight hours a day at the house caring for George, bringing him to doctor appointments, and doing light cleaning. She had become a great friend to Sarah over the years. She was compassionate and understood the challenges of Sarah's situation of having to care for a loved one with a prolonged illness. Sarah often confided in Linda about work and the boys. But, Linda didn't work nights or weekends. There was no way Sarah could leave for the weekend and go to Vegas without someone to care of her father.

"I don't know. I'd have to think about it."

"What if I booked you a flight and gave you no choice?"

She kissed his cheek. "Give me a few days to think about it."

He reluctantly agreed. Sarah loved that Jim was so protective of her. If it hadn't been for Jim, she never would have survived the last twenty-five years.

***

She pulled into the garage and turned off the engine of her Rav-4 keeping the radio on to hear the last chorus of her favorite Christmas song. Tears streamed down her face as she sang along to Faith Hill's *Where Are You Christmas*. It made her cry every time it came on the radio but the tears came harder now. She was trying so hard to make this year's Christmas memorable, but as usual it was all going unnoticed.

As the song ended, she sighed and wiped the tears from her cheeks with the back of her hand. She checked her face in the mirror and swiped away the black eyeliner that had puddled under her eye with a purposeful finger. Then she took a deep breath. She would need all of her strength to get through the rest of the day.

Shep and Sadie greeted her at the door, whining and wagging their tails. She patted them for a minute before she went to check on her father. Joe was splayed on the couch, still in the same clothes from yesterday.

"Dad, do you need anything?"

He looked pissed off as he turned to her. He waved his hand and shook his head.

"Where are the boys?" she asked.

"I don't know for Christ's sake! They don't tell me!" he roared.

"Why are you yelling at me? I asked a simple question."

"Just go cook or something," he said, as he turned up the sound on the television to drown her out.

She called downstairs to see if the boys were there.

"What?" Cam yelled.

"Where's Zach?" Sarah asked from the top of the stairs.

"Sleeping."

She went to the kitchen, poured herself a glass of wine and took her anxiety pill before she started to get everything ready for Joe's family to arrive. She thought about the photography conference that Jim told her about and took out the pamphlet from her coat pocket. She wondered how she could make it work but it seemed to daunting a task. She stuffed the pamphlet back in her pocket as the doorbell rang.

Joe's parents were always early and the first to arrive. Today, they were an hour early.

"Where's my Joseph?" Joe's mother Judy asked as she hugged Sarah. Judy had aged very well. She kept her hair stylish and dyed it blonde to cover the gray. She was dressed in a black skirt with fashionable black high-heeled boots that came up to her knee. The boots raised her small five-foot frame by three inches so she was almost eye-to-eye with Sarah. Her sweater was red for the occasion. *Cashmere*, Sarah thought as she hugged her mother-in-law.

Sarah sighed heavily as she said, "He's sleeping in the living room."

"What about the boys? I have presents for them!" Judy said excitedly.

"Zach is sleeping upstairs and Cam is in the basement," Sarah said, holding back the urge to make some snarky comment about how Zach hadn't come home last night.

"They need to come say hello to their grandmother," Mario commanded. When Mario spoke everyone was supposed to jump and do whatever he said—and mostly everyone did. At sixty-nine, Mario still had a full head of jet-black hair, which Sarah imagined he dyed. He was only a few inches taller than Sarah, maybe five-six. He'd put on some weight over the years but it was all in his belly. His legs were like twigs.

Sarah called out to the boys, but neither responded.

"Joe must have worked a lot this season. Poor guy," Judy said.

"Yeah, must've," Sarah said sarcastically, as she went to the kitchen. Truth was Joe had been fired from the home improvement store three months ago for not showing up. Sarah had only discovered that because she had gone to the store to see him and his boss told Sarah the truth. She waited for Joe to tell her about being fired but he kept the lie going for weeks, telling her he'd worked overtime or he made up some story about a customer from his day. Sarah went along with it, amused by his ability to lie with a straight face, until they couldn't pay some bills. When she confronted him, he shrugged and said, "I was going to tell you eventually." That was a turning point for her. Even though they'd had their fair share of hard times, she still cared about him. However, he didn't seem to care about her in the least.

"How about some wine?" Judy said.

Sarah got out a glass and filled it while Mario went to say hello to George. Sarah heard him wake Joe. *Let the party begin*, she thought.

She called down to Cam from the top of the stairs and told him to come say hello. He grunted frustratingly as he paused his game before coming up to say hello to his grandparents. As soon as he was done, he went right back downstairs to resume playing his Xbox.

Joe's sister Cristina and her husband Andrew arrived next with their three boys ages nine, seven, and five. They were wild and drove Sarah's father crazy. All day he yelled at Sarah to make them be quiet. Sarah ignored him. His sister Monica and her husband Rich came later with their teenage kids, Tyler and Grace. Their kids were both straight A students and played multiple sports. They were destined for greatness, or so their parents told anyone who'd listen. Both of Joe's sisters worked in the restaurants that Mario owned. Monica's husband was the head chef at the Oak Street location. Tyler and Grace both worked there too. Zach had bused tables for a few months but quit because "It was too hard." Mario never let him live that down. Cam worked as a dishwasher one day a week at the Main Street location but he hated every minute of it. He only did it because Mario insisted on it.

After dinner, they all opened presents. Sarah had her father go into his room so that everyone could be in the living room without him yelling at them to be quiet. She turned on his TV and got him situated before returning to the chaos in the living room.

Zach turned on his charm and was actually pleasant to be around. He always had such a way with people. He could make anyone feel important. Even though he might not have cared about Grace's softball scholarship to the University of New Hampshire, he asked her about it, congratulated her, and told her he'd come to her games. He played board games with the younger kids too. Seeing him laugh and smile made Sarah's heart happy but it made her wonder why couldn't he talk to her like that. Zach was always quiet around her and he always seemed angry.

As everyone was getting ready to leave, Cristina handed Sarah a small rectangle present wrapped in red and green plaid paper. Sarah didn't hide her surprise; the adults didn't exchange gifts.

"Just something little," Cristina said.

Sarah carefully opened the wrapping paper. It was a picture frame. Inside the frame was a photograph of a ruby throated hummingbird in flight. Its wings were blurry as the creature fluttered at lightning speed hovering in front of a vibrant red flower.

"I took it last summer," Cristina said. "I know how much you love them. Those are the flowers on my front porch." Cristina had been taking photography lessons at the studio for a while now. The photo was really beautiful.

"Thank you," Sarah said, as she hugged Cristina. "I love it!"

"Why do you love hummingbirds so much?" Cristina asked.

"My aunt once told me that hummingbirds represent freedom. Something I never had much of as a little girl."

"*Please*…you had freedom," Joe said, rolling his eyes.

Sarah shot him a look. She wasn't in the mood to fight with him.

After his family was gone, Sarah was in the kitchen putting away the remaining dishes. Joe came into the room and sat down at the kitchen table.

"Today was good," he said.

"Well this morning sucked, but yes, the rest of the day was good," Sarah said.

"Oh my fucking God! Can we just move on? Why the fuck do you have to drag everything out!"

"Oh! OK, I'll sweep everything under the rug like your *mother*! I'll go on pretending that you are perfect and that our life is perfect!"

"I give you everything! And all you do is disrespect me! I work my ass off and you never appreciate me!"

She folded her arms in front of her chest and faced Joe who was now standing next to her. His arms were folded across his chest too with his hands tucked under his armpits. It was how they fought now, face-to-face, arms tucked away. No more evidence.

"Give me things? You've been in and out of work for years! All of *this* is because of *me!*"

"Don't be a fucking cunt," he yelled. He got close enough so that his nose touched hers. He breathed heavily like a bull about to charge.

Sarah had vowed not to fight with him anymore. The first time it happened was when Joe was laid up with a broken leg. He hurled a tennis ball at Sarah as she put groceries away in an effort to get her attention. The ball hit her in the temple, startling her. Without thinking, she whipped the ball back at him. "Don't ever throw anything at me again!" she said.

Joe had laughed and demanded a beer. After that it was small pushes or slaps to the back of the head or shoulder. Sarah didn't fear him the way she feared her father so she fought back. Then one day, he shoved her head so hard that Sarah fell to the floor. She immediately got up and fought back. It was instinctual. No one had ever pushed her like that before.

Their fighting escalated until one day the boys came home from school and witnessed their parents shoving and slapping each other. Sarah would never forget the looks on their faces; their eyes wide and mouths hung open. Cam was on the verge of tears. Zach stared at Sarah, narrowing his eyes as if he was mad at her. At the age of eleven, they were used to her and Joe arguing but they'd never seen them be physical. She couldn't imagine what they were thinking. She immediately went to them and pulled them close but Zach pushed her away. Cam leaned his head into her chest.

Joe pushed by them, got in his truck, and drove away. Sarah tried to talk to the boys but Zach went to his room and slammed the door. Cam just wanted to know if Sarah was hurt. She assured him she was fine, but she was lying.

She would never have predicted she'd end up in an abusive relationship. She was smart and educated. How could she have let things get to this? She knew in that moment that she couldn't allow the abuse to continue. That night she packed her bag. It was time to end the charade.

Joe came home and found her in their bedroom with her suitcase open on the bed. He grabbed her arm and leaned in close to her ear. "I've been keeping pictures of the bruises you give me. I've been documenting it for years. If you leave me, I will expose you for the abusive bitch that you are. I will make sure that you get nothing. I'll make sure you never see the boys again."

The last thing she wanted was to lose the boys. Besides, would anyone believe that they were both participants in the abuse? The fighting stopped for a while after that day but soon they just became much better at hiding it: grabbing arms, pinching, shoving. All things that left bruises but that could be hidden or explained easily.

Now, as she walked away from him, he grabbed her arm.

"Let go of me!" Sarah yelled.

"You know what your problem is? You don't know your place!"

"My *place*? What the fuck are you talking about? My place has been taking care of all of you. When have you ever wanted for anything? When have I ever *not* taken care of you?"

"I haven't had a blow job in years," he laughed.

She reached up and shoved him away. "Fuck you, Joe! You didn't come home last night. How do you think that makes me feel?"

"I got home this morning. We could have had a great day but you were the one who pitched a fit and went to *the studio.*"

"You weren't at Brian's last night were you?"

"Oh, *come on,*" Joe said, rolling his eyes.

She shoved him on his chest with both hands. He stumbled back catching himself on the counter and then he lurched at her and grabbed her neck. She put her hands up to block him.

"STOP! I mean it! STOP!"

She wondered if her father was listening. Before his stroke he would have come in and defended Joe. The stroke had its benefits.

"I'm tired of living like this," she said with desperation in her voice. "Please, I can't live like this anymore. Let me go. Just let me go."

"We aren't getting divorced. I'm Catholic, we don't get divorced."

Sarah laughed. He was a Catholic who hadn't gone to Mass in the eighteen years they had been together. Their marriage had been at city hall, so technically it wasn't even recognized by the church, which Judy reminded them of whenever she got the chance. Joe didn't care about divorce, he was more afraid his father would cut him out of his will. As hardheaded and old fashioned as her father was Mario Rossi was worse. He was an old school Italian and believed in family and the institution of marriage. "People don't divorce," he once said. "They stick it out until they die."

"Stop using religion as an excuse. We don't love each other anymore. I'm not sure we ever did. It's time to end this," Sarah said.

"No divorce!"

"Oh, but cheating and lying are OK?"

Joe shook his head.

She heard her father calling her from the other room. She straightened her shirt and fixed her hair before she looked in the living room to see if what he wanted.

"Stop yelling at him," he said, pointing his crooked finger

at her.

She fought the urge to throw something at him.

"Mind your own business," Sarah said.

Then she went into her office, slammed the door shut, and cried.

9

The day before New Year's Eve, Sarah went to the movies with her friend Meg. Each year, they went to all of the movies that were getting Oscar buzz before the awards ceremony aired in February. Then they'd watch the show on TV together rooting for their favorites. She'd met Meg through the boys and baseball. Meg's son was one year older than the twins, but the boys were always on the same baseball and soccer teams. She and her husband, Mike, also had two younger daughters—one was in eighth grade and the other was a freshman at the high school

Meg had a way of making everyone in her presence feel important. Being friends with her was easy. Sarah and Meg talked about books and movies and went yard-saleing together on Saturday mornings, scouring for antiques. Sarah could tell Meg things that most people wouldn't understand. Meg listened, rather than judged, and offered thoughtful advice when needed. She told Meg about what had happened over Christmas as they rode to the movie theater.

"Maybe it's time to get away like you've always dreamed of doing," Meg said.

"You have no idea how close I am to doing it."

"Then do it. For once, do something for you," Meg implored.

Sarah told Meg about the photography conference.

"But, I don't know. I have school and the boys, my dad...," Sarah trailed off.

"You overthink everything—that's why you're stuck here. Look, I know I've said this to you before but you really need to listen to me. You gotta stop putting everyone else first. People like your father and Joe are only taking advantage of the fact that you can't say no. It's time to stop living in fear."

She knew that Meg was right, but she didn't know how to change who she was. She'd been doing it forever, and it wasn't something she could just stop.

"You've told me how you always dreamed of traveling the country and taking pictures. Why not go to Vegas for a few days and see where life takes you?" Meg asked.

"I don't know..."

"You're allowed to be happy, Sarah."

Sarah looked out the car window and watched drops of rain run down the glass. If she went away, she would have to spend a week preparing meals that the boys could put in the microwave or that Linda could heat for her father before she left for the night. She'd have to get all the laundry done, pay the bills, and clean the house. It was so much work for a few days. Then there would be all that work when she got home: dishes piled high, laundry to do, cleaning. Never mind how she'd have to prepare lessons for a substitute at school. She imagined Joe's reaction when she told him she was leaving for a few days. He'd get angry, sulk, make her feel guilty for leaving, and even resort to jealousy. "Who are you meeting there? Will guys be there?"

Ugh, she thought, *too much hassle*.

"I'll think about it," Sarah told Meg as they went into the theater.

***

On New Year's Eve, Sarah reluctantly got ready for the

party her friend Jen was hosting. The thought of going to a party and pretending that everything was fine between her and Joe was draining enough, never mind having to deal with Jen.

Jen had lived in Sarah's neighborhood when they were little until she moved to the next town over when they were freshman in high school. They had tried to keep in touch, but Jen became boy-obsessed and started doing drugs, so Sarah stopped answering her calls.

Jen moved back to Lincoln a year ago because she got divorced. Sarah bumped into her at the gas station in town, and they seemed to pick up where they left off in high school with Jen needing constant reassurance and Sarah offering it. Jen didn't have any children and was hell-bent on showing her ex that she could find another guy to love her since he'd left her for a much younger woman.

Jen begged Sarah to go with her to concerts and bars, which Sarah did, but she never told Joe where she was going. He'd never let her go to a bar without him. She had to lie and say she was going to the studio or out with friends from work. Jen would often meet a guy while they were out and leave Sarah alone. Therefore, when Jen suddenly stopped the constant calls and texts Sarah took it as a blessing and never questioned her. Tonight would be the first time Sarah had seen her in few months.

Sarah stood in front of her closet in her bra and underwear. She pushed her clothes from side to side looking for something to wear. After trying on and discarding several different outfits, she settled on a black dress she'd worn to many parties and weddings in the past. She looked at herself in the mirror. The lumps, bumps, and rolls were getting harder to hide with clothes. She vowed to work out in the New Year.

She threw a scarf around her neck, grabbed her gold wedges, and went downstairs. Joe was at the kitchen table playing a game on his cell phone. She told him she was ready. He didn't bother to look at her as he got up and went outside to the truck leaving her to follow behind him. She made sure her father had everything he needed before she left.

"I'll be home right after midnight. Will you be OK?" Sarah asked her father.

"I'll be fine," he said without taking his eyes off the police drama he was watching.

They drove the twenty minutes to Jen's house in their usual silence. Jen greeted them at the door and handed them glasses shaped like '2013'. Jen said she was too busy entertaining to talk but the beers were outside on the deck. Then she fluttered off. Sarah wondered if Jen's new fuck-buddy was at the party. Sarah assumed that was why Jen wasn't calling her anymore, because she was busy with some new guy.

Sarah and Joe parted ways, each quickly finding other people to talk to. Other husbands and wives seemed to be joined at the hip but Sarah was used to being alone.

She kept her eye on the clock willing it to midnight. They'd only been at the party for ten minutes and all she wanted was to go home, get out of her uncomfortable dress, and stop acting as if she liked any of these people.

As midnight approached, people poured fresh drinks for the midnight toast, gathered hats and noisemakers, and found their kissing partner. Sarah stood alone in the corner of the room. Joe was nowhere to be found. She walked outside to the deck, figuring he was out there smoking pot, but he wasn't. She went all around the house searching for him.

Someone shouted "One minute!" and everyone gathered by the TV to watch the ball drop. Sarah went to the basement but Joe wasn't down there either.

"30 seconds!"

Sarah wished she could disappear.

"20 seconds!"

Sarah made her way through the crowd. No one seemed to notice her, never mind ask her where she was going as she grabbed her coat from the closet and went out the front door.

She ran down the front steps as the house erupted in

cheers. "HAPPY NEW YEAR!"

She approached the truck and narrowed her eyes trying to process why the windows were fogged up. Was the truck moving? She pulled open the driver's side door. Sarah's jaw hung open. Joe and Jen were tangled up in the backseat, naked with sweat pouring off them; they both turned and looked at Sarah.

Her entire life flashed in front of her. The lying, the cheating, her father's demands, her mother's illness, her lack of childhood, and now her boys drifting further and further away. Meg was right—she was allowing all of this to happen. She was to blame.

"Get out of the car!" Sarah screamed maniacally, her body shaking uncontrollably.

Joe and Jen scrambled to gather their clothes and cover up their nakedness. As soon as they were out of the truck, Sarah got in the driver's seat and left them standing together. Neither said a word to her as she pulled away.

All of the other times he'd cheated, she'd somehow managed to pretend it didn't happen because she would have had to admit that her entire life was a lie. Now the image of the Joe and Jen naked, in this very truck, made feel her sick.

She pulled over and threw up.

***

Sarah flew into the house and stormed upstairs. She ignored her father, who asked what she was doing. She dug her pre-packed suitcase out of the closet and flung it on the bed. She threw in more clothes and shoes without thinking about what she was putting in. She went to the bathroom, gathered her makeup and other necessities and put those into the suitcase too. She looked at all of her medications lined on her nightstand, but decided to leave them there.

The image of Jen and Joe together came rushing back. How could she have let this happen? Not only was he cheating again but he was cheating with *Jen*! She sobbed and pounded her fists as she screamed into her pillow. It was an ugly cry.

When she finally calmed down, she looked at herself in the mirror and saw the shell of the person she had become with such clarity. "You are a *fool*," she said. Adrenaline ran through her veins like quick-moving lava, and suddenly her mind was clearer than it had ever been. It was time to go. She unzipped her dress and left it in a heap on the floor. She pulled on yoga pants and a sweatshirt, and tugged her long brown hair into a low bun. She took off her wedding ring and threw it on her bureau.

She went to her office and emailed her principal.

Dear Tony,

I won't be returning after vacation. I'm sorry to do this to you. I don't know when I will be back. Something has happened and I will be unreachable for a while. I'll get in touch when I return.

Sarah

She took a piece of paper and wrote a note for Joe that she taped to the refrigerator.

I will be gone for a while. YOU can explain this to my father and the boys. Have fun with that.

She couldn't even think about the boys. If she did, she would never leave. She'd call them when she had time to process everything. Right now, she needed to put as much distance between her and Joe as possible. She went into the living room and asked her father if he needed anything.

"Where's Joe?"

"I'm sure he's still at the party. Do you need anything?" Sarah asked, trying to steady her voice so he wouldn't realize she was upset.

"What happened?"

"Nothing, Dad. Do you need anything?" Sarah said, annoyed with his questions.

"What's wrong with you? You in a hurry or something?"

Frustrated, Sarah stormed out of the room. "You have two minutes to tell me if you need anything. Otherwise you're on your own!" Sarah called out.

She let the dogs outside, then went to her office, and packed her camera equipment, including the new lens she'd bought for Christmas. She piled everything in the kitchen before she went in one last time to see her father.

"I'll take a soda," he said.

Sarah brought him a soda, kissed him on the head, and tucked the blanket around his legs. She left the room without saying a word.

She brought her things out to her car and went back in to let the dogs inside. She kissed Sadie on the head and rubbed Shep's back. "I'll miss you two the most," she said.

She sat in the car and stared at the house. They'd moved in when the twins were one. They were being evicted from their apartment and needed a place fast. When the realtor showed them the house, it was a mess. It hadn't been cleaned in years and it smelled like cat piss. Sarah hated the house—it was too big and needed too much work inside and out—but Joe put in an offer anyway. When he came home and told her that he'd bought it, she cried. It wasn't her dream home and she had wanted to keep looking, but the offer was accepted within hours and the house was theirs. Over the years, she'd grown to love the house that was the place where she'd raised her boys. It had history. Now, as she stared at it, she felt detached from all that had been. Life had changed and so had she. She had sacrificed everything she ever wanted by marrying Joe.

Sarah pulled out of the driveway and didn't look back. She drove all night, determined to put as much distance between her and home as possible.

10

Sarah checked-in to a hotel in Ohio and took a long, steamy shower before calling Meg. Even though she'd dreamed about running away her entire life, it didn't feel as freeing as she thought it would. All she could think about was what would happen to her when she returned. How her father and Joe would make her pay for humiliating them. It wouldn't matter that she'd caught Joe having sex with her friend. All that would matter was that she abandoned them and her *duties*.

Fuck my duties, she thought as she toweled dry. Her breath came faster as her body reacted to the anger that swelled inside her.

"I didn't do anything wrong!" she yelled into the mirror. "I put up with all of their crap for way too long. I couldn't care less what they think!"

She dressed and called Meg.

"I can't believe you actually left!" Meg said.

"I'm surprised it's not the talk of the town."

"We were away, remember? I just got back today. I called your house, and Linda said you haven't been seen or heard from in two days!"

Sarah took a deep breath and filled Meg in on what had happened on New Year's Eve.

"Shit, Sarah. What's your plan?"

"To get to Vegas for the conference, then I don't know. I just need some time to clear my head. Don't tell anyone that you heard from me. I'm going to call the boys next but they probably won't answer their phones anyway."

"I never understood that. You're their mother, they should be required to answer the phone, or they get the phone taken away."

"Meg…," Sarah pleaded. It wasn't the first time Meg tried to give Sarah parenting advice, but she just wasn't in the mood for it now.

"I'm sorry," Meg said. "Keep me posted and stay safe. Let me know if you hear from Joe."

"I threw my old phone out the window in New Hampshire. He doesn't have this number. And, I deleted my Facebook."

"Great, that means he'll be calling me," Meg said.

"Please don't tell him you heard from me."

"I can't lie. You know that."

It was true; Meg was the worst liar that Sarah had ever met. It didn't help that Meg was a huge believer in karma and thought bad things would happen to her if she lied.

"You know how hard this was for me," Sarah beseeched.

"I know. You're right. I told you to do this, and I support you. I won't tell Joe anything. Just keep me posted where you are so I know you're all right. OK?"

"Keep an eye on the boys for me, please," Sarah said, her voice breaking.

"You got it."

She hung up with Meg and called both boys and, as predicted, neither answered. She sent them texts and waited for them to reply. She fell asleep waiting.

The next morning she woke at five a.m. and checked-out of the hotel. Neither Zach nor Cam had texted her back yet. She imagined all the men in her life sitting around in the living room, discussing the fact that she was gone. She wondered if Joe had told them the truth about his cheating, or if he'd conveniently left that part out.

She sent Jim a text. She knew he would worry about her.

I'm sorry I left without saying goodbye. Things are complicated. I'm going to Vegas for the conference.

Jim responded immediately.

Good job, kid. I heard what happened. Been in touch with Linda. Take as long as you need.

Sarah's eyes welled. His encouragement gave her the resolve to keep going.

After eight hours of driving, she got off the highway and found a shopping plaza that had a couple of discount stores, restaurants, a movie theater, and other shops. She parked her car in the last row of the lot near the far end of the shopping plaza. She didn't think anyone would bother her there. She reclined the seat, got a blanket from the back, and slept.

She woke up three hours later cold and hungry. She went into one of discount stores where she changed her clothes in the bathroom and brushed her teeth. She bought some bottles of water to keep in the car, and then she drove over to one of the chain restaurants where she sat at the bar and ordered dinner. She called Linda.

"Oh, I wish you hadn't called me," Linda said. Her voice was low as if she'd just been caught doing something she wasn't supposed to be.

"Why?" Sarah asked, confused.

"I really don't want to be in the middle."

"In the middle?"

"Yes, of you, and your father, and your husband."

"I'm sorry," Sarah said. "I just needed to know how things were going there. The boys won't answer their phones."

"If I were you, I'd keep going wherever it is you're going,"

Linda said.

"What? Why?" Sarah said, confused.

"It hasn't been good here. Your father is mad as hell that you took off like that. It's all he talks about. Joe hasn't even been here in the last few days, and the boys are in and out. Zachary is staying with a friend, and Cameron been here but he's not saying much."

"I should come home," Sarah said, imagining the chaos.

"No! Don't!" Linda insisted. "I talked to Jim, and he told me what happened at the New Year's party."

"How does Jim know?"

"Someone told him, I guess. He called to make sure that your father would be taken care of while you're gone. He said he would pay for everything your dad needs."

Sarah drew in a sharp breath as tears filled her eyes. Jim. He was always taking care of her like that.

"But the boys...," Sarah said, choking back tears.

"The boys are seventeen, almost eighteen. It's high-time they grew up," Linda said. "They'll find a way to push through. Cameron is a lot stronger than you think, and I have a funny feeling Zachary is too."

Sarah wiped the tears from her eyes, hoping no one was watching her, although there weren't too many people in the bar who seemed to care about her right now.

"How long do you think you'll be gone?" Linda asked.

"I don't know. Maybe a week. I'm heading to Las Vegas for a photography conference. After that, I really don't know."

"If you want my advice, stay away until you feel strong enough to make the tough decisions you've been putting off for a long time."

"But my dad...," Sarah said.

"Your father will be fine. I mean it. It's time for you to get stronger. Come back when you're ready to face all of this with a clear head. The boys will be OK, trust me."

Sarah had spent her entire life doing the right thing for everyone else. Maybe Linda was right. It was time for her figure out what she really wanted.

11

Sarah approached the "Welcome to Fabulous Las Vegas Nevada" sign, and a wave of chills went down her spine. She let out a squeal of excitement that she had finally made it.

Over the last week she'd thought about turning around several times, but then the image of Joe and Jen all sweaty and naked in Joe's truck would pop into her mind and propel her forward. The boys were still ignoring her texts and calls, but their mother left them; she couldn't blame them for being upset. Mothers don't leave their children. But she wasn't leaving them for good. She'd be home after the conference. She would explain everything to them when she returned.

She drove slowly down Las Vegas Boulevard with the people behind her honking their horns. She didn't care though; she wanted to take it all in! She passed the dancing water fountains, the Eiffel Tower, and the Italian-inspired canal complete with gondolas. It was hot, and there were hundreds of people walking along the strip. The energy was intoxicating. She found the hotel where the conference was being held and pulled into the valet area.

"Welcome to the MGM!" said the hot, young valet as he opened her door. He wore tan shorts and navy blue short-sleeved shirt that looked like it was one size too small but it accentuated his muscles in all the right places. He was clean-shaven and his teeth gleamed white.

"Thanks!" she said, as she got out of the car trying not to stare at him.

She drew in a deep breath as she looked around. Sarah had a few hours before the conference started, so she checked-in and then went to the casino.

Sarah walked down a long hallway towards the casino, passing all of the high-end stores. She stopped and looked in the windows, wondering if the people inside shopping had just won big. The lights and sounds of the casino bombarded her as soon as she entered it, along with the faint smell of smoke, even though there was a sign that said the casino was "non-smoking."

She stood behind the crowd gathered at the craps table, trying to understand the game, but she ended up leaving even more confused. Everyone cheered as the dice rolled to reveal the numbers they'd bet on. Too afraid to join in, she moved over to the blackjack table. Even though she'd played blackjack with her father many times before, Sarah had never been to a casino. She watched for a while before deciding to move on.

She walked through rows and rows of slot machines. The jangly sound of music and hum of wheels spinning and levers snapping drew her in. She sat down at a machine next to an elderly woman. She put some money into the penny slot machine and pulled the lever. She watched as the cherries and sevens rolled around at lightning speed. As they stopped, she sighed. She didn't win.

"Keep tryin!" said the elderly woman sitting next to her. She wore a visor and had a heavy sweater on because, as Sarah learned later, the casino was always so cold. The woman's purse was across her body, and she held it tightly on her lap. She had a southern accent.

"OK!" said Sarah, excitedly. Then she pulled the lever again.

"I've been here all day. I won a hundred bucks!" the

woman said.

"Wow! That's great!" Sarah said not knowing if that was great or not. It seemed like very little for sitting there all day.

"Ah, well, I'm waiting for the big pay out. My daughter is over there," the woman said gesturing to her daughter who was sitting at a machine down the line. The woman Sarah was talking to was in her eighties and her daughter appeared to be in her sixties.

"That's nice that you two are here together," said Sarah, feeling sad that she never got to do anything like this with her own mother.

"We're both retired, so we come here every day."

"Every day?" Sarah asked.

"But we only play the penny slots because we live on a fixed income."

Sarah nodded. She suddenly felt sorry for them, wondering what kind of life that was, coming to a casino day after day to play penny slots. It seemed dismal, and yet, probably better than sitting at home watching hours of daytime television like her dad. At least they were out and socializing a little bit.

The woman gave Sarah tips on how to play and after a while, Sarah began to win. An hour later, she realized it was time to check-in at the conference. She was up by ten dollars. Happy with her winnings, she cashed out.

"You can't leave now," said the elderly woman. "You just put in all that money. That machine will pay out big soon!"

"Oh well, maybe next time," Sarah said. As she walked away, Sarah saw the woman slide over to her machine and put some money in. She stopped and watched, secretly hoping the machine would be a winner. The woman pulled the lever four times then slid back to her machine.

She walked through the lobby of the hotel on her way to the conference center, passing another casino and the pool. The hotel was bustling with activity. Kids were running around, couples walked hand-in-hand. The conference attendees were easy to spot with their tote bags and lanyards around their necks.

She found the registration booth and got in line. There were three lines arranged by alphabet. She listened to everyone talk to each other as if they were old friends. It made her feel uneasy, as though she didn't belong.

A large sign welcomed conference attendees. It read, "Get ready to change your life!" Sarah smiled. The conference was geared towards wedding and portrait photographers, which she wasn't. Although, Jim thought it was the direction she should go if she wanted to make a career from photography. It wasn't that she was opposed to doing weddings or portraits; it just wasn't her passion.

"What's the name of your business?" asked the woman behind the table when Sarah got to the front of the line.

"Oh, I don't have a business. I'm just here to learn," Sarah said, self-consciously.

"Don't be ashamed of that! That's why we're all here!"

Sarah gave her name and the woman handed her a badge and a bag full of freebies: pens, notepad, lanyard, and a small flashlight. Sarah quickly checked her itinerary. Her first class started in an hour. She checked the map to find her classrooms and then decided to explore the vendor hall.

She looked around the exhibition room in awe at the number of vendor booths. She walked down the first aisle, stopping to look at photography books, camera equipment, and software. At the Canon booth, her jaw dropped at the amount of equipment on display.

"Impressive, isn't it?" a woman asked.

"Definitely," said Sarah, looking at all the cameras, lenses, and other accessories.

"What do you shoot with?"

"Oh me?" Sarah said, embarrassed. "I'm just an amateur."

"It's OK," the woman said, putting a hand on Sarah's shoulder. "We all start out as amateurs. What do you use for a camera?"

"Oh, um, a Nikon D7000."

"Great camera. Do you have it with you?"

Sarah held up her bag indicating that she had it.

"Can I see some of your shots?"

Sarah turned on the camera and scrolled through the pictures to find one she felt was good enough to show the woman. She settled on a shot of the mountains just after a fresh coat of snow. It was sunrise and the sky was a lovely mix of pink and purple. She handed her camera to the woman and watched as her eyes lit up.

"I love the composition in this photo! You've done a nice job with balance too."

Sarah smiled feeling proud.

"What's your name?"

"Sarah Rossi."

"Well, Sarah, you're definitely not an amateur. These photos are absolutely stunning!"

"Thank you," Sarah blushed.

"If photography isn't your business, it's time to make it your business. You could have a great career. Here, let me show you some of our equipment."

"Oh, I don't have any money."

"I'm not here to sell you anything. Just to show off our products and get people excited about them. We encourage people to test the equipment too. I mean, sure, if you bought something that'd be great, but mainly we're here to show everyone what's new."

Sarah felt embarrassed. She had never been to a trade show before.

She followed the woman into the booth and listened as she told her all about their line of cameras and lenses. She even let Sarah try a few. After about an hour of walking through the exhibit hall, it was time for Sarah's first class. She had signed up for basic courses that could apply to any area of photography: lighting, finding your creative style, and how to start a photography career.

She took a seat in the middle of the room, on the aisle. She was the third person to arrive. The other two were busy on their smartphones. She took out a notebook and a pen and waited as everyone else began to arrive. The room filled quickly. As she looked around, she felt as if there was a neon sign pointing at her in screaming lights that read: AMATEUR!

Then the instructor began, and Sarah forgot all about feeling out of place. In fact, she had never felt a greater sense of belonging in her life. It was as if she'd finally found the tribe she didn't even know she'd been searching for—people who, like her, saw what she saw when looking through the lens. The people who took classes at Jim's studio were doing it for fun, not because they had a passion for photography. Here she felt as if she belonged.

She discovered she knew much more than she gave herself credit. When some people asked questions, Sarah mumbled the answers to herself before the instructor responded. Soon, she had the confidence to shout out the answer. At the break, she went to get a bottle of water.

She texted Jim:

I made it to the conference in Vegas. It's incredible here! Thank you for telling me about it.

Within a minute, she got a response:

Jim: Glad you like the conference. I knew you would. Hang in there kid. And have some fun. =)
Sarah: I am. ;-). Be home soon.
Jim: Don't rush back. Take some time for you. You deserve it.
Sarah: Thanks.

Sarah's eyes filled with tears. Jim was always telling her to have fun—maybe it was time for her to do just that.

"How'd you like the class?"

Sarah looked up to see a man standing next to her. He was very tall with broad shoulders. He had dark hair and dark eyes with long eyelashes. He was good-looking but not in an obvious way. She was drawn to his cool, calm energy. She wiped the tears from her eyes.

"It was great! I really liked the teacher," said Sarah.

"Yeah, she was great. I'm Jack. Jack Morrissey," he said, as he reached out his hand.

"Hi, I'm Sarah. Sarah Rossi," she said.

His hand enveloped hers. He squeezed it but not too hard. Something inside her stirred. She pulled her hand away as she blushed.

"Where are you from?" Jack asked.

"New Hampshire."

"Whoa! You came a long way!"

"I did," she said. "How about you?"

"Arizona."

They both nodded as they stood in awkward silence. His eyes pierced hers, forcing her to look away. Jack looked a little younger than Sarah but not by much. He told her he was a high school teacher and had come to learn some new techniques to show his students. Jack, like Sarah taught, as a means to pay bills, but it wasn't his passion either. *We have something in common,* Sarah thought.

"What class do you have next?" Jack asked.

"Oh, I'm taking the Master Class next."

"Me too!" Jack said.

Sarah smiled. She checked his left hand for a wedding ring. Nope. No ring. Then she wondered if he was gay. Why else would he be talking to her? But as the day went on, Jack sat next to her and flirted with her, and Sarah flirted back.

At the end of the day, Jack asked Sarah to join him for dinner.

"No strings. We can talk about photography," Jack said, smiling at her.

His entire face lit up when he smiled. It was hard to say no to that face.

***

Sarah woke thirsty and needing to pee. The clock read 3:23. She could still feel the effects of the alcohol she'd consumed earlier. She wasn't sure if it was day or night; her room was so brightly lit. She pulled herself out of bed and went over to look outside. It was dark, yet bright lights illuminated the boulevard. The street was filled with cars and there were loads of people everywhere as if it was the middle of the day, not the middle of the night. She turned around and saw Jack lying naked in her bed. His body was lean and sexy. His muscles weren't bulging but Sarah could tell he spent some time in a gym.

Earlier they had a delicious meal in the steakhouse restaurant and drank two bottles of wine. They talked about photography and swapped stories about teaching. Sarah learned that Jack was a widower. His wife had breast cancer and died eight months ago, just two years after their wedding. They didn't have any kids. Sarah shared that she'd recently discovered her husband was having an affair with her friend. She told Jack she had left home but she left out the part the twins. She didn't want to explain everything and ruin the night because they were having such a good time. Jack was genuine and kind, and it was refreshing to talk to someone who shared her passion.

After dinner, Jack offered to teach her how to play craps. Sarah took him up on the offer. At first, they watched other people roll the dice while he offered commentary in an attempt to help Sarah understand the game. Everyone cheered and clapped with each roll of the dice. The game, although still confusing to Sarah, was incredibly exciting. The camaraderie between the people surrounding the table was infectious.

Then Jack took a turn rolling the dice while Sarah stood next to him. He asked her blow on the dice for good luck. When he rolled a seven, Jack turned and kissed her on the lips, sending electricity down her spine. He picked up the dice and had her blow on them again. He seemed unfazed that he'd just kissed her, so she brushed it off as innocent.

After an hour, Jack was up by five hundred dollars and he decided to cash out. They left the craps table laughing. He had his arm around her shoulders as they cashed in his chips with the cashier.

"Did you have fun?" Jack asked.

"The most fun I've had in a very long time." Sarah said, not wanting the night to end but it was close to midnight, and she was feeling very drunk now after all the wine she had drank at dinner not to mention the free drinks she indulged in at the craps table.

They stood close in the elevator as they ascended to their respective floors—he was on the ninth, she was on the fourth. The elevator stopped at Sarah's floor and she stepped out of the elevator, saying goodbye to Jack, but he followed her out.

"Is it just me or do we have...a connection?" he asked, as the elevator doors clapped shut.

Sarah smiled. "It's not just you."

Then he stepped towards her and pulled her to him. Jack kissed her lips and lingered there. Sarah relaxed into the kiss. His lips sent a jolt of electricity shooting through her body. She couldn't remember the last time she kissed Joe. They barely spoke never mind made-out. Then the image of Joe and Jen flashed in her eyes. What was she doing? She pulled away.

"I'm sorry, I can't. I'm...married."

"I know. I'm sorry," Jack said. "It's just...you're so sexy. I can't help myself."

Sexy? Sarah thought. No one had ever called her that before. He reached for her hand and looked into her eyes. His thumb rubbed the back of her hand.

"Well...when you put it that way," she said smiling.

"I'm just sayin...," he said, staring into her eyes.

People came and went from the elevator as they stood holding hands and staring at each other. His smile lit up his eyes and made her heart thump. It'd been a long time since she'd even thought about sex. Would she even know what to do? She wasn't even sure when she last shaved her legs. She thought about Joe again. Why was it so easy for him to cheat?

Why had she been so faithful all these years? Didn't she deserve pleasure too? What was holding her back? She didn't know.

"Let's go," she said, pulling Jack towards the hallway that led to her room.

"Really?"

"What happens in Vegas stays in Vegas," she said, laughing.

The door to her room was barely shut when he pulled her to him again. His arms wrapped around her as he kissed her. She'd never been kissed with that kind of desire before. She felt light as air as his tongue played with hers. She lifted his shirt and ran her hands up his back. Jack pulled off her shirt and kissed her neck, sending chills down her spine. It had been years since another human being had touched her like this. Her mind was spinning. He unhooked her bra and slid it off, exposing her breasts. He ran his thumbs across her nipples causing her legs to grow weak. Then he led her to the bed. He sat down while she stood over him. Jack looked up at her, rubbing her back.

"Are you OK?" he asked.

"Yes," she said breathlessly.

"I just want to make sure—"

Sarah stopped him with a kiss. She was sure. Having sex with Jack was exactly what she needed in this moment. If she thought about it anymore, she might not continue. She kissed him and pushed him down onto the bed. He held her and they kissed again.

"I have a condom," Jack said, as he pulled it out of his pocket.

"Oh, right," Sarah said, feeling silly for not thinking about protection. She wondered why he had one and if he planned to pick up some woman at the conference. She decided to let that go. "I don't do this very often. I mean, I do *this* but not…well…pick up guys and—"

Jack stopped her with a kiss. He slid off her pants and soon they were both naked, their bodies pressed together.

Sarah felt safe in his arms. Jack took his time, kissing her neck and everywhere else on her body. She'd forgotten how amazing sex was. Sex with Joe was rushed and there wasn't any foreplay. He never cared if she was satisfied. Jack definitely cared. Sarah's body reacted in ways she forgot were possible. Although, she couldn't help but wonder what he was feeling. Was she the first woman he'd been with after his wife died? Even if she weren't, she appreciated that he was being so tender with her.

Now, as she watched Jack sleep, Sarah wondered if she should wake him. Was she obligated to spend the day with him now? She really wanted to wake him and have sex again, to touch his body and to feel his touch again, but he was snoring lightly, so she decided to let him sleep. She, on the other hand, was too keyed up to sleep. She scribbled a note to Jack letting him know she'd be back soon. Then she dressed, put her hair in a ponytail, and went down to the casino. She played the slots for a few hours, feeling happy.

Going to the conference was the best thing she'd ever done for herself. Just being around all these people, who loved the art of photography as much as she did, was invigorating. She learned new techniques, made connections, and met Jack.

Still, she wrestled with guilt. She felt guilty for leaving New Hampshire like she did, and ashamed that she'd had sex with a stranger. She looked around. Even though it was seven in the morning, the casino was full of people. What was she doing here? The ride to Las Vegas had taken a week, and it was exciting. She had a destination. Now, she had to drive home. Back to face Joe, her father, the boys…The thought of going home now was equal parts scary and depressing. She cashed out her small winnings and went up to her room.

Jack was sitting up in bed, watching TV.

"Good morning," she said.

Sarah handed him the coffee she'd bought downstairs and sat on the other side of the bed.

"Morning. Thanks for the coffee."

"I didn't know how you took it, so I got it black. I think there's cream and sugar in here somewhere," she said, as she stood.

"Black is fine."

Sarah sat back down.

"You OK?" Jack asked.

Sarah sighed. "Yeah."

"Well, that didn't sound too convincing," Jack said.

Sarah turned to face him.

"The conference ends today, and that means I have to go home. And…it's just…," she said, trailing off. It's just that home was the last place she wanted to go.

"And…home is complicated," Jack said.

"Exactly."

"You don't have to rush back," said Jack.

Sarah shrugged. He made it sound so easy.

He reached out and held her hand. "I know. We made things more complicated last night. Don't get me wrong, last night was incredible, but I'm not looking to make your life more complicated," Jack said, smiling at her.

"Last night was pretty incredible," she said, thinking about his body against hers.

"You're the first woman I've been with since my wife died. On one hand, I feel guilty about that, but on the other, I'm really happy it was you."

Sarah smiled. She felt the same way.

"Look, any man that can't see how great you are doesn't deserve you," Jack said. "You're smart, funny, incredibly sexy, and you deserve the best. Maybe you don't have to go home just yet," Jack said, reaching for her hand.

No man had ever said she was sexy before. It made her giggle. She'd never seen herself that way. The fact that Jack did made her wonder what sexy really meant to him, but she didn't ask.

What *if* she didn't go home yet? Where would she go?

"What about going to California?" Jack asked, as if reading her mind.

"I've always wanted to go there," she said.

"Well, there you go! It's only four or five hours from here. Go for it!" Jack said.

Sarah smiled at the thought. Jack leaned in and kissed her neck sending the familiar jolt down her spine. She pulled him to her and he rolled on top of her. Sarah pulled off her shirt while he shimmied off her pants. He kissed her from her toes to her neck until she couldn't resist him anymore.

Sarah thought about the idea of going to California as Jack went to the bathroom after they finished making love. She could drive four hours towards home...or, four hours to get to the one place she'd dreamed about going her entire life.

"I'm going to head to my room to get ready for my class at nine," Jack said, as he came out of the bathroom.

They compared classes, and unfortunately, they didn't have any together.

"Thanks for a great night," he said, as they hugged near the door.

"No. Thank you," Sarah said, kissing him. "You were so sweet to me and I'll never forget that."

"No, really. This was the first time I've laughed and felt this alive in a long time. Thank you for that," Jack said.

Sarah told him she felt the same way about him.

"I won't forget you," Sarah said, meaning it. She was relieved that he didn't seem to want anything else from her, like a phone number or to see her again.

"Maybe I'll see you next year?" Jack asked.

"Maybe," she said, smiling. "You can always find me at the slots," she laughed.

"Oh, come on! Have I taught you nothing? Craps is where it's at!"

They laughed. Then he kissed her.

"Take care of yourself. And go to California, will ya?" Jack teased.

"I just might," she said.

He kissed her one last time and then he was gone. Sarah took a shower and got ready for her next class. Jim and Jack were right; it was time for Sarah to have some fun. She was this close to California; it would be silly not to go. Besides, what's another couple of days? Life back home would wait just a little longer.

12

Sarah left Las Vegas on Monday morning on a mission to get to California. Going home wasn't an option just yet. She'd only just begun to feel free. When she started to see the signs along the highway for Laguna, she turned up the music a little louder, and danced to the beat.

She arrived in Laguna, giddy with excitement. She ran across the street to the beach. Volleyball nets waited for someone to play. The basketball courts were empty too, as were benches along the path. She walked for a while on the beach before she took off her shoes and stepped onto the cool sand. She couldn't help but smile when her feet hit the Pacific Ocean. The cold water shocked her; she hadn't expected that. Then again, it was January.

She walked along the beach for a little while before her stomach growled and she began to feel lightheaded. Sarah went back to her car and continued driving through town on the Pacific Coast Highway.

The town reminded her of any seaside town in New England with its quaint shops except here palm trees lined the street. Sarah couldn't help but look up at each one to admire them. She made mental note of the many art galleries, one after another, and couldn't wait to explore them. She turned up the radio and smiled from ear to ear as she danced to a Katy Perry song. After all these years, she was finally in California!

She spotted a hotel overlooking the ocean and pulled in the driveway. The Inn at Laguna Beach was located in the heart of downtown atop a bluff that overlooked Main Street Beach. Sarah went inside and asked for a room. They only had one room available—the Sunset Vista suite. It was expensive but the manager said it was the perfect place to get lost in the sunset. That sounded perfect to Sarah so she told her she'd take it.

Sarah ate a quick breakfast in the hotel's restaurant before going up to her room. The large suite had two bedrooms, a small kitchenette, and a bathroom as big as her kitchen back home in New Hampshire. A deep tub built for two sat in the middle of the bathroom. The shower, also built for two, had two showerheads on each side and one rain showerhead in the middle. It seemed a little too extravagant for one person, but Sarah told herself she deserved it.

She opened the doors to the balcony and stepped outside, taking everything in with all of her senses—the sounds and smell of the ocean, the warm air grazing her body, the scenery. To the left was the beach she'd walked earlier. She grabbed her camera and snapped some photos.

She couldn't stop smiling. She'd dreamed about this moment, of being in Laguna Beach, her entire life. She stripped naked; as if she was removing the suit of armor she'd been wearing her whole life. She didn't care if anyone was watching. The cool air brushed across her bare skin. She danced and shouted "I'M FREE!" Before anyone could look up to see her, she ran inside and into the bathroom to take a long hot shower before she went to sleep.

Sarah awoke midafternoon, thirsty and hungry. She went down to the lobby and took a free apple and a granola bar from the coffee station, and then went out to sit on the beach to read. She was reading *Anna Karenina* by Leo Tolstoy again.

When she first read the book in college, it didn't speak to her. The book was difficult to understand and relate to then. However, when her mother was dying and Sarah was spending endless days sitting in the hospital by her mother's side while she had chemo treatments, Sarah found the book in the hospital's library. This time, the story hooked her in from the first sentence: "All happy families are alike; each unhappy family is unhappy in its own way."

Suddenly, the book took on a completely new meaning for her. Anna, stuck in her situation and realizing that the only way out was to take her own life. Sarah could relate to that. It was one of her all-time favorites; since college, she had read it four more times. Her favorite quote by Tolstoy was "If you want to be happy, be." Today, as she sat on the beach in Laguna, she was happy, truly happy for the first time in her life.

At dinnertime, Sarah asked the concierge for a place to eat. The young woman gave her directions to a restaurant within walking distance.

Sarah spotted the Mexican restaurant that the concierge said had the best margaritas and guacamole. It was a five-minute walk from the hotel. The restaurant's large full-length windows were fully open to the outside. As she walked by, she could smell warm corn tortillas. A waiter stood at a table by the window, making guacamole for his guests. Sarah's mouth watered as she inhaled the smell of garlic. She went in and took a seat at the bar. Even at eight o'clock on a Wednesday night, the restaurant was quite busy.

Sarah caught a glimpse of herself in the mirror across the bar and chuckled. She still wasn't used to seeing herself like that. She had long, straight brown hair for most of her adult life, but now her hair had blonde highlights and was cut into a bob style. While she'd waited for a flat tire to be fixed—somewhere in Iowa—she'd found a salon and told the young girl to do whatever she wanted. The girl took her literally, but Sarah was OK with it. She played with her hair while she waited for the bartender.

"What can I get for you?" the bartender asked, as she set down a cocktail napkin.

"Margarita on the rocks."

"Sure thing."

Sarah watched the attractive bartender pour her drink. The girl's thick blonde hair draped down to the arch of her back. Her flawless twenty-something body didn't have an ounce of fat on it, and her legs were long—they seemed to extend on forever. Her skin was tan and her breasts were clearly not God given; they were two perfect circles. The bartender put the margarita in front of Sarah, along with a bowl of warm, salty tortilla chips and fresh salsa.

"Is it always this busy on a Wednesday?"

"Oh yeah," the bartender said. "We're going non-stop around here. During the summer, you have to make reservations weeks in advance. This is our slow season."

Sarah nodded and took a long sip of her perfectly mixed margarita.

"How is it?" the bartender asked.

Sarah gave her the thumbs-up sign.

"Are you here on vacation?"

"Um, yes," Sarah replied. She wasn't sure how long she was staying, whether it was a few days or more.

"Where're you from?"

"New Hampshire."

"New Hampshire, huh? What do you think about Laguna?"

"No comparison! It's so different here."

"Well, we do have the most beautiful people, sunsets, and beaches. You'll love it."

"I hope so. I've risked a lot to be here," Sarah said. Why did she just say that? Maybe the tequila had already gone to her head.

"Really? Did you leave your *man*?" the bartender said in a tone indicating she ready to hear a juicy story.

Sarah thought carefully about her answer. "You could say that. I was tired of dragging through life and not really living it. I wanted more, he didn't."

"I can totally understand that. Good for you for making the change! Do you have a place to stay?"

"I'll be at a hotel for the next couple days. After that, I don't know."

"Brandon!" the bartender yelled across the bar to a guy who was staring down at his cell phone.

He raised his head of thick dark hair and smiled. Brandon appeared to be a few years older than Zach and Cam.

"Does your father still have the cottage available?"

Sarah's eyes widened. *What is she doing?*

"Yeah, he can't find anyone acceptable enough for him to rent to," Brandon called back.

Sarah sensed a hint of sarcasm in his tone. The bartender turned to Sarah.

"I just found you an apartment! Take this number and call Will tomorrow," she said, as she grabbed a pen and a napkin and wrote a phone number on it. "He's Brandon's dad. Great guy. His place is about a twenty-minute drive from here, in Laguna Hills, but his apartment's cheap and clean and the best part—furnished. He only wants to rent to older people, no offense. But, you know, people who are responsible." She pushed a napkin across the bar to Sarah.

Sarah picked it up looked at it before she put it in her purse. *I won't be needing that.* Sarah smiled, trying to recover from the "older people" comment. Her birthday was just a few months away, and she was feeling less and less okay with it. There was still so much living she had to do.

She ordered guacamole and pulled out her book.

13

The next morning, Sarah asked the woman at the front desk for ideas of places to photograph. Heisler Park was at the top of the list, so she made it the first stop of the day. She walked by the restaurant where she had eaten the night before and remembered the napkin with the phone number on it that the bartender had given her. Getting an apartment seemed too permanent, she thought. But...she'd already spent more than she'd intended and wouldn't be able to afford hotels much longer. Maybe it made sense? She shook her head. No, she had to go home soon. This was just a vacation, nothing more than that.

She turned the corner and the ocean came into full view. The park, which was perched on a cliff above the ocean, had spectacular gardens, many palm trees, and footpaths that stretched north to south. On the plush green grassy area, there was a group of women doing yoga. It was bright, yet hazy out, with a soft breeze blowing as she walked along Cliff Drive. She breathed deeply and felt her entire body relax.

She watched the ocean roll in peacefully. Joggers quietly padded the pavement, bikers whizzed by like flashes, and elderly couples strolled in their quiet way. On the benches, a few homeless people slept under palm trees, but she decided they were harmless. She photographed the gardens, and then attached the telephoto lens to capture the view that stretched down to Laguna's Main Street Beach. She thought about how much Jim and the others at the studio back home would love it here.

She walked to Monument Point, the veteran's monument, and took more pictures. The area around the monument had concrete benches and a coin-operated telescope. Seeing the telescope gave Sarah a pang in her heart. Her boys would have run straight to it when they were little. Her eyes welled with tears. She quickly wiped them and kept walking.

After an hour, Sarah began to feel dizzy and in need of food. At the main road, she looked around unsure of which way to go. A woman walking hurriedly with her dog stopped at the crosswalk and pushed the button to change the light so she could cross. Sarah tried to get the woman's attention but the woman didn't notice.

"Excuse me," Sarah said, a little more loudly this time. The dog barked startling Sarah and his owner.

The woman pulled ear buds out of her ears. "Can I help you?" she asked, breathlessly.

"I'm looking for a place to get some breakfast. Can you point me somewhere?"

The chocolate lab sniffed Sarah's shoes. She couldn't resist bending down to pat his velvety ears. The woman pointed to the camera in Sarah's hand and said that she might love the Garden Café across the street.

"The food is yummy and they have an impressive garden hidden in the back that might be great for taking pictures."

Sarah thanked her for the suggestion. With that, the woman put her ear buds back in and crossed the street. Sarah ran across the street in the opposite direction.

Sarah stopped in front of the Garden Café. It was a small, fairy-like house. She pushed open the small white gate and entered a yard that was covered with vases and gnomes of all shapes and sizes. Plastic pink flamingos, life-size garden angels, glass globes, potted plants, and fairies were everywhere. She walked slowly, taking it all in.

As she got to the porch, she saw that the front door, painted a bright indigo blue color, had a "CLOSED" sign on it. Sarah sighed and turned to leave when suddenly a man came barreling out of the door holding a large sign that read, "OPEN." He let out a yelp at the sight of Sarah.

"Ohmygoodness! You scared the *crap* out of me. I thought one of those creepy statues had come to life!"

"Sorry," Sarah said, holding back a giggle.

He was average height and appeared to be in his late forties. He had thinning brown hair with wispy blonde highlights. His jeans were rolled up on the bottom like the Rat Pack in the fifties. He wore shoes with no socks and a white button-down shirt rolled up at the sleeves and unbuttoned to the middle of his chest. He reminded Sarah of someone on TV, but she couldn't place whom.

"No, no, no!" he said waving a hand above his shaking head. "Don't apologize honey, I'm just losing my mind is all. We open at eight and since it is now eight-oh-five we are officially open, and I am *late* getting out the sign." He covered one side of his mouth with his hand and leaned into Sarah. "Please don't tell Michael. He'll *kill* me. I'm late every damn day getting the sign out, and he swears we lose business because of it! God, he is such a drama queen."

He replaced the "CLOSED" sign with the "OPEN" sign and told Sarah to follow him inside.

"I'm David, by the way," he said, as he went behind the counter.

"I'm Sarah," she said, smiling at David, whose energy seemed boundless.

"So, you want some breakfast, I assume? Maybe I shouldn't assume. You do want breakfast, right?"

Sarah nodded.

"Well, Michael is in back and ready to go, so what would you like?"

"Well, coffee and I'll take a suggestion on what to order."

"Honey, if you don't get the green apple pancakes, you'll regret it. Then again, the California omelet is delicious too."

"OK, I'll go with the apple pancakes and coffee."

David directed her to the garden then walked hurriedly toward the kitchen. "I'll bring the food out when it's ready," he called back to Sarah.

Sarah followed the sign that pointed towards the patio. She rounded the corner and stepped down onto the cobblestone path. Her eyes lit up as she took in the most impressive, tranquil place she'd ever seen, breathing in the fragrant smell of flowers in bloom. A large lemon tree at the back of the garden towered over the space. Other plants had pops of bright lavender and cobalt blue flowers. Purple salvia lined the walkway, and bursts of orange flowers sprouted up from behind. A red flower she'd never seen before caught her eye, so she snapped a few pictures of it. Ferns and grass helped to cover the fences and buildings to the left and right. Birds chirped and butterflies fluttered past. Then, out of nowhere, she heard the familiar whizzing sound of hummingbird wings.

The bird hovered over a red flower as it began to drink the nectar. Careful not to move too suddenly, she brought her camera up to her eye and began clicking the shutter as fast as possible. It's bright purple head and green iridescent body was so different than the red-throated hummingbirds she was used to seeing back home. Within seconds, the bird was gone, but for that fleeting moment, an intense feeling of peace came over her.

A fountain on the other side gurgled, as did a small man-made pond next to it that was filled with lily pads and koi fish. The memory card on her camera was almost full after she clicked some shots of the pond, so she chose a table toward the middle of the garden and looked through her photos.

She jumped when David called out to her as he entered the garden.

"I'm sorry, I was lost in thought," she said, apologizing for her reaction.

"I saw that. I was only asking if you'd like some more coffee," he said, swirling the hot pot.

She nodded her head, and he poured her a cup.

"So, you're vacationing?" David asked.

"Did this give it away?" she asked as she held up her camera.

They laughed as David sat down across from her. Sarah poured two creams and two packets of raw sugar into her cup and stirred slowly. David tilted his head as he stared at her.

"There's something about you I can't put my finger on," he finally said.

"Do I look like a long lost relative or something?"

"No. No. That's not it," said David sitting back, crossing his legs, and folding his arms across his chest. "No, there is something. I just can't put my finger on it."

Sarah liked his candor so she decided to play along.

"Ax-murdererish?"

David let out a loud "HA!" and laughed. "Hardly, darling. No, more like a cat that ate the canary."

"I did not eat a canary today, or any day for that matter," she teased.

A voice yelled from inside that there were customers waiting. David rolled his eyes.

"OK, Mr. Bossy. I'm coming! I'm coming!" David shouted, as he got up and left Sarah alone.

A few minutes later, a group of five women, all dressed in yoga clothes, entered the garden. Every one of them had perfectly tight bodies and perky boobs. They were all talking at once. Sarah wondered if anyone was actually listening to each other or if they even cared what each other was saying. Thankfully, the women settled on a table in a distant corner of the garden far enough away from Sarah.

David came back to the garden with two plates in his hands. Green apple pancakes for her and a blueberry muffin for him. He set the plate full of pancakes in front of her. The sweet and spicy scent of the cinnamon filled her nose, making her mouth water. He sat down across from her and began picking at the top of his muffin. Sarah didn't know whether she should be annoyed by his company or grateful for it.

"Shouldn't you be out front waiting for customers?" she asked.

"Yes, but you seem lonely. I can deal with Michael later. Besides, he's busy now with all of their orders," he gestured over to the large group of women. "And, *Miss Nosy Pants*, I made sure to put the bell on the door knob, so when someone comes in, I'll know and he won't have a conniption fit. Anyway, back to you. How are the pancakes?"

She'd just taken a large bite. The pancakes tasted even better than they smelled. The gooey texture of the cinnamon sugar mixed with the fluffy pancake and green apple was delicious. The pancakes didn't even need syrup, but she put it on anyway. Her mouth was still full when she answered, "Delicious! Good choice."

"You know," David said, tilting his head to the side and pointing his finger at her. "I think I just put my finger on it."

"On what?" she asked.

"You remind me of me."

"In what way?"

"Well, about twenty-five years ago, I left my wife."

Sarah swallowed hard and coughed.

"God darling, don't choke. It's shocking, I know, but I had a wife once. We married right after college. She was the first girl I had ever been with, and the last for that matter." He let out a snort. "I asked her to marry me because people were starting to question my sexuality. I wasn't ready to be outed yet, so I asked the girl to marry me to distract people. Sadly, she said yes. Her prospects were slim I'm afraid, still are I'm even more afraid to say. Anyway...," he said as the bells on the door began to clang. "Hold that thought," he said as, he hurried to the front.

Sarah laughed. David was like a breath of fresh air. It was strange, but she felt an instant connection with him. Yet she couldn't help but wonder, what was the point of him telling her all that?

She ate her pancakes slowly, savoring each bite as she waited for him to return. She finished her coffee and found herself wishing she had a cold drink. Whenever she had too much coffee, her head began to throb. She rubbed her temples and put on her sunglasses.

She sat back in her chair, full from breakfast, and wondered where David had disappeared to, when suddenly the place erupted in a flurry of activity. Various sized parties of people entered the garden, and David ran out holding a large tray over his head filled with food for the group of women behind her.

On his way by Sarah's table he leaned in and said, "Sorry love, but our conversation will have to wait. We just got a bus full of people, and I'm the only one here today. The girl that usually works here left the other day to move to Hollywood—not that she has a chance in hell of becoming a star, but *whatever!*"

Sarah looked around. There was no way David could handle all of this by himself.

"I don't have anything going on today. Maybe I could help," she said. She'd never worked in a restaurant before, but she had waited on several people her entire life. How different could it be? Besides, she hadn't felt useful in weeks; it might be fun.

"Oh darling, Michael will kill me, but I'm taking you up on your offer. You're going to have to be the runner. Come on, grab your plate and cup and I'll show you where to put them. Come on! Chop, chop!" he said, rushing off.

Sarah hurried behind him, trying to keep up. They went into the kitchen where a tall, brawny guy moved around quickly, banging pans. He wore jeans and a sleeveless black shirt with a red bandana tied around his head. His full head of black hair was peppered with gray.

"Michael," David called out, but Michael either didn't hear him or he ignored him. Sarah couldn't be sure.

"MICHAEL!"

Michael turned around quickly only to turn back just as quick to continue scrambling eggs on the hot top. Sarah only had a second to take in how handsome he was with his intense blue eyes and Tom Selleck mustache.

"What's the emergency!" he called from the stove.

"I just want you to meet Sarah. She's going to help me today."

Michael turned around again, this time lingering a little longer as he focused on Sarah, who waved at him tentatively. He turned back around and said nothing. As comfortable as David made her feel, Michael made her feel equally as uncomfortable. His eyes were penetrating and he seemed annoyed by Sarah's presence. David pulled Sarah over to the warming station and told her to ignore Michael.

"He's intense, don't worry about it." Then, he explained how everything worked in the kitchen. "He works very efficiently, so you won't get too confused. When you hear the bell, put the plates on a tray, then carry them out to the garden. Each table will have a number on it, so just look for the number on the food ticket and there you go. Sound easy enough?"

Sarah nodded. Michael continued to work and didn't look up again as she and David talked.

"OK. Here, put on this apron," David said at the precise moment that Michael banged the bell. "God, Michael! Couldn't have you just told us the order was ready? We're standing right here for God's sake!"

"Customers are waiting!" Michael roared.

Sarah flinched; she'd heard that tone one too many times. It stirred something inside her and her heart began to race. Memories of her father and Joe demanding things from her bubbled to the surface, and she wondered if she'd last an hour.

Since leaving New Hampshire and making decisions based on her wants, her needs, she was acutely aware of the control her father and husband had on her. They constantly criticized her. Everything from the orange juice she liked and they didn't, to her new clothes, to the curtains she bought for the kitchen was all up for scrutiny. And it was constant. Even the twins had started to treat her that way. She decided she wouldn't let Michael rattle her.

As the morning went on, time flew. Sarah waited on tables, poured coffee, and chatted with customers. The job was much more fun than teaching fifth grade math that was for sure. As the morning ended and just before the lunch crowd began to trickle in, David pulled her outside and handed her a glass of water with lemon.

"So, you think you'll be back tomorrow?"

"Oh, I don't know. I—" she said.

David laughed. "I'm just saying you really did a great job today."

Sarah relaxed. "I didn't realize it would be as busy as it was!"

"Well, we never know. Summer is our busy season, but during the winter each day is different. Chances are tomorrow won't be as busy, but then again we're coming towards the weekend, so who knows…"

Sarah nodded her head and took a sip of the water.

"OK, we have about thirty minutes before the lunch crowd gets going so spill it. What's your story?" David asked.

Sarah had thought about what she was going to tell him all morning long, but she still didn't know what say. The truth? A version of the truth? A lie? A combination of all three?

"Well, what do you want to know?" Sarah asked.

"Let's start with your last name."

"Rossi."

"OK, Sarah Rossi. Are you on vacation or new to town?" David asked.

Sarah looked up toward the sky thinking of how she wanted to answer. David stared at her, his eyebrows stretched up towards his hairline. She didn't know why, but he made her feel as if she wanted to spill her whole story to him. At the same time, she was afraid he would judge her, or worse talk her into going back.

"Let's just say I'm taking it day by day for now," she said, honestly.

David lowered his eyebrows and smirked at her.

"Ah, I see. Well, that just brings me back to my story that I started telling you earlier," David said.

Sarah pulled her feet up on the chair and hugged her knees close to her chest to listen.

"Well, as I said before," David began. "I was married…to a woman. And, if you haven't already figured out, I'm gay," he said, laughing.

Sarah laughed too. "Well, I never like to assume," she said.

"After the wedding, we settled into this 'Happy Town, USA' life. Married, bought a house, got a dog, and then she started talking about having kids. Listen, we were barely having sex because I just couldn't stomach it. I tried to close my eyes and pretend it was Brad Pitt I was fucking, but then she'd say something and ruin it for me. That's when I knew I had to get out of the marriage. The last thing I wanted was having a child with this woman. Even worse, I could not imagine telling my Evangelical father that I was gay. It was outta the question. So, I packed my things one day while she was at the grocery store, and I left."

"You left?" Sarah's mouth hung open.

"Now don't get all judgy on me," David said, waving his hands. "Maybe I'm a coward, but I had to do what was best for me. I'm pretty sure I would still be living in Virginia with five kids by now because I never could have looked her in the eye and told her I'd been lying to her all those years."

Sarah tried to decide whether to tell David her story. Then, Michael came into the garden.

"So, Miss Sarah," Michael said. His formality was unnerving.

Sarah sat up straighter.

"We really didn't have time to meet formally. Michael Inwood, owner of the café," he said, holding out his hand for her to shake.

"*Co*-owner," David corrected, as he pointed towards

himself, indicating he was the other owner.

Sarah shook Michael's hand. She sensed he was angry, or maybe just stressed. Sarah couldn't really tell. He looked as if he had the weight of the world on his shoulders.

"Thank you for the help this morning," Michael said.

"No problem. I had nowhere else to be, and David looked like he could use some help, so I jumped in."

"Appreciated," said Michael. Then he took a deep breath and took his glasses off, folding them and crossing his arms across his chest. "Can I be frank?" he asked.

Sarah nodded, unsure of what he was about to say.

"David here loves to save lost puppies."

Sarah looked back and forth at the two men confused.

David rolled his eyes. "Michael, please. Don't go there," he pled.

"Well," said Michael, returning the rolled eyes. He put up his hand as if to dismiss David. "He does, and I'm tired of taking care of those puppies. He finds them, takes them in, and I get stuck picking up the shit."

Picking up the shit? Sarah thought. *Wow, this guy is a piece of work.*

"Listen, I'm not here to cause problems," she said defensively. Not understanding what a *lost puppy* was or why he was telling her this.

Sarah looked at David who gave her a sympathetic look. Michael stared at her with a furrowed brow.

"I think I'll just go," said Sarah.

"I think that's—" Michael started but David interrupted him. The two exchanged a look and then David asked Michael to join him on the other side of the garden. Michael sighed and the two walked off.

Sarah could hear them talking, but couldn't make out what was being said. After two minutes, they came back and both stood in front of her. Sarah sat taller. David looked as though he'd burst with excitement, but Sarah still felt uneasy because Michael looked so serious.

"I'm sorry. I think we got off on the wrong foot," Michael

said.

Sarah immediately noticed that the angered tone he had just minutes before had now softened. He explained that they really could use a waitress for a few days, and it would be great if she could stay to help them.

"Um…," Sarah said, unsure of what to do. She didn't want to create problems between David and Michael, and now she wasn't sure if she wanted to continue to work for Michael. But, she looked at David, who was smiling and begging her with his eyes to stay. Something just felt right here at the café.

"I could help you for a couple of days, I suppose," she said. She wasn't sure what made her say it, but there it was.

That was all David needed to hear. He jumped up and down and hugged her.

Michael's eyes softened and Sarah saw a hint of a smile.

"OK then, just until the weekend would be great. If you don't mind me asking, where are you from?" Michael asked.

"New Hampshire," Sarah said. Then added, "I arrived in town yesterday and I'm living day by day right now."

Michael folded his arms across his chest and sighed. "Fine, I'll get the application." Then he walked away leaving David and Sarah together.

"We've been burned before by waitresses," David said. "That's why he's being overly cautious. It's fine. He's just a stick in the mud!"

Sarah smiled, although she still felt uneasy at the way Michael looked at her and spoke to her. His distrust made her want to prove to him that she wasn't a lost puppy, whatever that was. Yet, she wondered if she'd done the right thing by agreeing to stay. *It's just a few days*, she thought. Besides, she could use the distraction. She wasn't ready to drive all the way back home just yet.

A few days at the café might be just want she needed. She'd been gone from home for almost two weeks. She couldn't even *think* about going back—between the long drive ahead, the shit-storm she'd face when she arrived, and the fact that she just couldn't imagine resuming a life she hated. She didn't even recognize her old self, the afraid and insecure Sarah. That girl was fading away. The new Sarah— the one that had been suppressed all these years—was on her own now and just beginning to find her voice.

14

On Saturday, Sarah got up early and drove to San Clemente, a small town south of Laguna. David told her it was a great place to photograph surfers. The last few days at the café had been fun, yet exhausting. David and Sarah worked so well together. It was as if they'd known each other for years and could read each other's minds. He brought out Sarah's silly side, which helped make the days fly.

Even after just a few short days, Sarah knew some of the customers by name. David made sure he introduced her to all the regulars. She loved chatting with the people who came in, whether they were tourists or regulars. No one knew her past and didn't even ask about it. At the café, she could just be Sarah, the waitress.

The Garden Café was a magical place. Everyone was so positive and upbeat that it was hard *not* to be happy there. Besides, there wasn't anything difficult about the job. David took the orders and Sarah brought out the food. Working also kept her mind busy, so she wasn't thinking about home too much. On Friday, Michael asked if she could come back the following week.

"If you can help us out a little longer, we'd really

appreciate it," he'd said.

Sarah tried to hide her shock that he'd asked her to stay. She was certain he hated her. He barely spoke to her—only when he needed her in the kitchen. But she knew, from David, that there weren't a lot of applicants and they desperately needed the help. The weather was getting nicer and people seemed to be coming in droves. Besides, getting some pocket cash from the tips was helpful. The money she'd put aside for a rainy day (aka her escape) was draining fast. They agreed she would stay on until they hired someone more permanent.

Sarah parked her car near the train station in San Clemente, then crossed the tracks and headed toward the pier. Large brown and white pelicans flew above her and dived into the water to catch fish. She turned on her iPod and searched for a song before finally stumbling across an old favorite—a live Jack Johnson album. It seemed perfect for a day at the beach watching the surfers. Sarah adjusted the sound as she breathed in the salty air and walked to the pier.

A sea of black wetsuits bobbed up and down on their surfboards as they waited for a wave. Sarah took pictures as she watched the surfers wait patiently for the perfect wave to swell. Then, in unison, they began paddling out further in the water.

Out in the distance, Sarah spotted the wave they were all looking to ride. As they got out towards the end of the pier, they sat up on their boards and waited. After several minutes, they began to paddle furiously. Suddenly, all the surfers jumped up on their boards just as the wave reached its peak. She raised her camera to her eye and began snapping pictures. She was in awe that no one crashed into anyone else as they rode the wave in. They all seemed to have an unspoken rhythm between them. If it weren't for the colorful surfboards, it would have been hard to tell the surfers apart.

A herd of seals surrounded the pier. They were playfully vying for her attention as if they were putting on a show just for her and the camera. She snapped some photos of them—

how could she disappoint those little buggers?

She spent the rest of the morning walking the pedestrian path along the beach, marveling at all of the luxurious homes and dreaming of one day owning one. She thought about the boys and how much they would love to see all of this. Both of them snowboarded and would probably be out there trying to surf. She'd texted them every day and their continued silence was killing her. Neither one had texted back or returned a call in the two weeks she'd been gone. Not even a text to tell her to stop texting them. Nothing. She worried they weren't going to school and thought about calling Linda to check in, but both Linda and Meg had told Sarah not to call, that they would call her if needed.

A little after noon, she found her way back toward the pier where she had begun her journey in the morning searching for a place to eat. There were a few restaurants to choose from, but she settled on a small pizza place near where she had parked her car. Sarah ordered a small cheese pizza and sat down to look through the photos she'd taken throughout the morning.

"Are you a professional photographer or just a hobbyist?" asked a woman sitting next to Sarah.

"Oh, hobby, but I'd love to make it a profession someday," Sarah said. Admitting that to strangers was getting easier. Not one person ever told her it was a silly idea.

"Do you live around here?"

"In Laguna," Sarah said, surprising herself how casually that slipped off her tongue.

"Oh, so you must go to Leslie's then?"

Sarah furrowed her brow and shook her head.

"You don't know Leslie?"

Sarah shook her head again.

"Leslie owns a camera shop in Laguna but it's much more than a camera shop. It's a gallery and a place for photographers to gather and help each other with problems. You can print and mount your photos there. It's awesome. Leslie holds classes and arranges group outings too."

"Oh, no, I just moved to the area. I'm not familiar with it. I'd love to know where it is though."

The woman reached her hand over and introduced herself as Allana Moore. Sarah shook her hand. Allana was in her early thirties and had a sleeve of colorful tattoos on her left arm. Her hair was pulled up into a messy bun on top of her head, creating a colorful mix of brown, blonde, and red. She had multiple piercings on her face and ears. Allana told Sarah all about Leslie's shop and the photographers club that Leslie ran.

"I try to go on as many outings as I can. They meet twice a month at various locations. Leslie *loves* the desert, so she plans a lot of trips there. I usually make a point to go on the trips up north in Santa Barbara, because it's so beautiful up there."

"More so than here? Because I'm from New Hampshire, and I'm just in awe of the beauty here."

Allana laughed. "Every area of California has its own beauty. Think about the East Coast from Maine to Maryland and how different everything is in between. Each state has its own beauty, right? California's the same way, except it's all one state."

"Are you from the East Coast?"

"Mostly everyone here is," Allana laughed. "I'm from Rhode Island, actually."

They talked for a while about life on the East Coast versus the West Coast. Allana had migrated west for a job as a graphic designer when she graduated from college and never looked back.

"I don't miss the snow one bit," said Allana. "I was nostalgic for it when I first came here but now, whenever I go home to visit my parents, I like the snow less and less each time. Now I crave the warmth and the sunshine. California, especially SoCal, has such a magnetic pull."

Sarah nodded; she felt it too. Allana asked to see some of Sarah's photos. Sarah handed her the camera and watched Allana as she clicked through the pictures.

"These are striking photos. You should show them."

Sarah laughed. "Show them? They aren't *that* good."

"Go to Leslie's today, if you aren't busy. Look around her shop at her photos. She's won prizes for a lot of them and has showings all the time. I would say your pictures are as good as hers if not better, and Leslie is a mastermind behind the camera. No kidding, you're *that* good," Allana said.

Sarah scrolled through her photos on her camera as she listened to Allana. She had always loved her own pictures, and Jim gushed over them, but she always thought he was just being nice.

"The club meets again next weekend," Allana said, interrupting Sarah's thoughts. "We're going to Limestone Canyon. It's a great place to shoot. We'll meet in the morning, hike, have lunch, and be back by early afternoon."

"Hike?" she asked remembering her last hike in New Hampshire with the dogs. It was just before Christmas. She'd taken them on a short hike but had fallen and twisted her ankle. It wasn't a bad sprain but it took her a while to get back to the car.

"It's not like you're thinking. Back east hiking means mountains; here it means mostly hilly trails. Limestone is the Grand Canyon of southern California. It's gorgeous there. You have to come."

"It sounds like fun!" said Sarah. "I'm definitely going to stop in at Leslie's on my way home so I'll ask about it. Thanks so much for all the info. I'm so glad I met you!"

"It was great meeting you too. Now I need to get a move on. I have a big project for work that's due tomorrow. I just came down for a break and a bite to eat."

"You live close by?"

"About a block away in a small—a *very* small and *very* expensive—one-bedroom. But I love the sound of the ocean, and couldn't possibly live anywhere else."

Sarah was beginning to feel the same way.

***

Sarah found Leslie's shop just off the main street in

downtown Laguna. The building was hard to find at first. She circled around the block a few times before she finally spotted the unpretentious sign that read "Leslie's Camera and Gallery" just before she was about to give up.

A high-pitched voice greeted Sarah, but her eyes were adjusting from being outside, so she couldn't see where it was coming from. As her vision came into focus, she saw a woman approaching her.

Leslie Sullivan introduced herself. She was petite and had flawless skin making it hard to figure out how old she was. Sarah couldn't help but notice the enormous diamond ring on her left hand though, probably at least three carats. Sarah told her that Allana suggested she come check out the shop.

"I just love Allana! She's the best and so sweet to send you here. I will definitely need to send her a thank you note," Leslie said, as she grabbed a piece of paper and a pen from behind the counter and scribbled a reminder for herself.

Leslie told Sarah all about the photography club and the smaller groups that met at the store to develop pictures or to help each other with camera issues. Sarah thought about how much she missed her own photography club, and Jim. *Maybe I'll call him later*, she thought. Then Leslie told her to look around and let her know if she had questions.

The store was very eclectic and there was a lot to take in. Photographs hung on the walls for sale, cases with Leslie's handmade jewelry (another one of Leslie's hobbies) lined the counters, and shelves of sculptures that Leslie and other people had made were scattered throughout. There was an entire wall full of books about photography, cameras, and art. Sarah got lost in the small store for almost an hour. When she was done, she waited to say goodbye to Leslie, who was helping someone at the counter. Leslie introduced the woman she was talking with to Sarah.

"This is Anita. We run the club together."

Sarah and Anita shook hands.

"Would you like to join us tomorrow for our trip to Limestone? We leave here at six a.m.."

"I would love to!" Sarah said. She had hoped that Leslie would have mentioned it earlier.

"Great! Come here for six and you can ride with us. You'll definitely want your telephoto lens, but bring any others too."

"I keep everything in one bag, so I'll have it all."

"OK, you might want to get a backpack if you don't have one. We usually eat a picnic lunch in the canyon. And bring a lot of water. It gets hot in there."

Sarah agreed to meet them in the morning and drove to the store to buy a backpack and some good hiking shoes.

***

They arrived at the canyon and were greeted by a docent, John White, who led the group through the canyon for the day. He told them that Limestone was a wilderness preserve and a gift from a real-estate developer. A landslide had carved the sinks, but no one was sure if it was a storm or an earthquake that helped to create the magnificent rock formations. When he finished speaking, he turned to address the group crowded together behind him.

"Deer," John whispered, pointing to four deer standing conspicuously behind a tree. Cameras raised and clicking noises were heard in concert. Sarah had deer and moose living in her backyard at home so she wasn't quick to raise her camera. Instead, she pointed hers towards the lush greenery and flowers that popped with neon green color. There was a soft murmuring among the group until Sarah squealed as a rather large lizard scurried in front of her. The deer that everyone was photographing scattered, and the group turned to see what the fuss was about.

"It's a lizard," she said, awkwardly. The lizard had stopped and remained motionless on the trail in front of her. Sarah pointed to it.

"Get used to those," John laughed. "They're everywhere in the canyon."

Sarah skulked away, apologizing for ruining everyone's shots.

"I'm not used to seeing lizards," she said to Allana. Sarah had been very happy to see Allana when she arrived at the canyon. She spotted her right away and went over to say hello. Allana was alone, although she seemed to know just about everyone in the group.

"I will never get used to the lizards. Don't worry about it," Allana said, laughing.

This made Sarah feel a little less embarrassed, but she couldn't help noticing that some of the others were staring at her, probably upset that they didn't get to ogle the deer longer. The lizard ran onto a rock and stared at Sarah with a sideways eye. She adjusted her camera and took a close up of it. The lizard sat perfectly still as she clicked away. There really wasn't anything scary about the lizard it just looked creepy.

As they continued, the docent pointed out mountain lion tracks.

"Mountain lions?" Sarah asked nervously.

"Not to worry, they scatter when we come through," John said.

Sarah wasn't convinced. She kept looking around and jumping at every little noise she heard but, thankfully, they didn't see a lion all day.

They gathered for lunch at the top of the canyon. The docent lingered with the group in the back to make sure they made it to the top. Sarah and Allana continued, not ready to eat just yet. Sarah was in awe of the desert beauty—all of the cacti, colorful flowers, and strange plants. It was unlike anything she'd ever seen. Once they reached the sinks, Sarah gasped.

"This is breathtaking!"

"I told you," said Allana.

In the dipping springs, the rock face was covered with bright green moss and ferns. Sarah couldn't stop commenting on its beauty. Allana had to drag her away to meet the others for lunch. Leslie and Anita asked to see Sarah's photos. She handed them her camera apprehensively. She hadn't looked through them yet and wasn't sure if she had anything good enough to show them.

Leslie and Anita leaned their heads together as Leslie scrolled through Sarah's photos.

"These are fabulous!" Leslie said.

"Have you ever showed your work?" Anita asked. "Or, better yet, sold it?"

"Oh, God no! I still have a lot to learn," Sarah said, blushing as people hovered over Leslie's shoulder to view the photos on the camera's tiny screen. Sarah bit her nails resisting the urge to pull her camera back.

"You do realize you have a great eye, don't you?" Leslie said.

Sarah shrugged and nodded shyly.

"We'll have to work on her confidence," Leslie teased as she handed Sarah her camera. "You really are a great photographer. You need to allow yourself to see that because we do."

"Thank you," Sarah said.

"They're right, you know." Allana said.

"I'm just not used to people gushing over me like that. Makes me uncomfortable."

"Understandable. But everyone needs to learn to take compliments. Sometimes those words are what we need to hear to help us grow. If you continue to believe you aren't any good, then you will never be good. You have to allow yourself to believe it."

Sarah cocked her head to the side and thought about that. Her entire life all she ever wanted was someone to gush over her photos. She scrolled through her pictures, seeing them for the first time. They were good, really good in fact. Jim tried for years to get her to enter her pictures in various contests, but Sarah never felt her work was good enough to win anything. Now, she was curious if she could win a contest or sell her photos. She'd seen a lot of paintings and photos in the galleries in Laguna that were, in her opinion, just OK. Yet, those artists put their work out there. Why couldn't she?

Sarah arrived back at her hotel late in the afternoon, exhausted yet invigorated. She took a long rejuvenating shower, ordered a burger and fries from room service, and sat on the balcony waiting for it to arrive.

15

A week later, Sarah and David were preparing for the lunch crowd, filling ketchup bottles and wrapping silverware in napkins. Her shift was over, but she liked to stay and wait for the afternoon waitress, Jess, to arrive and relieve her. It gave her more time with David. Michael was in the background preparing food. He still made her uncomfortable mostly because he was very serious about his work and didn't participate in the chitchat that she and David engaged in. Whenever she was in the kitchen, Sarah made sure to keep her teasing and giggling with David to a minimum. She didn't want to poke the bear. She couldn't help but wonder what Michael would think about her situation, about her running away from her family. Therefore, whenever David asked her questions about home she kept her answers vague. She didn't want to jeopardize her job at the café just yet. She was enjoying life...for once.

"So, we want to invite you to dinner tomorrow night," said David, gesturing to Michael.

So, they are a couple. She hadn't been able to decide. Michael gave a small but noticeable smile before he went back to stirring something.

"Sounds great. What can I bring?" she asked. She'd been eating in restaurants for weeks so the thought of a home-cooked meal sounded wonderful.

"Nothing, just you," Michael called out without turning around. He was always listening, even if he didn't appear to be.

"Are you sure?" Sarah asked. "You guys have done so much for me already."

Michael turned and peered at her over his glasses that hovered on the end of his nose. For the first time, Sarah saw a softer side of him, and she knew he was genuine when he said, "No, you've helped us. Just come ready to have a good time. David invited Jillian."

"Jillian?"

"She's my friend. I think you two will hit it off. She's in the middle of a divorce right now so she could use the company. I can come pick you up if you want," David said.

"No, then you'll have to drive me home. Besides, I'm a big girl. I think I can handle the drive to Dana Point."

Dana Point was a twenty-five minute drive from Laguna.

"OK then, eight o'clock. And don't bring anything or he will kill you!" David said, nodding his head towards Michael.

Sarah smiled. Michael turned and smiled too, and winked at Sarah. It was the first time she'd seen a playful side of him.

***

Sarah spent the afternoon on the beach reading and relaxing. Even though it was a little chilly, it was nothing compared to the snowstorm that was happening back home. Whenever she thought about home, the image of Joe and Jen would flash in her mind. She tried not to think about home.

She left the beach just after four. She had plans to meet Leslie at the shop to look over the pictures she'd taken at Limestone and choose a few to put up for sale in the shop. At first, Sarah was apprehensive about it but now she was excited about the idea of selling one of her photos.

As she dressed, she spotted a napkin on the floor. She

picked it up. It was the napkin that the bartender had given her about the apartment. She stared at the name—Will—for a while wondering how the napkin had gotten on the floor.

However, her bank account was draining fast and she wouldn't be able to afford the hotel much longer. She picked up her cell phone and dialed the number listed on the napkin, but she got the voicemail. She hung up. *I can't do this!* Getting an apartment was too permanent. No, she had to go back home soon. She shook her head as if to snap her out of the fantasy of staying in Laguna and finished getting ready to meet Leslie.

Before she left, she closed the doors to the balcony. As she did, she came eye to eye with a hummingbird sending chills down her spine. It hovered there, its wings fluttering, and its eyes shifting back and forth. She felt like it had something to tell her. A message, or a sign, her Aunt Donna would have said. She waited motionless for the hummingbird to fly away, but it didn't. It stayed at eye level with her, its tiny body suspended in flight. She wondered if she was seeing things and reached her hand up to touch it, but the hummingbird disappeared in an instant. This was the second hummingbird she'd seen since arriving in Laguna. It was rare to see hummingbirds in January back home but maybe Southern California was different. Or maybe…it was her aunt sending her a message…

She spun around grinning ear to ear. She dug through her purse to find the napkin, and dialed Will's number again. His voice was smooth as he said hello. Her body covered in goose bumps.

Will said his son had told him she might be calling.

"My kids are always trying to get this place rented," said Will.

"If it's not available that's OK," Sarah said awkwardly.

"It's available. Why don't you come and take a look at it?" he asked.

Sarah's heart pounded. What was making her so nervous?

"How about tomorrow afternoon around four?" Sarah

asked. Figuring she could go there before she went to David and Michael's.

"Sounds great. I'll see you then," Will said. He gave her his address before they said goodbye.

After Sarah hung up, she stood holding the phone close to her chest and the familiar feelings of guilt washed over her. What was she doing agreeing to look at an apartment? She sighed as she thought about Zach and Cam and how they still weren't calling her back. She thought about her father but quickly pushed the thought out of her mind. She was tired of thinking about everyone else. It was her turn now and time for her to do what felt right for her. Everything about being in Laguna just felt right. She wasn't ready to go home yet.

She called David next.

"I think I might be staying in Laguna for a little while longer. If you still need me to work, I'm available."

"Are you kidding? Yes, of course I want you to work here!" David shrieked.

"What about Michael?" she asked. At first, he'd agreed for Sarah to stay for a few days but it'd been a couple of weeks now and he didn't seem to be able to find anyone to fill the position. Either that or he wasn't trying all that hard.

"What about him? We can't find anyone else, and even he's said that you've worked out brilliantly. I'll talk to him. I'm so excited!"

Sarah laughed. "Me too. Thanks for everything you've done for me, David. I'll see you tomorrow at your house. I'm off to meet Leslie at the shop."

She hung up with David and sat down on the bed, feeling nervously excited. Laguna was drawing her in more and more.

16

She met Leslie at the shop as planned. Sarah arrived a little early and the shop was packed with people. She recognized some of the people from the photographers club who were talking to Anita. Leslie saw Sarah and came running over to hug her as she entered the store. People were huggers in California. Sarah wasn't used to it yet. Leslie reintroduced her to a couple who had their arms around each other.

"Sarah, this is Brad and Adrienne. They're two of my students."

Sarah said hello and shook their hands. Brad and Adrienne were in their sixties, Sarah estimated. They stood close together. Adrienne rubbed Brad's back in a loving way.

"We were just looking at some of the group's pictures from the trip to Limestone," Adrienne said.

"Show her your photos, Sarah," Leslie said.

She handed the camera to Leslie, who scrolled through before settling on some to show Brad and Adrienne.

"Wow! These are fantastic!" they exclaimed in unison.

"Oh, I still have a lot to learn. I'm sure yours are great too."

"Not like yours. You have a great eye," Brad said.

"You really do have something special. You have a tremendous grasp of visual weight. Look here," Leslie said showing them a photo of the sinks. "See how the red flower here in the foreground balances the expanse of the blue sky against the sinks? Just stunning. And look at this yellow flower at the bottom of this photo. The flower in the corner with its vibrant color balances the gray rock beautifully."

Brad and Adrienne nodded and agreed with Leslie. Sarah felt proud listening to her photos be critiqued.

"I would love to see you show these in the Art Festival in March," said Leslie.

"Oh, I don't know," said Sarah. What she really didn't know was if she'd still be in Laguna in March.

"Do you have a portfolio?" Anita asked.

"Not really," Sarah said.

Leslie and Anita exchanged a look. Sarah wondered what they were up to.

Then Sarah and Leslie went into the back and looked at Sarah's photos on the computer. They chose five to mount and put up for sale in the store. When they finished Leslie asked Sarah if she'd like to join her and her husband for dinner in Newport.

"That sounds fun. Sure!" Sarah said. She hadn't met Leslie's husband yet. She wondered if he'd be as full of life and down to earth as Leslie.

"Well then we should get going. Don't want to keep Nathan waiting," said Leslie.

Sarah followed Leslie out to her car—a cream-colored Bentley—that was parked in front of the store.

"This is a beautiful car," Sarah said, trying not to sound overly excited, but it was the most expensive car she had ever seen in person, never mind been in.

"Oh, Nathan bought this for me. Frankly, I can't stand driving it. It's so pretentious. I'd be happy in an old fashioned bug."

The soft cream-colored leather seat enveloped Sarah as she sat down. "This is so soft," she said, as she rubbed leather.

"Yes, the seats are extraordinary aren't they?" Leslie said, looking left and pulling out of the parking spot just outside the store. "I know it's a great car, but to spend as much as he did on it was so silly. I mean, do you know what I could do with two hundred thousand dollars?"

Sarah's eyes widened. *"Two hundred thousand?"*

"I know. Ridiculous. But, Nathan insisted that I should have something nice after I pulled through the cancer."

"Oh, I didn't realize," said Sarah.

"It's fine. I had a brain tumor. We tried the chemo and radiation for a while, but it wasn't working. I wouldn't wish chemo on my worst enemy. It's that awful. Your body goes through hell. Anyway, my husband, God bless him, did some research and found a doctor in Massachusetts who was doing an experimental surgery to remove tumors like mine. That's all Nathan had to hear! Before I had time to think, we were on a plane to Massachusetts. They removed the tumor successfully, and then I spent several months in rehab and long hours of physical therapy to get my fine motor skills back."

"Wow, I'm so sorry," said Sarah. She admired Leslie's openness about her illness.

"Well, thank you. But, it's OK. I go for testing every six months to see if the tumor has returned. So far so good! Each day is a blessing."

Sarah thought about her mother who never talked about blessings, or joy, or anything at all really. It made her sad that her mother never got to experience the happiness that Sarah was feeling in California. Back in New Hampshire, Sarah hadn't been able to find joy in anything. Now she felt as if each day was a blessing. Probably because she knew, the rug could be pulled from underneath her at any minute.

"I'm happy you pulled through it. My mother died of bone cancer."

Leslie offered condolences.

"It was a long time ago, but watching her suffer in the end

was horrible," Sarah said.

"Cancer sucks," Leslie said, as they waited at a red light. Sarah agreed.

"Do you have children?" Leslie asked.

"Yes. Twin boys. They're almost eighteen."

"We had twins too!" Leslie said.

"Oh, wow! That's great," Sarah said, smiling at their shared experience.

"We had a boy and girl. They're in their thirties now. Drew lives in Tokyo because of his job. He's very a successful businessman. Amanda lives in New York City. She's a lawyer working for a publishing company."

"Impressive! I worry my boys will never find their way."

"Oh, give it time. They're still young."

They talked the rest of the way about the boys and Sarah danced around the reason she was here and not back home with them. She told Leslie they were home with their father, which wasn't a lie, but she still felt like she was being dishonest. She was grateful when Leslie didn't press her for more details.

Two valets flanked the car and opened their doors as they arrived at the tapas restaurant. The valet said that Leslie's husband hadn't arrived yet. *They must be regulars*, Sarah thought. Inside, the dimly lit restaurant was bustling with activity. They waited at the bar for Nathan to arrive.

"Must be stuck in surgery," Leslie said, cynically.

Sarah could tell that meant he was always late. They ordered martinis and found a place to stand out of the way.

A few minutes later, Leslie's husband arrived. As soon as he walked in the door, Sarah knew it was Leslie's husband. Nathan Sullivan was five-foot-nine, had perfectly styled brown hair (obviously dyed), gleaming white veneers, and tight tanned skin. He came over and kissed Leslie hello.

"I got stuck in surgery," he said. Nathan was a plastic surgeon with offices in Newport and Beverly Hills.

Leslie rolled her eyes as if to say, *see what did I tell you?* Then Nathan turned to Sarah. He smiled as he looked her up and down. She felt as if he was sizing up all of her flaws and making a mental note of the procedures she could benefit from. Leslie introduced them and Nathan reached out, taking Sarah's face in his hands and kissing each cheek.

"So nice to meet you! Welcome to California!" Nathan said, as if he were the welcoming committee. "I hear you're a wonderful photographer."

Sarah smiled. "Oh," she said feeling awkward. She wondered what Leslie had told him about her. "Thank you."

"Shall we sit, ladies?"

Nathan motioned to the hostess that they were ready. As they walked through the restaurant, he commanded the room. He stopped several times to say hello to various people. He seemed to know everyone in the place. He finally came to the table a few minutes after Sarah and Leslie were seated and looking through the menu.

The waitress came to the table and Nathan ordered a bottle of wine. After Sarah saw the price of the bottle he ordered, she was nervous that she hadn't brought enough money. They probably made more in a month than she ever did in a year. When the waitress came back with the wine, Nathan tried it and gave his approval before the waitress poured everyone a glass. Then, he began ordering food. He consulted Leslie for suggestions, but not Sarah. When he finished ordering, he turned to Sarah.

"We ordered a little bit of everything!" Nathan said.

"Can't wait to try it all," Sarah said.

Nathan smiled at her, making her feel self-conscious again. She touched her face nervously.

"So, Leslie tells me you're from New Hampshire. What brings you to California?" Nathan asked.

"I needed a change and California was always some place I wanted to go."

"I really think we have a pro in the making here," Leslie said.

Sarah flushed. "Oh, I don't know," she said.

"If you're good, own it!" Nathan said.

Sarah sank in her chair.

"He's trying to say that you shouldn't say you aren't good, because you are," Leslie said, coming to her rescue.

"I'm sorry. I'm not used to people gushing over my work."

"You think we're just being nice?"

Sarah nodded.

"You have something special, Sarah," Leslie said. "I really think you should pursue this as more than a hobby."

"It's what I've wanted to do my whole life. To be a photographer," Sarah said.

"But life got in the way?" Nathan asked.

Sarah nodded again. "Yes, that. And I had a very domineering father, who told me that photography was a hobby, not a profession. He said I needed a career that would be *suitable* for a mother. So, I became a teacher."

"Sometimes parents don't understand the mind of a creative child. Creative people don't think like "normal" people. We see the world in a different way, we live in our heads, and we are adventurous!" Leslie said.

Sarah agreed with that. She thought about Joe and how boring and predictable he was. She couldn't even get him to try a new restaurant, never mind travel.

Nathan looked at her with his devilish smile. It was as if he was stripping Sarah down to her soul. There was something about him that was equal parts terrifying and reassuring at the same time.

"I feel like there's more to the story," Nathan said.

Sarah took a sip of wine. Her heart beat nervously as they stared at her, eager for her to answer. There wasn't any sense lying to them, Sarah thought, but how much of her story could she tell without them urging her return home?

"I guess I just wanted to do something for me. I was tired of doing everything to please everyone else." Sarah smiled at her answer. It summed everything up nicely without revealing too much.

Nathan leaned in looking at her inquisitively with his head

tilted. "Do you have kids?"

"She has twins! Like us!" Leslie said.

Sarah smiled and nodded.

"So, you left your kids behind...," Nathan said keenly, sitting back in his chair folding his arms across his chest.

Sarah shifted in her seat not sure if she should answer him or not.

"Mothers don't leave their kids unless they have a really good reason," Nathan said.

Sarah's eyes filled. She felt like she was being interrogated. Leslie must have noticed that she was uncomfortable.

"Nathan, leave the girl alone. She—"

"No, it's fine," Sarah said, taking a deep breath. Even though Nathan was pushing her for answers, she sensed he was coming from a good place. "I left an abusive father and husband behind. My sons are following their pattern, and I have no control over them anymore. I left because if I didn't, I would have taken a bottle of sleeping pills with a bottle of wine to end the hell I was in. Oh, and I found my husband having sex with someone who I thought was a friend. There. That's the real reason I left."

Sarah finished talking and realized she was shaking. It felt so good to let all that out. It was as if a weight had been lifted off her chest.

"It takes a strong person to do what you did. If no one's said it to you, I'm proud of you for getting away from all that," said Nathan.

She wiped the tears on her cheeks with her napkin and laughed nervously. "Thanks..."

"I agree," Leslie said. "It takes courage to leave an abusive relationship."

"But there was nothing courageous about it. I left in a fit of rage," Sarah said. The first few days after she left were a blur. She hardly remembered those initial miles, or what she was thinking for that matter.

"But how often have you thought about leaving?" Nathan asked.

"Too many times to count."

"See? You reached a breaking point. Don't worry about the people you left behind right now. Focus on you. Get your footing so you can either go back a stronger person, or decide if you want to stay in Orange County."

Sarah shook her head. "I can't even imagine going home at this point."

"Well, take it day by day for now," said Leslie.

The waitress arrived, and thankfully, the conversation moved away from Sarah. Small plates of food rotated around the table and when they were empty, the waitress plonked down a few more plates. It seemed never ending.

The Sullivan's talked about their kids and Nathan's work. He had some astonishing stories to tell about being a plastic surgeon. Sarah marveled at how down to earth Leslie and Nathan were. They were regular people who happened to have a lot of money. She watched as Nathan talked to, and about, Leslie. Sarah could feel the love they had for each other. She had to hold back tears watching them. Nathan had such love in his eyes for his wife of thirty-five years.

"Everything was so good!" Sarah said, sitting back in her chair feeling fuller than she'd ever had before.

"What was your favorite?" Leslie asked.

"Oh, the rice balls were so good. And the braised short ribs were to die for. Oh and how about that lamb? I loved it all!"

"Glad you enjoyed it!" Leslie laughed.

The bill came and Nathan pulled out his black American Express card and handed it to the waitress.

"What do I owe?" Sarah asked.

Both Nathan and Leslie laughed, which made her feel childish.

"*We* asked you to dinner, dear. Our treat," Leslie said, patting Sarah's hand.

She'd never been treated to a dinner this extravagant in her life. "Thank you very much," she said.

"Our pleasure," said Leslie. "Now, you just give some

thought to entering your work for consideration in the art festival. It's only six weeks away, and applications are due by the end of the week. You could show some of your Limestone photos. I love the ones you took in San Clemente too."

Sarah nodded and agreed to everything Leslie said, which seemed to make her and Nathan happy. But the thought of showing her work was still terrifying.

"Leslie's right, you should show your work at the festival. It would be a great way to start your business," said Nathan.

"You mean a photography business?"

"Yes!" Nathan said.

Sarah blushed. She walked behind Nathan and Leslie as they left the restaurant. They were holding hands. She'd never had that closeness with Joe. She wondered if she would ever experience that kind of love.

After a few minutes, the valets returned with both cars. Nathan walked Leslie to her car. Sarah couldn't help but watch as the two kissed before Leslie got in the car. She still couldn't believe she'd opened up to them about leaving and her life back home. Even more shocking was that she'd opened up to them and they didn't tell her to go home. Instead, they supported her.

Nathan walked over to Sarah's door.

"Let me," he said, as he opened the door.

"Thank you," Sarah said, as she got in.

Nathan leaned in the car. "You'll know when you're ready to face everything back home."

Sarah smiled and nodded as Nathan shut the door. Except she couldn't imagine ever going back home.

17

Sarah drove to Will's place in Laguna Hills, blasting Dave Mathews. The ride through the canyon was breathtaking. The hills and red rock seemed to extend into eternity. The shadows and sun hit the rocks just right, making her regret not bringing her camera.

She followed the directions Will had given her. With each turn, the homes became more and more spectacular. Then she made the final turn onto Will's street. She drove down the road carefully, checking each house's number. 26095, 26148, 26242, and then finally 26258. Will's house was at the end of a cul-de-sac.

She stopped in front of the house and stared at it. The house wasn't what she was expecting. *Where is the apartment?* She thought as she eased her car into the driveway.

It was a large home situated on a good-sized lot. All the homes on the street had perfectly manicured lawns that were so green it was as if someone had painted them. There were three palm trees in his front yard and rows of green bushes lining the pathways. Pops of color peppered the flowerbeds. The house didn't look like the other houses on the street, which were white stucco homes with orange tiled roofs. Will's was brick with a dark tiled roof that reminded her of the Tudor style houses from back home.

Just as she was about to put the car in reverse to leave—because she had envisioned an apartment not a house—she spotted a man walking towards her. Two shiny gray Weimaraner dogs ran down the driveway alongside of him. The man waved at her, and so she put her hand up and waved it back and forth. She had no choice now. She put the car in park.

Will was in his late forties, maybe early fifties and was very attractive. He was tall and she could tell he was in great shape underneath his jeans and long-sleeved cotton shirt that hung just right.

Sarah let out a forceful breath and turned off the engine. She quickly looked in the mirror and swiped her finger underneath her eye to clean up the eyeliner that had smudged there. Will was close; she didn't have time to put on lip-gloss. She ran her hand through her hair and got out just as Will reached her car. Sarah extended her hand and introduced herself.

"Did you find it OK?" he asked, as he shook her hand sending electricity up into her chest.

He looked deep into her eyes, causing her to pull her hand away in embarrassment. *What is wrong with me?* She thought. She tried to steady her voice so she could respond.

"Yes, the directions you gave me were very easy to follow. Gosh, your home is gorgeous," Sarah said, as she took it all in.

"Thank you. We've lived here for almost twenty years. It's too big for us now with the kids all off on their own, but it's home."

"So, it's just you and your wife here then?"

"Actually, just me. Oh, and Rocky and Adrian here."

Sarah laughed at the dog's names and bent down to pat them. "They are beautiful dogs. I like the names. Movie buff?"

"Who isn't a Rocky fan?" Will joked.

She laughed as she rubbed the dogs for a while, not sure what to say or do next. After an awkward silence, Will told her about the apartment and gestured for her to follow him.

"It has its own entrance, so you won't need to come through the house or anything. It's completely furnished except I don't have any linens in there. If you want, I can supply them. The rent is cheap, just four hundred a month. I'm not looking for the money, I just want the space used, that's all. I'm not a creepy stalker guy. I'm not looking for a relationship, and I won't be knocking at your door looking for a booty call at three a.m.," Will laughed nervously.

Sarah laughed too. "Well, phew because I was worried," she joked, but it was a relief to hear.

They passed a three-car garage. One of the bays was open and inside was a small sports car with its hood up. In front of another bay was a two-seater Mercedes. Sarah wondered what Will did for a living.

She followed him along the path that went along the backside of the main house. As they rounded the corner the cottage, as he referred to it, was a smaller version of the main house. It was brick, had large windows, and a garden that she could tell would be pretty come spring when all of the flowers were in bloom. He stopped at the entrance of the house and turned to her.

"So, what brings you to Orange County?"

"Uh, well," she said, stumbling on her words. "I was looking for a change and decided Laguna was the place that could help me do that."

"I can't place your accent. Where are you from?"

Sarah blushed unaware she had an accent. "New Hampshire."

"Wow, OK."

Sarah sensed Will was apprehensive about something.

"Is that a problem?" Sarah asked.

"Well, no. It's just…I'm not looking for trouble. If you're running from the cops or from some husband who will come searching for you with his rifle, I'd rather not rent to you."

"Well, I'm not running from the cops, nor do I have rifle-wielding husband," Sarah said trying to lighten the moment. She'd lied about the rifle. Joe had several, but the chances of him finding her here were slim enough to justify the lie.

Will smiled.

"I'm just looking for a new start," she said.

"Fair enough. Come on in."

Sarah admired the window boxes that hung by the front door. The flowers in them were purple and white and spilling over the edges. She didn't know what they were, but made a mental note to look online for them later. The entryway to the cottage was small and opened up to a living room/kitchen combo. It was bright and airy and Sarah loved it instantly. She admired the shabby chic décor and wondered who had decorated it. She took note of the small bathroom in the hallway on the way to the bedroom suite complete with walk-in closet and bathroom. It was homey.

When she finished looking around, she went back to the door where Will was standing. She told him she loved it.

"I can offer a short-term lease of three months with the option to renew after the second month," he said.

Sarah didn't want to sign a lease. That definitely seemed too permanent. "Oh, I'm not sure how long I'm staying. I don't think a lease will work for me. I'm really sorry I wasted your time today," Sarah said.

"Think about it if you need to. No pressure. The place is available if you want it; just call me if you change your mind," Will smiled. "Do you like horses?"

Sarah nodded.

They walked to the back of the property where Will showed her the horse paths that stretched for miles behind his house. He told her that it was all his property, but the neighbors around him, who also had stables, used the paths to exercise their horses. Will said he had two horses stabled at his neighbor's barn, but he rarely rode them anymore.

The dusty pasture was much different from the sprawling green grassy pastures from her hometown. She could see a large barn down below and thought how great it would be to get back to riding. She hadn't ridden since she was a teenager.

She asked about the horses. Will didn't answer at first. Sarah wondered if he'd heard her, or if he was ignoring her. Should she repeat the question or let it go?

"I'm divorced. She left me for our dentist," Will said. He turned to her and began laughing. He laughed so hard that it made Sarah laugh nervously.

"I'm sorry, but I don't really talk about this. And, it's been two years!" he said, as he laughed until tears spilled out of his eyes.

Sarah laughed along with him but didn't really know what was so funny.

"You come along and here I am blurting out my deepest secrets," Will said, wiping his eyes.

"I'm so sorry, I didn't mean to...," she said, although she wasn't sure why she was sorry.

"Stop. It felt good. Actually, it didn't hurt a bit."

"Well, then...you're welcome?" She smiled awkwardly at him.

He smiled too and explained that the horses were his ex-wife's. His tone grew somber as he told Sarah about the last two years of trying to avoid talking about the fact that his wife cheated on him.

"Everyone knows, but I don't like to talk about it. Hurts too much."

Sarah understood what he meant all too well. "I caught my husband having sex with my friend," she blurted.

Will raised his eyebrows. "No kidding," he said.

Sarah nervously kicked the ground. "Yup. I found them on New Year's Eve out in his truck. I went home, packed a bag, and drove as far away as I could."

Will shook his head. "I'm sorry," he said.

"Don't be," she said. "It wasn't the first time. Just the first time I actually saw it with my own eyes."

"We should swap stories sometime," Will said.

Sarah smiled. "We should," she said.

An awkward silence fell between them. They both looked around as if they were hoping to find what to say next out in the air.

"I'm gonna go," Sarah said, as she began to walk away. Will followed behind while the dogs ran beside her. She patted the dogs one last time then got in her car. She played it cool, taking her time getting situated in the seat. Will held the door as she buckled her seat belt. She waved awkwardly as she pulled out of the driveway. Will waved back.

She rolled the car along slowly, thinking about the apartment—the cottage—or whatever it was. A place she could call home. No, she told herself, home was in New Hampshire. Home was where she was everyone else's maid, nurse, and cook. Home was where she didn't matter, where she was invisible, where she was miserable and sad.

She wondered if Jen and Joe were together now. She shuddered at the visual of them having sex in Joe's truck. Then Sarah stopped her car. He heart raced with excitement as she pulled a U-turn and went back to Will's. Rocky and Adrian came out barking as she walked towards the garage, announcing her arrival. Will turned and smiled.

"I think I'll take it," she said.

Will laughed. "What changed your mind, the horses?"

"No. I've been told I overthink things sometimes, and I decided I should just go for it. I mean, living at the hotel is nice but it's expensive."

Will agreed. "We can take it month to month for now, if that's a better option for you."

"Are you sure? I mean, that would be great!" Sarah was nervous and excited all at once. She had to pinch her side to make sure this wasn't a dream. They agreed she could move in right away.

"Do you need any help moving in? I can get my sons to help you if you do," Will offered.

"All I have is one suitcase. I'll buy sheets and towels though, and groceries, but I think I'll be all set."

"You travel light, that's for sure. I look forward to having you as a neighbor."

She smiled as she walked back to her car. Will waved with one quick pass of his hand before stuffing it back in his pocket. As she pulled away, she glanced in her rear view mirror to see if he'd gone back to the house. She smiled when she saw Will standing at the end of the driveway, watching her leave.

18

Sarah arrived at David and Michael's house a little after seven o'clock. She stood on their doorstep shivering with a bottle of wine and a bouquet of flowers. She regretted not bringing a sweater. Their house was sandwiched between two others. It was hard to tell where one ended and the other began. All of the houses in southern California were so close together, unlike back home where people had more land than house. Their front porch was small and homey with a small white bench and two large flowerpots blooming with white Christmas roses.

Michael answered the door. "Hello, Sarah Rossi."

He always said her first and last name. There was something about it that Sarah thought was endearing. He wore dark jeans and a light blue button-down shirt with the sleeves rolled up to his elbows. He smiled and seemed relaxed, which made her feel at ease. She hoped she'd see a different side of Michael tonight. She couldn't imagine David would be with someone as angry and serious as Michael was at work.

"Hello, Michael Inwood," she said.

He gave her a hug and took the wine from her. He smelled

like green apples and mint.

"You can give David the flowers, he'll love them."

He led her inside where the lights were low and candles lit up the entire house, making it feel warm and cozy. She could hear music playing, but couldn't place the song. She admired the art on the walls and wondered if they were paintings by local artists. Michael led her to the kitchen in the back of the house, where David was busy preparing food. The large kitchen was to the left and on the right was a living room area with a huge sectional couch and big screen TV that hung over a massive fireplace. Along the back wall, there were large doors that led out to the patio.

"I'm so glad you came!" David said, as they entered the kitchen.

"I wouldn't miss it," Sarah said, handing him the flowers. David hugged her as he gushed over the bouquet, and then took them over to the sink where he began snipping the ends off with kitchen shears. Michael stole pieces of cheese from the platter that David had been arranging. He gestured to Sarah not to let David know. Sarah laughed.

The doorbell rang and Michael excused himself. When he left the room, David put down the flowers and came over to Sarah.

"I want you to tell me how it went with *Will!*"

"It went great. He seems really nice and the apartment, well guest house, is so charming and perfect," she said. She hadn't been able to stop thinking about Will since she left him. Those eyes…and how he'd opened up to her about his situation. They had something in common; they'd both been cheated on. She decided not to mention that part to David.

"Are you going to take it?"

"I think…I'm going to take it," she said.

David jumped up and down and hugged her.

"Wow…putting down some roots. I'm impressed. I thought you were only here for a *mini-vacation.*"

"I was. I am. I really don't know what I'm doing anymore."

"We'll talk more later," David said, as a woman entered the kitchen behind Michael, who was telling an animated story. When he was done, introductions were made.

Jillian was dressed in black pants and a gray knit poncho-style sweater with fringes on the end and black flats. Her look was sophisticated, polished, and yet casual and comfortable.

Michael poured wine and led everyone out to the patio. Sarah immediately went over to the heat lamp, drawn to the heat like a lizard. She stood under it soaking up the warmth. David brought out the cheese tray and an assortment of hot appetizers and set them down on a long teak table set with candles.

Sarah watched Michael carefully. He joked, told stories, and Sarah discovered how he loved using sarcasm. It was so nice to see a different side of him.

"So, David says you're new to Laguna. Where are you from?" asked Jillian.

Sarah gripped her wine glass with two hands. "New Hampshire. I arrived in Laguna about two weeks ago."

"Oh, that's nice. Why did you do leave New Hampshire?"

Sarah steadied her breath and let out a nervous laugh. "Well, that might be too long of a story. Let's just say, I came here because I was looking for a change."

"She left her husband," David said, smirking at her.

Sarah's jaw dropped and her face grew hot. She hadn't told David her story yet, even though he begged her every day to tell him. She'd been waiting for the right time. She didn't want to tell her story in front of Michael for fear of what he'd say. She thought about lying and telling them that her husband had died or something, but she knew there'd be too many follow up questions.

"Actually…" Sarah said, figuring there was no use it trying to hide it. "I did leave my husband."

David's eyes widened. "I knew right away—that first day I met you. Right, Michael? I said, 'she left her husband,'" David said.

Sarah shrunk as she waited for Michael to answer. He

nodded his head slowly, staring at Sarah.

"Are you divorced?" Jillian asked.

"No, but we should be," Sarah said. She turned away from all the eyes staring at her. This conversation was quickly going somewhere she wasn't ready to go. She glanced over at Michael, who was sitting next to David. His arms and legs were crossed, and he had a scowl on his face.

"Sarah's getting an apartment," David said.

"Really?" Michael asked. "No more hotel?"

Sarah steadied her breath as she nodded her head.

"She's going to live in Will Donovan's cottage."

"Oh! That's great!" Jillian said.

"Will is a great guy," Michael said.

Sarah watched him intently, searching for meaning behind his words. Was he being sarcastic or sincere? She wasn't sure.

Michael stood, shook his head, and went inside. *David likes lost puppies,* she remembered him saying.

Sarah thought about following him to apologize, but she wasn't even sure for what. For being a lost puppy, maybe? Then she wondered why his approval was so important to her? She'd been living out from under the control of the men in her life for a couple of weeks and felt so free. She liked making decisions on her own and answering to no one. Michael wasn't demanding answers, but she still wanted to know what he was thinking.

Sarah finished her wine and looked around for the bottle so she could refill her glass. Thankfully, David jumped up and filled her glass.

"Do you have kids?" Jillian asked.

Sarah flinched.

She let out a forceful breath and decided what the fuck. If they weren't going to like her, so what.

"Twins," she said. "They're seventeen," she blurted before they could ask.

Michael came back out to the patio with another man following behind him. Sarah hadn't heard the doorbell ring, but she wondered if that was why he'd left the conversation and not because he was upset with her. He introduced this new addition as Brett. Sarah figured Brett to be in his thirties, but he was dressed like a twenty-something in blue plaid shorts and a brown pullover sweatshirt that said Billabong across it. Sarah smiled when she panned down to his neon green Chuck Taylor sneakers. He hugged everyone, including Sarah. She was starting to get used to all the hugging in California. Brett smelled like patchouli.

Sarah hoped the conversation would move away from her now.

"Brett works for Will," Michael said to Sarah.

"You know Will Donovan?" Brett asked.

"I just met him today, actually."

"Great guy. I've worked for him for ten years," said Brett.

"What do you do?" Sarah asked.

"Construction. I'm one of Will's foremen. We're working on a project out in Coto, remodeling a house on a golf course, and let me tell you, it's unreal," said Brett.

"Coto De Caza is private community west of here. I'll take you out there someday and you can take some pictures," said David.

"Are you a photographer?" Jillian asked.

"Yes," said Sarah. And for the first time, she didn't feel the need to say that she was just an amateur.

"Do you just take pictures for fun, or is it your profession?" Michael asked as he rejoined the group.

Sarah sat up straighter.

"Fun for now, but I hope to make it my profession someday."

Michael locked eyes with her. "What did you do for work in New Hampshire?" he Michael.

"I was a fifth-grade teacher. And no, I didn't love it."

"Why not?"

"It just wasn't something I ever wanted to do. My heart wasn't in it."

"And photography was?"

"Yes, since I was nine. That's when I got my first Polaroid

Instant Camera for Christmas."

The camera was as big as a toaster. Sarah used a whole pack of film within minutes of opening it. The pictures flew out of the front of the camera, and Sarah would shake each one gently, blowing on it to help it dry faster. After each picture revealed itself, she'd take another. She'd never seen anything so magical before!

Then her father yelled at her in front of a house full of guests for using up all the film so quickly. He said she was "wasting" it on meaningless pictures. Sarah was crushed. To her, the pictures weren't meaningless, even though whenever she looked back through those old picture albums, she had to admit that maybe her father had a point. She took pictures of pictures hanging on walls, the space under her bed, the toilet, the cat...loads of pictures of the cat. The point was that the pictures weren't silly to her. She was seeing those things in a different way. For her, things came to life through the lens of the camera, but to everyone else, those things were ordinary.

Michael finally looked away from her and her body relaxed. He clapped his hands together and stood.

"Who wants salmon and who wants a filet?" Michael said.

His abruptness in changing the subject made Sarah wonder what he was thinking about her. Not being able to read him was driving her crazy. Sarah told Michael she'd love a filet and then she excused herself to use the bathroom. She needed to get out from under the spotlight to gather her thoughts. Jillian jumped up and said she'd show the way. When Sarah returned to the kitchen, Jillian was helping David toss the salad. Brett was outside talking to Michael by the grill.

"Is there anything I can do to help?" Sarah asked.

"No!" David said. "You're the guest of honor. There will be no work for you tonight."

"I feel special then...and useless. I'm not used to people doing things for me."

"Well, then enjoy," David said, winking at her.

Jillian laughed and nudged David. Sarah could sense they

were great friends.

"How long have you two known each other?" Sarah asked.

"Going on seven years I think, right Dave?"

David agreed and told Sarah how the two had met at a gallery event that Jillian ran. Sarah learned that Jillian had only been married for three years when her husband came home one day and said he didn't want to be married anymore. Jillian said it was because she wanted kids, and he didn't. They'd been trying for months and the trying had become a chore.

"I guess I should've realized he really didn't want a baby and stopped pushing him so much."

"Paaahleease…," David said, rolling his eyes. "You've got to stop blaming yourself. You were trying to have a baby for three years. If he didn't want kids, he should've said so sooner."

Sarah agreed.

"Yeah, well, he *said* he wanted a baby. The miscarriages and the IVF just became too much for him I guess. I think he just freaked."

"Freaked? No, he was an asshole. He cheated on you. Remember?" David asked.

Jillian looked down. Sarah could tell she was hurting, so she changed the conversation and asked about Jillian's job as a gallery manager. She worked at one of the largest galleries in Laguna. Before long, Michael came in holding a platter.

"Dinner's ready!" Michael called out.

Michael didn't take his seat right away. He asked Sarah to join him in the wine room nestled into the area under the stairs leading up to the second floor.

Michael ducked his head as they went in. The room was small, only large enough for three or four people to be in at a time, yet it held a couple hundred bottles of wine. In one corner, there was a small shelf built into the wall with a tall wine opener mounted on the shelf.

"What do you like, Sarah Rossi?" Michael asked, rubbing his hands together as he looked around.

"Oh, I'm not really qualified to choose wine," she said. She drank wine but never really cared what kind it was.

"That's all right. Just pick something," Michael said looking around the space.

Sarah could tell he was proud of his collection. She thought about the wine she had with Nathan and Leslie at the tapas restaurant. "I tried Malbec the other night and that was really good. But anything is fine."

"Malbec it is!" Michael said, excitedly pulling out two bottles of Malbec from the top rack. He showed one bottle to her. "This one is from our trip to Washington State last year, we toured some wineries there. Washington has been producing Malbec since the eighties. It's very hard to find up there, but if you know where to look you can find some beauties. We've been saving these for a special occasion."

"Oh, I'm sorry. You can pick something else," Sarah said.

"No, no, no. Don't apologize. It's a really great choice and this is the perfect group to share it with. Come on," Michael said leading them out to the dining room.

Sarah blushed. "I feel bad if it's a special wine."

"Don't ever feel bad for making a choice," he said looking deep into her eyes. "Besides, everyone deserves to drink nice wine." Michael smiled, as he put his hand on her shoulder.

Sarah relaxed. She couldn't help but feel they'd made a connection.

They emerged from the wine room together, laughing. David smiled at Sarah and signaled for her to come and sit next to him.

The rest of the night, she was able to relax because they didn't ask her any more questions about her past. Jillian was definitely someone she wanted to get to know better, and couldn't wait to go and see her at her gallery. At the end of the night, David walked her out to her car. It was a little after two in the morning.

"So, did you have fun?" David asked eagerly.

"I had *the* best time. Thank you so much for having me."

"If you haven't already figured it out, mostly everyone in

California comes from somewhere else. Most of us are transplants, so we all know what it's like to come to town and not know anyone. We take care of each other. It's what we do here."

She smiled. "Well, thank you. Very much," she said, as she hugged him.

"Listen, you. I know we've only known each other for a short time, but I feel like we're kindred spirits or something."

"I feel the same way about you," Sarah said.

"Well, just know that if you need anything, you can count on me."

"Thank you," she said. "And you can count on me."

"Call me tomorrow if you need help moving into *Will's*," he said making quotation marks with his fingers.

"What is *that* supposed to mean?" she laughed.

"Nothing. I just don't know why you won't look for something a little closer to us here in Dana Point…"

"I'm going with the flow. I took the job with you on a whim, and I was given Will's name by chance. I'm just trying to let destiny guide me, instead of overthinking anything. It feels right, and I'm excited about it. Besides, if it doesn't work out, then maybe you'll be stuck with me."

"Hmmm…I get it; you don't want people telling you what to do. I can live with that," David said.

Sarah hugged him again.

"Thank you for everything," she said.

As she drove back to Laguna to spend the last night in the hotel, she thought about Will and wondered if he had a good night too.

19

The next morning, a tiny bit of sun found its way through the window, catching her just right as she opened her eyes in her hotel room. Today was the day she was moving into Will's cottage. She had left New Hampshire in a hurry with only one goal: to get as far away from Joe as possible. Now, her little get-away was turning into a completely new life.

Part of her felt guilty about that. It seemed unfair to the boys for her to be living a life without them. She had finally stopped her daily calls them. They still hadn't responded to a single one. She wondered what they thought about her leaving and if they knew the whole story. Not just Joe's version of God knows what. They saw the verbal—and physical–abuse that Sarah had suffered. They experienced it too. She hoped they would understand why she left. She sent them each a text even though she knew they wouldn't respond. She had to keep trying.

There was a loud knock at the door. "It's Carlos!" he called from the other side.

Sarah quickly tugged on yoga pants and a sweatshirt then pulled her hair into a ponytail, as she opened the door. Carlos smiled back at her.

"Buenos Dias!" he said, as he rolled the cart full of breakfast items in the room.

Each day he put more goodies on the cart: pastry, eggs, fruit, and sometimes a huge Belgium waffle—all complimentary because she was in the Sunset Room. She asked him to set the cart out on the balcony, explaining that this was her last day at the hotel.

"So sorry. I don't have you on my check out list," said Carlos apologetically.

"No, you wouldn't. I just made the plans to leave yesterday."

"OK then. May I pour your coffee today?" Carlos asked, as he had every day since she arrived, but she'd always said no.

Sarah smiled. "Yes, that would be nice."

Carlos beamed. "That's it! Sometimes you have to let people do things for you, huh?" He wasn't asking a question; it was more of a statement. He poured the coffee and set it down in front of Sarah.

"Anything else, Miss?" Carlos asked.

She breathed in the ocean air. There was haze over the ocean, and the visibility was low. Some days the haze would lift and the blue sky would appear, and other days it lingered in the sky. It had only rained once since she arrived. Sarah thought about the endless gray days back home that made the winter months almost unbearable. Not seeing the sun for days on end did something to her soul. She hated all the bare tree limbs and dirty snow on the side of the road. Sarah smiled as she looked at the green palm trees and sandy beach, already scattered with people enjoying some exercise.

"Carlos, is it ever cloudy in California?"

"Hardly ever, and when it rains, it passes very quickly."

Sarah nodded.

"Thank you, Carlos. I really appreciate what you've done for me during my stay here," she said.

He blushed. "I'm just doing my job, Miss. Have a great day."

She took her time eating the giant, juicy strawberries, sweeter than any strawberry she'd ever had back home, before picking at the cranberry orange muffin savoring each bite of the crumbly top. She read for an hour before getting dressed and going for a walk on the beach.

She slipped off her shoes when she reached the cool sand, watching a woman throw a ball into the ocean while her dog ran into the water to retrieve it. Two elderly women, both wearing large-brimmed hats to shield the sun, laughed as they enjoyed a morning stroll along the ocean's edge. She'd seen the two walking side by side on the beach almost every day. Their arms were locked together, helping to balance each other on the uneven sand. Some days they walked in silence and other days they laughed so hard they had to stop to hold each other up. Sarah wondered if they were old friends, sisters, or maybe lovers. She couldn't take her eyes off them. She'd never had a relationship like that with another woman, one where you could be together in silence one day and laughing so hard you needed to pee the next. She pulled out her camera to capture the moment. When she looked at the photo in the viewer tears filled her eyes. She longed for closeness with someone like these two women shared.

Sarah walked all the way to the Main Street Beach, soaking up the sun.

***

Sarah left the hotel just after noon to move in to her new place.

Her new place.

On the way, she stopped at the store to buy some groceries. She arrived at Will's just after two in the afternoon. Will was in the garage, working on his car again. He came out and directed her into the third garage bay that he had cleaned out for her.

"Welcome, neighbor!" Will called out as she emerged from her car.

She felt her face blush as she took things out of her car.

Why did he make her feel this way?

"Want some help?" Will asked.

"Nope! I got it. Thanks," she said nervously, as she loaded her arms with bags. She hoped her face wasn't as red as it felt.

"You aren't used to people helping you, are you?" Will asked.

"Um, well, I guess not. How do you know that?"

"Well, because my selfish princess of an ex-wife would have said yes in a heartbeat and walked away without carrying one thing in herself."

"Ah...," Sarah said, as she tried to picture Will—who seemed so down to earth—with someone so entitled.

"I insist," Will said, as he reached into her trunk.

She couldn't help but notice his large biceps as he pulled out her suitcase. She stopped herself before her thoughts could go any further. *He's my landlord, nothing else.*

Sarah grabbed the bag of groceries and the bouquet of colorful flowers she'd bought for herself, and followed him to the cottage.

"Mariella's still inside giving it a good cleaning, but I think she's almost done." Will said as they reached the front door.

"Mariella?" Sarah asked.

"She's my housekeeper."

"Housekeeper...," Sarah said tentatively. Even though she knew there were housekeepers at the hotel cleaning for her, it felt different here.

Will laughed, making her blush again.

"I'm sorry. I'm not laughing at you. I just find you very refreshing is all," he said, then added, "In a good way."

"As long as it's in a good way, I won't worry then," she said.

A petite, older woman dressed in denim Bermuda shorts and a white short-sleeved three-buttoned shirt appeared from the bathroom.

"Sarah, this is Mariella," Will said.

"Nice to meet you," Sarah said.

"Very nice to meet you, Miss Sarah. I'm glad that this

space will finally be used again," Mariella said with a heavy Spanish accent.

"Mariella was our nanny for the kids when they were young. Now she's taken on more of a household manager role," Will said, winking at Mariella.

Sarah smiled when she saw him wink. Clearly the two had history.

"Yes, household manager covers it," said Mariella. Then she turned to Sarah. "I do everything here Miss Sarah, including washing this man's clothes. You'd think that a grown man would know how to throw in a load of laundry, but no, no, no. He waits for me to arrive on Monday and then complains that he couldn't wear his favorite jeans because he got them dirty while he was working on his car on Saturday. Shah!"

Sarah laughed.

"Yeah well, if I did my own laundry then I wouldn't need you and then what?" Will teased.

Mariella swatted him with the towel she was holding and they both laughed, just as old friends do.

"Mariella will come in and clean for you once a week."

"I won't do your laundry though. Sorry Miss, that's where I draw the line," Mariella smiled at Sarah.

"Oh, it's OK. I can clean. Really," Sarah insisted. "It sounds like you have your hands full with this guy," Sarah said nodding her head towards Will. "I don't mind cleaning. In fact, I find it relaxing."

Will smiled at her.

"I like this girl," Mariella said. "Good job finding a tenant this time!"

"This time?" Sarah asked.

"Mariella didn't like the last guy I rented to. He was a real jerk, very disrespectful. Not only did he treat Mariella poorly, but he also used my home as his party house. I'd come home to fifty half-naked people in the pool, which some people would love I'm sure, but I'm not a partier. I mean, I like to have good time don't get me wrong, but these people had zero respect. One time I left the main house open by accident, and when I got home, there were people everywhere, including my bedroom. It wasn't good."

"No, it wasn't," Mariella said. "It took a long time to get rid of the guy, but he finally left. That was what? Last summer?

"Wow, just last summer?" Will asked, looking to the sky thinking about it. "I guess you're right. It was when Lauren went off to school. I was thinking it was right after Tiffany left."

Mariella shot Will a look questioning him with her eyes. Sarah turned away so they could have their moment.

"What?" Will asked.

"You just said Tiffany's name. Never mind you said it in front of a total stranger. No offense, Miss Sarah."

Sarah unpacked groceries, trying to pretend she wasn't listening.

"Well, a new me, perhaps," Will said.

"OK," Mariella said, holding up her hand. "That's fine, I'll leave it be. Miss Sarah, it was very nice to meet you. If you ever need anything, anything at all, you just ask, OK?"

"Thank you, Mariella. I appreciate that."

Mariella pushed Will aside kiddingly and walked out of the house, leaving Will and Sarah alone. Sarah started opening cabinets, trying to decide where to put things.

"Is there anything else you'd like me to bring in for you?" Will asked.

"No, thank you," Sarah said. Although she did have a couple bags in the car to bring in but it felt strange to ask him to get them.

"OK, then. I'll get back to the garage. If you need anything, let me know."

"Sounds good," Sarah said, but what she really wanted was for him to stay and talk. The connection she felt to him was intense, like she knew him from a previous life or something.

Will walked toward the door, and just before he was all the way out, he said, "There is a barbecue at the beach tonight.

Would you want to come?"

He smiled at her, but Sarah sensed he was nervous. Was he asking her out? She wanted nothing more than to be able to say yes, but she already had plans with Jillian.

"Oh, um…," Sarah said, as she searched for words. "I'm meeting a friend in a little bit, and I'm not sure what our plans are for later."

"Oh, sure. I understand," Will said looking disappointed. "No worries. Have fun unpacking," Will shut the door before Sarah could respond.

Sarah waited a minute, hoping he would open the door and come back in, but he didn't. She took a deep breath and smiled.

She walked to the bedroom and unpacked her suitcase, hung clothes in the closet, and put her toiletries in the bathroom. She lingered on her reflection in the mirror for a minute. "How the hell did you get here?"

She shook her head, snapping herself out of it. Her cell phone buzzed in her pocket—it was David. Hearing his animated voice instantly brought a smile to Sarah's face.

"I came to the hotel to get you for lunch, and you were gone! Some friend you are," he said playfully.

"Wait, did we have plans?" Sarah quickly ran over in her mind whether or not she had made a lunch date with David last night. It was possible that she had enjoyed too much wine and didn't remember.

"No, I just thought I'd surprise you," David said. "I worked breakfast this morning and took the afternoon off. Michael likes to live at the café, but I need my time off."

"Oh! Here I was thinking I was too drunk last night and didn't remember making plans with you."

"You weren't drunk! If you were, you're a really controlled drunk. Anyway, Jillian said you're meeting her later at the gallery. What time do you think you'll be in town?"

"Maybe an hour or so. I'm just finishing unpacking now. I'll head out when I'm done."

They agreed to meet at Jillian's gallery in an hour.

20

The gallery Jillian managed was in the heart of downtown Laguna, just across from Main Street Beach. Sarah walked in and her eyes darted around the room at all the paintings. A variety of pastels, watercolors, oil paintings, and sculptures filled the space.

A couple waited for Jillian who was behind the counter talking on the phone. On the other side of the room, two women were looking at a painting and discussing it. Sarah overheard one of them say she wanted the artwork for her bedroom. The two were standing in front of an enormous watercolor of Egyptian mummies in tombs—a rather odd piece to put in a bedroom, Sarah thought. Jillian finished her phone call and came over to Sarah.

"Just give me a few minutes," Jillian said in a hushed tone. "These are some of my best customers. Figures they both come in on a day when I'm trying to sneak out early. Look around, you'll find the photography in the back to the left."

Sarah told her to take her time. She listened to Jillian talk with the customers, quickly impressed by how much Jillian knew about the artists and their vision for each piece. Sarah made her way around the gallery until she got to the photography collection, which was smaller than the other collections. One group of photos was particularly mesmerizing. The photographer captured everyday moments: birthday parties, dinner with friends, a family at the beach. Even though the photos seemed ordinary at first glance, Sarah couldn't stop looking at them. It was as if she was in the room when the photo was taken and could hear the conversations. Jillian came up beside her and asked what she liked.

"I really like this photographer here. What's the name?"

"This is Jacqueline Teixeira's work. She's local and a good friend of mine, actually. She started doing photography for fun, but she's really started to make some great money selling her pieces here."

Sarah nodded trying to imagine what it would be like to sell a photo.

"What type of camera do you use?" asked Jillian.

"A Nikon D7000. I just got a new telephoto lens for Christmas that I've tried out a few times. I have yet to see the prints though. I have a macro lens too, which I use the most, and I have a speed light but I never use it." She left out the part that she'd bought the telephoto lens for herself.

"I'd really love to see your work sometime. What do you like to photograph?" Jillian asked.

"I really love capturing people when they don't know I'm shooting them. In those moments, I feel like you can almost see into someone's soul because they aren't posing or putting on some mask, if you know what I mean."

"Do you like the pictures you take?"

"Yes," Sarah said.

"That's all that matters," Jillian said. "When the artist's passion comes through in their work, it's really magical. It's almost as if the photograph has energy or a vibe that draws people to it."

"Wow, I love that." Sarah could feel the energy in the room now that she was aware of it; she had subconsciously felt it as soon as she entered the gallery.

"Exactly. Now you know why I love my job!"

Sarah nodded.

"Well, I'm free to go now. David is waiting for us at the beach," Jillian said.

"OK, I'm ready," Sarah said.

They walked across the street to the beach. The sky was the perfect shade of blue and the sun felt warm on her skin. They snuck up on David as he sat on a bench overlooking the ocean. His face pointed towards the sun, and his eyes were closed.

"Boo!" Jillian said as she grabbed his shoulders.

"God! You scared me!" David squealed.

Then he got up and hugged them both.

"I'm so excited! Today will be fun, right Jill?" David asked.

"Yes! So here's what I'm thinking…Let's drive up the coast and show Sarah Newport and Balboa Island. Then we can hit the barbecue on the beach later. We'll stop at Trader Joe's to pick up some snacks and wine."

Sarah's heart jumped. She wondered if it was the same barbecue that Will had invited her to.

"A barbecue on the beach in January?" Sarah asked.

David laughed. "We do it all the time. Corn dogs, hot dogs, anything you can cook on a stick over the fire."

"I didn't bring a warm coat for later. I didn't think we'd gone so long," Sarah said.

"No worries, we can stop at my place before we get going and pick up sweatshirts and blankets for later. I'm just a few minutes down the road that way," Jillian said.

***

Sarah turned off the Pacific Coast Highway onto a small access road. Jillian's house was at the end of the road. It was built on the edge of a cliff, overlooking the ocean. The front of the house had windows from top to bottom, so no matter where you were inside you had a perfect view of the ocean.

"Wow, your house is beautiful," Sarah said, as she entered the house.

"Thank you. The art business has been very good to me."

"Yeah, that and a little help from Daddy," David said under his breath to Sarah.

Two cats swirled around Sarah's legs, meowing. She scooped the fluffy white one up into her arms. It purred loudly while the gray and white cat stood up on its back legs, trying to crawl up her pants. She bent down to pat him. She thought about Shep and Sadie. She hoped someone was taking care of them.

"Balboa Island is mostly closed down for the season," Jillian said, breaking Sarah's train of thought. "But I still think you should see it. You could get some great shots there."

"Well then, let's get a move on," David said. He gathered the blankets and took them out to Sarah's car.

Jillian got a sweatshirt for Sarah and they met David at the car. David offered to drive, so Sarah threw him the keys. Michael was meeting David at the beach later, and Jillian was going to get a ride home with her friend, Trevor. Sarah wondered if he was more than just a friend but she didn't ask.

***

The highway ran along the coast with wonderful views of the ocean. Even though Sarah had driven the highway many times since arriving in Laguna, she had never been able to take in the scenery.

"So, how did the move go?" David asked.

Sarah told them how Will helped her bring things in and about Mariella.

"So...what do you think about Will?" Jillian asked.

Sarah wondered what she was getting at. "He seems nice," she said. "And lonely."

David snorted. "Yeah well..."

"Do you know much about him?" Jillian asked.

"Not really," Sarah said, deciding not to tell them how awkward it was when Will told her about his ex-wife.

"He owns half the town," Jillian said.

"Oh?" Sarah asked, intrigued.

"Oh, yes really," David said. "Every strip mall from San Clemente to Newport Beach is owned by Will Donovan. He doesn't need a tenant in that cottage any more than I need a ticket for the Titanic."

Sarah laughed.

"About a year ago, a friend of his convinced him to let John Butler move in. Which was a huge mistake," Jillian said.

"John Butler—the actor?" Sarah asked.

"That's the one," Jillian said.

"He told me that after his wife left he had a tenant that was a bit of a partier," Sarah said.

David nearly drove off the road and Jillian gasped.

"He told you about Tiffany?" they yelled in unison.

"That's HUGE. It's almost an unwritten rule not to mention her in front of him," Jillian said.

"Why?"

Jillian told Sarah all about Tiffany. The daughter of a super successful real-estate developer from the eighties. Tiffany was a daddy's princess, accustomed to living a certain lifestyle at a young age. She went to college only to drop out because she couldn't stand the college life; it was too boring for her. Tiffany wanted to be up in Beverly Hills, where she intended to find a husband and settle there.

"Her daddy cut her off because she dropped out of school without telling him," David said. "He said he wouldn't pay for anything until she got herself back into college. He wouldn't even let her live at home. Tiffany begged her mother to get her father to change his mind, but all her mom could do was get him to agree that Tiffany could live at home if she got a job. Then one night she met Will Donovan at a beach party. He was twenty-four and making a name for himself as a real-estate developer. He bought his first apartment complex in Mission Viejo using some money his father, a plastic surgeon, had given him after he graduated from USC. Tiffany latched onto him, and they got married on the beach six months after they met."

"They had kids right away," Jillian continued. "Although,

Tiffany wasn't really cut out to be a mom."

David laughed. "You can say that again. She had a lot of help: nannies, housekeepers, assistants. Tiff was always dressed to the nines with her nails manicured, and her hair done. Then, there was Will. Rough and tough guy with his dirty jeans and rough hands from working construction. Complete opposites."

"He worked, she spent the money, and occasionally they attended functions together," Jillian said.

Sarah conjured up the image some reality TV housewife. "Why did you think Will fell for her if they were *that* different?" she asked.

"Because she was good in bed," Jillian laughed and so did David and Sarah.

Sarah knew she was kidding but she couldn't help but wonder how Tiffany and Will ended up together. Then again, she and Joe were complete opposites too.

"Tiffany started having an affair with her dentist a few years ago. I think Will knew about it the minute it started but maybe he chose to ignore it. Who knows…," David said.

Sarah knew what that was like. Ignoring those subtle changes that happened, like when Joe stopped sleeping in their bed and she found receipts from restaurants an hour away on days he should have been working. And not wanting to mention it because you could be wrong or worse, right.

"Will finally kicked her out one day after catching Tiffany having sex with her lover in their pool," Jillian said.

"She moved up to Beverly Hills with the dentist and Tiffany finally got the life of her dreams," David said.

"Wow…," Sarah said. She couldn't help but wonder what Will was doing right now.

"Will Donovan is a great guy, really genuine. Tiffany didn't deserve him," Jillian said.

"So, why is it so taboo to mention Tiffany?" Sarah asked.

"I really never understood that either, but right after she left he went into depression or something. Which no one understood because Tiffany was hardly ever home when they were together she was always off traveling somewhere, and if she was home they didn't spend time together. When she left him, he went into hiding. No one saw him around town and if they did, he'd barely spoke to anyone. I think his employees started the drama about not mentioning Tiffany after he finally came back to the office. I think they were afraid that if they mentioned her, he wouldn't come back," Jillian said.

Sarah watched the ocean as it followed them, thinking about Will, secretly hoping she'd see him later at the barbecue.

***

David pulled into the municipal lot at Balboa Island twenty minutes later.

"Here we are!" he said excitedly.

While they walked toward the beach, David explained how busy Balboa Island was during the summer months and how it was nearly impossible to find a parking spot. Sarah looked around imagining throngs of people scurrying to the beach with coolers, bags, and kids in tow.

The sun was high in the sky and shined brightly as they walked along the beach and then up on the pier. Sarah took pictures of everything: the birds, the pier, the waves, the seals that were diving about at the end of the pier, the surfers. Surfers were everywhere in California. It didn't seem to matter what time of day or what the weather was like, you could always spot a surfer in the ocean on any given day.

They walked to the end of the pier to the 1940s inspired diner overlooking the ocean, and ordered milkshakes and French fries to share.

"OK, Miss Sarah," David started.

Sarah braced herself for what was coming.

"You've been so mysterious since you arrived. I just can't stand it anymore!" David said, as soon as the waitress turned away from taking their order.

"Why did I leave my husband?" she asked, trumping him.

He nodded. Sarah sat back and sighed. It was time.

"I caught my husband having sex with a friend of mine—his third affair that I know about. Something inside me snapped when I saw them fucking in his truck and I left."

David and Jillian's jaws hung open.

"I'm so sorry," David said.

"Don't be," she said.

"What about your sons?" David asked. He had concern in his voice. "Have you talked to them?"

She sighed. "Zach and Cam haven't returned one of my calls or texts in weeks. At this point, I think they want nothing to do with me."

"You're their mother. Of course they *miss* you," Jillian said.

"It's so complicated, Jillian."

Sarah told them about her life as a little girl, taking care of everyone in her family, and getting pregnant after a one-night stand. Then she told them about her life with Joe; how he turned out to be even worse than her father ever was.

"Why did you stay all those years?" David asked.

"I guess I believed I could always do something to make things better."

"But to run away like you did, I mean, don't you think you should go back...for the twins?" Jillian asked.

The waitress brought their food. Sarah waited for her to leave before she answered Jillian. Tears filled her eyes.

"I'm not a bad person," Sarah said.

"I don't think you are, but I can't help but worry that you're running away from something that you're too afraid to face, and that always backfires. Trust me, I know," Jillian said.

Sarah didn't mention that before she left she had begun to have episodes of anxiety attacks, and that the thought of ending up like her mother—depressed and confined to bed because of it—scared her to death.

"I was so lonely," Sarah said, wiping the tears from her eyes. "If you can imagine being surrounded by people all the time and yet feeling a hole of emptiness in your chest every day, that was me."

"I can tell that all of this didn't just happen," Jillian said. "I'm not trying to sound judgmental. I just hope you know what you're doing."

Truth was Sarah had no clue what she was doing. She knew she'd have to go home eventually, but for now, she was trying to live in the moment and do what felt right for her.

"Will you go back there eventually?" asked David.

Sarah took a sip of her strawberry milkshake. She swallowed hard as the cold liquid slid down her throat.

"I guess," Sarah said. "It's just…I've never been this free in my entire life. I don't know how to go back at this point…"

"But what about Zach and Cam?" Jillian asked.

"They're fine. I'm sure," Sarah snapped.

Jillian looked at Sarah with equal parts pity and disgust. David must have sensed the tension.

"OK, look. I think it took tremendous courage to do what you did," David said. "But Jill's right. You have a lot of unfinished business back home. You need to face that sooner than later."

"You have no idea how awful my life was! I can't do it! I won't go back!"

The small restaurant quieted as people turned to look at Sarah.

"I'm sorry," Sarah said, as she got up and went outside. She walked along the pier for a minute then she stopped to look out at the ocean. She leaned up against the railing and cried. It took her a lifetime to get away from the life she never wanted. She couldn't go back now. It would be like giving a caged animal an hour out in the wild, only to capture it again. That would be cruel.

Jillian and David walked towards her. Sarah wiped her eyes. They surrounded her and David hooked his arm into hers.

"Here's what I know," David said. "Whatever you need to do, whether it's going back home or staying right here, I will do whatever I can to help."

Tears streamed out of Sarah's eyes. She buried her head

on David's shoulder. Jillian leaned in and hugged them both.
"I'm sorry if I sounded judgmental. I didn't mean to upset
you. I just—" Jillian said.

"No, it's OK. I know I need to face all of this. I'm just so
scared that if I go back there I'll be stuck there forever."

"Well," Jillian said, hooking her arm into Sarah's free arm.
"We'll help you through it."

Having their support meant the world to Sarah. She wasn't
sure what they could do to help, but it was nice to know she
had friends. Real friends who cared about her.

They walked on the beach for a while and then went to
the boardwalk. Sarah tried to act as if she was having fun, but
inside she was struggling with her emotions. She knew they
were right, she had to go home and face Joe and talk to the
boys. Sarah snapped pictures of the cottages along the beach
trying to forget about home.

Most of the stores on the boardwalk were closed for the
winter, but there were some still open. They went into a retro
candy shop, where they had fun picking out candy they
remembered from when they were kids. Sarah found her
childhood favorites: Razzles and Lemon Heads. She bought a
few boxes of each. Then they walked passed an arcade that
was open on all sides reminding her of the arcades back
home at Hampton Beach. Inside, it was dark but the sounds
of games ringing and clanging drew them in. They played a
shooting game and Sarah played her old favorite, Centipede.
Afterwards, they debated about taking a ride on the Ferris
wheel, but then decided against it. Instead, they walked along
the harbor, looking at the boats and dreaming about which
one they'd like to own someday.

Sarah checked the time. It was almost one in the afternoon
back home. She told David and Jillian she needed to use the
bathroom. She dialed Cam's number on her cellphone. It
rang several times before going to voicemail.

"Hi, Cam. It's mom, *again*. Can you *please* call me back? I
know you're probably mad at me for leaving, but I need to
explain things to you and Zach. I don't know what Dad told

you about what happened on New Year's, but something happened and I want to talk to you about it. I went to a conference in Las Vegas—a photography conference. I learned so much. Then I ended up in California. I wish you could be here with me."

She stopped talking as she realized how ridiculous she sounded, as if she was on some fun adventure.

"*Please*, Cam. Just call me back. I know Grandpa's probably pissed at me and I'm sorry I left him too. Can you tell him that? I just need some more time. I need to figure things out. Life here is so..."

Sarah stopped again. She couldn't tell him that life here was amazing. She knew that would be a kick in the gut for Cam.

"Please. Just call me. OK, Cam? I love you and your brother. Call me back soon. Love you. Bye."

She ended the call and stared at herself in the bathroom mirror. She'd been gone for almost a month, and neither of her boys wanted to talk to her. She wiped the tears from her cheeks before she went back out to meet David and Jillian.

21

They left Balboa at four and went to the grocery store to get firewood and snacks for the beach party. They arrived at the beach just after five o'clock. The sun was making its way down to the horizon. Sarah took out her camera and took pictures of the boats as they headed into the marina.

"Is that the harbor where we were today?" she asked, pointing out across the ocean.

"Yes, Balboa is right in front of us, over there," Jillian pointed. "And, if you look, you can see the pier and the diner we ate at over there. Newport Beach is to the north."

Sarah took in the scene. The palm trees, the boats, the beach, the hordes of happy people all around. People greeted each other with hugs and caught up from their busy weeks. Even though she only knew two people, she still felt as though she belonged.

"Is the beach always this crowded on a Saturday night in January?" Sarah asked.

"Pretty much," Jillian said, looking around. She had rolled her jeans up to her shins and had a bulky, warm sweater on now that complemented her blonde highlights.

"This is awesome," Sarah said.

"It is. Come on, grab some blankets and let's go down," said David.

Jillian and David went around saying hello to friends. Sarah wanted to run after them when they left her standing alone but she didn't. People mingled, ignoring her presence, but at the same time, she couldn't help but feel as if she were on a giant Jumbotron and everyone was staring at the new girl trying figure out who she was. Soon people gathered around fire pits, cooking hot dogs on the open fire. The sound of the waves crashing against the shore was rhythmic and Sarah became less and less aware of the people around her. She closed her eyes and listened to the ocean.

"Fancy meeting you here."

She opened her eyes, catching her breath as she turned to see Will standing in front of her, holding a beer in his hand. He was dressed in dark jeans and a black pullover half-zip sweater. He looked relaxed.

"I would say so," she said, thinking about what David and Jillian had told her about Will. She felt awkward knowing his story.

"Did you have a good day today?"

"I had a *fantastic* day. I saw Balboa Island and a little bit of Newport."

"Different from New Hampshire, huh?"

"Have you ever been to New Hampshire?"

"I have," Will said. "I'm a skier and I once went on a quest to hit the top ten best mountains in the U.S."

"I didn't think New Hampshire had a mountain on that list," Sarah said.

"Ah, you're a skier then?" he asked.

Sarah nodded.

"Well, you're right. I went to Sugarloaf in Maine and then we decided to hit the White Mountains. We skied Cannon and Loon before we went to Vermont to ski Killington."

"Loon is practically in my back yard. How'd you like it there?"

"The trails were icy that day, but overall it was great. We

really enjoyed the New England trails."

"I've only ever skied in New England," Sarah said, looking at Will and noticing his eyes for the first time. They were brown with a golden tint, or maybe it was the glow from the fire.

"Well then, I'll have to take you Big Bear soon. The conditions are great."

Sarah blushed. "I didn't bring my skis with me."

"Are you kidding? I have enough pairs of skis to start my own ski shop. I'm sure we could find you a pair that would fit."

Sarah laughed imagining all the skis.

"Do you want a beer?" Will asked.

"Oh, well we brought some wine, but I can't seem to find David and Jillian right now." Sarah craned her neck, looking for a familiar face in the crowd. She was enjoying talking to Will, maybe a little too much. She needed David and Jillian to make this feel less like an awkward blind date.

"Well, I have ice cold beers right here if you want one. I'm going to get another one anyway, so how about it?"

Sarah nodded her head. "OK, why not!" she said.

Will pulled out two beers from the cooler and popped off the tops with an opener he had in his pocket. When he handed her the beer, his hand grazed hers as she took it from him.

"Thanks," she said, turning away so he wouldn't notice how nervous she was.

"Cheers," he said, holding up his beer.

Sarah tapped it. "Cheers."

"So, do you know anyone here?" he asked, leaning in so his mouth was close to her ear.

She couldn't help but laugh. He seemed nervous.

"No. Just you, David, and Jillian. To be honest, I feel a little out of place," Sarah admitted.

"You and me both. I never come to these things," Will said, smiling.

"Really? Why tonight then?"

"Michael Inwood insisted I come, and I was feeling… happy, so I thought, why not?"

Michael knows Will? He must've known that David was bringing her to the beach. She wondered if Michael asked Will to come because she was going to be there, but then she told herself she was reading into it. Michael was a hard person to figure out. One minute he seemed angry and impatient, the next he was sharing wine that he'd saved for years. Now, she wondered, was he playing matchmaker?

"Do you know anyone here?" Sarah asked.

"Define know…," Will said, laughing.

Sarah leaned into his shoulder, giving it a gentle push. He put his arm around her for a brief minute. She looked at him and smiled. He was so easy to talk with. She couldn't help but wonder what Will meant when he said he was feeling happy, but she didn't ask.

They talked for a while about their day, small talk, but it was nice. Sarah liked that he didn't take himself too seriously.

She spotted David coming towards them, holding Michael's hand. For some reason, Sarah got a knot in her stomach at the sight of Michael. She wondered if David filled him in about what Sarah had told him today.

Jillian trailed behind them, talking to a tall man who Sarah later learned was Trevor, Jillian's on again off again boyfriend. Apparently, things were complicated with his ex-wife. He'd recently moved back in with her to help with the kids and because it was better for him financially, at least until they could sell the house. He wasn't getting back together with his ex, but Jillian felt that he wasn't ready for a relationship just yet. Sarah watched them and thought they made a cute couple. Jillian was sophisticated and so was Trevor. He'd gone to Pepperdine University and was a lawyer now—not a high-powered defense attorney but a corporate lawyer. He reminded Sarah of Tom Brady, almost too good-looking. But, he seemed nice.

They had set up camp at a fire pit just a few yards away, so they all went over and sat down.

"Will, I'm glad you decided to come," Michael said, smiling like the Cheshire cat.

Sarah wondered what he was up to.

"Me too. I haven't been to a beach barbecue in years."

"Well, enjoy!" Michael said, raising his glass to the group who all yelled "Cheers!" in unison.

Michael seemed to know everyone on the beach. He was charming, friendly, and really seemed to care about everyone he talked to. Sarah got the sense that everyone loved him too.

David pulled the chairs into a circle around the fire and they all watched the sun set while they cooked hot dogs on skewers over the open fire and talked. Actually, they were tofu dogs, a first for Sarah, but they weren't that bad— definitely not the same as a good old traditional hot dog, but edible. Sarah took in the moment of being on the beach, in California, watching the sunset with new friends. She couldn't stop smiling.

22

Sarah sipped her coffee and breathed in the fragrance of the flowers from the garden as she sat at the table on her patio. She had Googled a map of California to find the next town to explore. She was looking forward to spending the day at Huntington Beach. Working at the café kept her busy during the week, so she hadn't had as much time to explore as she had originally thought she would.

She looked at the garden, wondering if Tiffany had a hand in designing it. She imagined a tall blonde with breasts too big for her frame and lips to match, and a designer dog under her arm as she bossed around gardeners and pool boys. She hated her and she didn't even know her.

Gosh, I sound like a jealous mistress or something, she thought.

She couldn't tell if Will was home or not. Her patio was on the far right corner of the main house, but she had a good view of his back yard and pool area. She hadn't been inside his house yet, but she assumed his kitchen overlooked the backyard. She imagined him in there now, having breakfast all alone and wondered if he could see her sitting in the garden from his house. A week ago at the barbecue, they had talked about books. Will had a love for books, just like Sarah, but he didn't have the same affinity towards the classics like she did.

"The thing about the classics…is that they were popular before anyone really knew there could be anything better," Will had said, teasing Sarah when she said how much she loved Hemingway.

"Oh, come on," Sarah kidded back. "Hemingway was a great writer and one of the most celebrated of our time. How can you not love his books?"

"It's not that I don't like his books," Will had said. "I just don't see why we have to put so much emphasis on the word classics just because they're old. Writers like Fitzgerald and Hemingway wrote great books, sure. All I'm saying is that there are much better books being published right now."

"Well then, what should I read? John Grisham? Or maybe romance novels, is that what you read?" she teased.

He laughed. "I don't limit myself to one type of book. I like to read everything."

"Everything except the classics."

"No, everything. I just don't limit myself to reading the classics. I like books that make me think. I love political thrillers, non-fiction books, self-help, and I really love Stephen King."

She laughed now, thinking about how they had agreed to read a book, her choice, at the same time and then discuss it over drinks. As she went inside to get more coffee, she thought maybe she'd pick up a classic for him today at the store, just to be funny.

***

Sarah spent the day exploring Huntington Beach. It was seventy degrees without a cloud in the sky. She walked on the beach, took pictures, and ate late lunch there. She returned home mid-afternoon.

Sarah was sitting by the pool soaking in the sun when she heard Will's car pull into the driveway. She checked the time; he was home earlier than usual. She wondered if something had happened at work. The engine purred as it slipped into the garage. She sat up and fixed her hair, ran her fingers under her eyes, and then checked her breath inside her cupped hand. She pulled her towel over her stomach. She was wearing a bikini—something she hadn't done since high school. She'd lost almost ten pounds since arriving in California, and she had felt brave enough to buy the bikini. However, she wasn't ready to wear it in front of anyone yet…especially Will.

Rocky and Adrian came running to see her first. She patted them as they fought for her attention. Will followed behind. He wore an expensive suit, a crisp white shirt, and a cobalt blue tie that gave him an air of importance.

"Sorry about the pups. They've been stuck in the office with my assistant. I've been in meetings all day."

"I just went to Huntington this morning. You could've left them here. I love them!" she said patting them.

"No work today?"

"I had the day off because I worked a party last night," said Sarah.

Will nodded as he loosened his tie then slid it off. Sarah drew in a breath. He looked so sexy.

"I'm gonna change. Would you like some company?" he said.

Sarah's heart jumped as if she were a freshman in high school and a senior had just asked her to the dance.

"Um, sure, that'd be great," Sarah said smiling up at him.

He gave her thumbs up and went inside. A few minutes later, music began to play in the pool area. Then Will arrived carrying a bottle of white wine and two glasses.

"I could use a drink. How about you?" he asked.

"I'd love one."

Will poured two glasses, handed one to her, and dove into the heated pool. Sarah watched as Will swam underwater all the way to the other end of the pool. He emerged, turned around, and did the crawl back to the other side. He did this a few times. She wondered what he was thinking. She'd never seen him so agitated. When he finally finished, he emerged from the pool, sat down next to her, and drank all of his wine.

"Did you have a bad day?" Sarah asked.

"You could say that," Will said, pouring another glass of wine.

"Sorry to hear that. Cheers," she said, holding out her glass. The glasses clinked together and they both took a sip.

There was an uncomfortable silence. Sarah could tell that Will was upset about something, but she hesitated to ask him about it. They hadn't made it past the small talk stage.

"It's Valentine's Day today," Will said.

"So I've heard," Sarah said. She wanted nothing more than to forget the day even existed.

"Not my favorite day. Never was," he said rubbing his head.

Sarah agreed. "So, what'd you do today?" she asked.

Will sighed. "Do you really want to know?"

"I asked," she said smiling.

He told her that he had spent the afternoon meeting with lawyers. Someone was suing his company and the lawyers were trying to settle out of court. They didn't make much progress.

"Oh, and I found out that Tiffany is getting married," he said. "The good news is that I don't have to pay alimony anymore. The dentist she ran off with can support her shopping habits now," he said bitterly.

"Seems fair."

Will laughed. "Tiffany doesn't care about fair. I'm sure she'll figure out some way to make me keep paying. She only cares about one thing, herself. She never cared about me."

"I'm sure she did," Sarah said. Even though she felt angry and bitter towards Joe, she did love him once and until recently cared about him. And, he had cared about her—at least she thought he did.

Will laughed again. "I'm not so sure about that."

"Well, you've got some great kids and if anything that

makes it all worth it," Sarah said.

Will's kids came to have dinner with their dad at least once week. He had two sons and a daughter. Sarah would see them sometimes when she got home from work and talk with them in the driveway. They were all very mature, hardworking kids who seemed to really love their dad.

"Thanks," Will said.

They sat in silence, sipping their wine.

"You never really told me about your life back home. Other than...let's see...your husband cheated, you lived near a mountain and skied a little, and you like to read," Will said.

Sarah was impressed that he'd remembered all of that. She knew all about his situation, but he didn't know hers. Her mind wrestled with what to tell him.

"Well...life back home was—is—complicated." She looked into his eyes but quickly turned away. It was the wine that was making her stomach flutter, she told herself. *Remember the last time you got drunk with a guy?*

"Well, I know complicated. Trust me," Will said.

"Well...," she sighed. Then Sarah gave Will her highlight reel: she talked about her mother, her father, her marriage. She talked about Zach and Cam, and when she did, she couldn't help but cry. Will listened carefully, nodding, saying things like, 'that's tough', but he wasn't judging her. He really seemed to understand.

"Sounds like we have a lot in common," Will said. "We both stayed in marriages we weren't happy in for the sake of others."

Sarah nodded and laughed. "Except you didn't run away like I did. You're a great dad."

"I don't blame you for running away. It seems like that was your only way out. People like us, who always do the right thing, sometimes get the shit end of the stick. What you did wasn't selfish, it was brave."

"Yeah, well. Some would say it was cowardly," she said, thinking of her father.

"Fuck 'em," he said.

They both laughed.

"How about a drive to the beach for the sunset?" Will said.

"Sounds like heaven."

Sarah ran to her house, grabbed a sweatshirt and her phone, and went out to the car. Sunset was in twenty minutes. She worried that they wouldn't make it in time.

"Don't worry; this baby can go pretty fast," Will said, as they got into the car.

"But we've been drinking, you shouldn't go too fast."

Will pouted, which made her giggle a little.

"You're right, Newport's too far. I have a better place to watch the sunset, but you'd better go grab that camera bag of yours. You won't want to miss this photo op."

Sarah ran out of the car and into her house to get her bag. *God, he is so hot*, she thought as she checked herself in the mirror.

Will tooted the horn and yelled for her to hurry or they'd miss it. She giggled again as she ran out the door.

Twenty minutes later, they parked the car in a residential area just off the Coast Highway. Will told Sarah to hurry as he grabbed her hand, which felt strange at first, but she told herself not to overthink it. After they had safely crossed the road, Will stopped in front of a large sign that read "Thousand Steps–Marine Protected Area."

"Ready?" he asked excitedly.

Sarah looked down at the set of stairs that seemed to lead to nowhere. "I guess so," she said hesitantly.

Trees surrounded the stairs, enclosing them into a tunnel. All she could see was darkness and never ending steps in front of her. The stairs were steep, and about half way down she realized that they would have to climb back up them.

"Is this really a thousand steps?" Sarah yelled to Will who ran down ahead of her.

He laughed. "No, there isn't really a thousand, more like two hundred or something, but it's worth it." Then he called back to her to hurry.

Her legs began to ache and Sarah wondered if she would ever make it to the bottom, if there even was a bottom. Suddenly, the trees cleared and she saw the ocean in front of her. The view was breathtaking and reinvigorated her to run down the final steps. She could hear Will calling out to her from the bottom. She emerged from the stair tunnel onto the beach, and Sarah immediately pulled her camera to her face, snapping pictures of the sun as it was falling to the horizon. Wispy clouds glowed orange as the large sun seemed to balance on the edge of the ocean.

"This is breathtaking!" Sarah said, taking in the beauty.

"I know. It's insane isn't it? You won't find anywhere else like it."

"Every time I go somewhere here, I can't believe it can get any more beautiful, and then it does."

Houses balanced on the edge of the cliffs overlooking the beach; each had a long, sometimes twisty, stairway leading up to it. The houses were tall and staggered and packed in like sardines. Will pointed to the trams leading up to some of the houses explaining that's how those people got down to the beach. There were so many homes up on the cliff. The only way to tell where one home ended and the other began was the color of the house. She took pictures of everything. Then she spotted a house that was actually on the beach, at the bottom of the cliff just steps from the ocean.

"Wow! Look at that!" she said to Will, who laughed.

He told her the house was once John Wayne's beach house.

"Cool!" Sarah said.

Large rocks scattered along the beach in such a way that they seemed to be placed there just so. Small tide pools were everywhere. She waited with her camera up to her face for a wave to crash over the rocks. Will stood by her quietly. Then he picked up a handful of small rocks and threw them one by one into the water. She turned her camera to him and clicked more pictures.

"OK, Annie Leibovitz, no more shots of me. Come on, I

want to show you something," Will said, reaching for her hand again. Sarah held it out, and when he clasped his hand around hers, her heart skipped.

He led her to a tunnel made of rock. Waves crashed over the rocks and the spray from the water tickled her face. The tunnel was filling with water as the tide was coming in.

"Wow!"

"I know. Come look," he said, as they peered through.

Sarah could see clear through to the other side although, since the sun was just about gone so it was getting hard to see.

"During the day, you can see so clearly over to the other side."

"Can we go through?"

"You can, but better to do it in daylight. It's rocky in there, and wet. We can come back another time and go through it if you want."

She loved that Will was offering to bring her back. She smiled at him and told him she would love that. She took more pictures, but the light wasn't cooperating and she didn't want to spend too much time fussing with her camera, she wanted to enjoy the moment, and Will's company. Sarah couldn't stop looking at the houses suspended along the edge of the cliffs above. They walked the beach for a while, talking and laughing.

"So when did you become interested in photography?" Will asked, as they sat on the sand looking out the ocean.

She told him about her first camera that her aunt had given her for Christmas one year and how her father thought that the pictures she took were a waste of film.

"That's too bad that he didn't see the value in it, or how happy it made you," Will said.

"He's never been concerned with my happiness."

She told Will how as a little girl she'd ride her bike around the neighborhood, secretly photographing her neighbors. She hid the pictures in a box under her bed and whenever she felt especially lonely, she'd pull out the pictures and fantasize what it would be like to live with them.

The Changs, who lived around the corner, fascinated her. Mrs. Chang and the tiny grandmother doted on the men and children, never too far from them. The children were always dressed neatly in crisp white shirts and tan chinos, even on Saturdays when they practiced math. Up the street lived a childless couple—the O'Briens—who always said hello to Sarah as she rode by them. They had nieces and nephews who came to stay with them all time. The O'Briens were always outside playing with them or riding bikes with them. Sarah had always wondered if they wanted a little girl. She'd go anywhere really, where a little girl wasn't expected to play the part of mom.

She told Will how she spent a lot of time at the McGilvarrys next door, where all eight children played outside all day until their Irish mother called them in for a boiled dinner. There were enough of them that they could have a baseball or football game without having to invite anyone else over. Mrs. McGilvarry never even seemed to notice when Sarah was there. She could be invisible at the McGilvarrys.

"You were lonely," Will said.

Sarah turned her head so he wouldn't see the tears in her eyes. Tears because he understood her like no one else ever had.

"Your dad sounds tough too," Will added.

"That's one way to put it. It was his way or no way. I loved being behind the camera because it was the one place he couldn't control. I could put the camera to my eye and suddenly the only thing that mattered was whatever was in front of me in that moment."

Will nodded and looked at her longingly. "Your parents obviously didn't realize that you have a real passion for photography."

"No, they didn't. It was silly to them."

"Well, I think it's awesome that you have a gift to see things in a way other people don't and can bring it to life for us to enjoy."

"Thank you," Sarah said, smiling.

They talked about Will's childhood and what it was like to grow up with older sisters.

"They were protective of me but mostly they wanted to make sure I knew how to treat girls. They never liked Tiffany so we stopped talking for a few years but we're fine now because I can finally see what they saw all along—how self-absorbed Tiffany really was. I didn't want to see it, I guess."

"You loved her," Sarah said.

"I did. At least I thought I did. I don't know anymore," Will said as he picked up a rock and threw it into the ocean.

Sarah understood. "I totally get it," she said.

He told Sarah how he played football in high school and was the star quarterback. "My father thought I was going to play for the NFL but I wanted nothing to do with that. When I quit playing in college, he was pissed and told me I was making the biggest mistake of my life. He got over it eventually. I know it sounds weird coming from a guy, but I just wanted a good job and a family."

"That doesn't sound weird to me," Sarah said.

Will shrugged. "I'm a simple guy I guess."

"Well, maybe, but there's nothing wrong with that. It's better than being a complicated guy," Sarah said.

"True," Will said smiling.

They stayed at the beach until the last bit of sun fell down into the horizon. Sarah started to shiver and Will suggested that they go home.

They climbed the stairs quickly at first until their legs began to burn. Will teased Sarah for being slow whenever she stopped to take a break but he waited for her. Joe would have run all the way up and never looked back.

When they finally got the top, Will reached for her hand. She put her hand in his, feeling his fingers wrap around her hand. She couldn't help but smile as he led her across the busy street. She didn't ever want him to let go.

When they arrived at home, he walked her to her door.

"We should do this again. I had so much fun!" Sarah said.

"I did too. I haven't laughed like that in a very, very long time. Thank you for that."

"This was the best Valentine's Day I've ever had," she said.

"Wow, I forgot it was Valentine's Day! Me too, then," Will said.

They both stared their feet. Sarah felt the urge to kiss him but resisted.

"God, you make me nervous," Will said. "You're so easy to talk to, but it's disarming."

Sarah's heart beat faster. She made *him* nervous? If he only knew how she was feeling.

"Well, thank you, I think?" she said.

Will moved toward her and accidently stepped on her toe. They both burst out laughing. He started to lean in again. Sarah braced herself, unsure if he was going kiss her, but instead he reached out to hug her.

Sarah held him, probably a little tighter than she should have, but he felt so good. She breathed in his scent deeply. He smelled liked like the ocean.

Will ended the hug, his face inches from hers. They're eyes locked. Her heart beat fast. Then, he pressed his lips onto hers. She returned the kiss. It was tender, as if they were both savoring it. His mouth parted slightly and she felt the warmth of his tongue against hers. It lasted just a few seconds and when he pulled away, she wanted to pull him back.

"I'm gonna go before we get into trouble," Will said, backing away as he held her hand.

Sarah didn't want to release him, but her fingers were slipping out of his hand. She wanted to pull him into her house—into her bed—but she let her fingers drop.

"See you tomorrow," he said.

She nodded but pleaded with her eyes for him to come back. When he was far enough away she turned and went inside, closing the door slowly as she watched him walk away. The door shut and she leaned her head on it. It was the happiest she'd felt in a long time. She sat on her couch, thinking about the afternoon. Her feelings for Will were intense. He was easy to talk to and funny. Not only that, but he seemed to really understand her and her reasons for leaving home. She wondered ...did she deserve to be *this* happy?

23

The next day, Sarah got up early and went for a run, something she started doing soon after she got to California. The crisp morning air filled her lungs. The deeper she breathed in, the more at peace she felt. She was never one for exercise in the past, but she felt compelled to exercise in California. Not just to have the perfect body, which she gave up on in her thirties, but because the weather was always nice and she felt that she should be outside doing something active all the time. She loved running in Will's neighborhood—*her neighborhood*—in the early morning hours when the only sounds were the sprinklers watering lawns and dogs barking as she ran passed their domains.

She hardly slept the night before, tossing and turning, fading in and out of sleep watching each hour go by as she thought about her night with Will. She'd never met anyone that made her feel the way he did. Her life in California felt like a dream and she was terrified that if she fell asleep someone would wake her up and all of it would be gone.

After her run, she tiptoed to her place hoping that Rocky and Adrian wouldn't hear her and start barking, which they didn't. She made coffee, showered, and arrived at work earlier than usual. Michael's car was the only one in the parking lot. He and David took separate cars because David liked to sleep in.

Sarah shut the car off deciding to wait for David. She wanted to tell him about her night with Will, but not in front of Michael. She reclined her seat and put the radio on.

A few minutes later, Michael came outside with a full trash bag. He stopped when he saw Sarah and gave a slight wave. Sarah rolled down her window.

"What are you doing here so early?" Michael asked.

"Couldn't sleep last night," she said.

Michael gave her a doubtful look, which made Sarah feel uncomfortable. It was as if he could see through her. He continued walking to the dumpster. Now that she was discovered, Sarah decided to go inside. She got out of her car and followed Michael through the back door into the kitchen, where the wonderful smell of cinnamon filled her nose. Michael poured two cups coffee and sat down next to her.

"Couldn't sleep last night, huh?" he asked, looking over the top of his glasses.

She nodded her head as she sipped her coffee. Michael had put a vanilla bean in it again. She loved that.

"Want to talk about it?" Michael asked.

"Oh, no. I'm fine," Sarah said. Telling David about Will was one thing, telling Michael was another. Her relationship with Michael was purely business. They rarely talked about anything except work and never talked outside of work.

"Fair enough," Michael said, and then he went back to where he was peeling potatoes.

Sarah sat by a table where stacks of fresh bread in paper bags were piled high. She asked what the bread was for.

"Panini's for the luncheon today," Michael explained, as he put his ear buds in. He always listened to music when he cooked in the morning. A few minutes later, he took the ear buds out, went over to the oven, and pulled out another tray of cinnamon rolls.

"Those smell yummy." Sarah's mouth watered as Michael

cut one and lifted it out of the pan. The glaze dripped down the sides of the hot bun.

"You can have one." He put the roll on a plate and handed it to her. He started to walk away then he turned to face Sarah. "Can I be honest?" Michael said.

"Sure," she said.

"David filled me in on your story."

Sarah blinked at him unsure of what to say.

"OK…," she said, wondering what he was getting at.

"I hate to say it, but I knew you were running from something. I just need to know one thing…" He trailed off.

Sarah shifted on the stool. She wanted Michael to like her, even though she wasn't sure why—maybe because he was important to David, or maybe it was something else. She decided she would be as honest with him as possible and whatever happened, happened.

"What do you want to know?" she asked.

"If you plan on taking advantage of David, or me, I would prefer it if you just left quietly. I can't have drama here."

Her throat clenched in the same way it had when her father reprimanded her. She had so much to say yet the words were lodged in her throat. She fought back tears and the urge to run out of the café and never come back.

"I would never hurt you! Or, David! You both mean the world to me. I'm not here to hurt anyone or anything," she said.

"Don't you still have an unfinished life in New Hampshire?" Michael asked.

She took a deep shaky breath. "I do."

He nodded, and then went back to his potatoes, peeling them with vigor. Sarah was unsure of what to say, or do, next.

"Here's what you don't know," Michael began as he spun around to face her.

She couldn't imagine what he was about to tell her, but could tell from his expression that it was serious.

"The girl you replaced? She didn't go to Hollywood like David initially thought.

"There was something about her that made me uncomfortable from the beginning, but David kept telling me I was paranoid. He believes everyone is good, which is why I love him, but this girl was a mastermind. She was a great liar—even fooled me.

"She stole money from the café a few times, but David wanted to keep giving her the benefit of the doubt. After the second time money went missing from the cash register, I did some investigating on my own. Turned out she had a rap sheet, warrants, and a huge drug problem. The day I was going to let her go, I found her going through my wallet. So I fired her and told her to get as far away from Laguna as possible."

Sarah wondered why David had lied about the girl going to Hollywood. Maybe he was too embarrassed. Michael wasn't done.

"And, the one before that? Her ex-husband put David in the hospital for nine days."

Sarah's mouth dropped as she stared at Michael in disbelief.

"One day, out of the blue, a woman came in asking for a job," Michael continued. "She seemed a little desperate, and so of course David was drawn to her. He insisted we hire her, which we did, even though we didn't really need another waitress. Joelle worked at the café for four months before things started happening. She began calling in sick or not showing up at all. If she did show, she was frazzled and out of it.

"One minute she would be full of life, happy and sociable, and the next she'd be an angry bitch. We never knew what was going to set her off. It drove David crazy that he couldn't figure her out.

"One day a guy came to the café asking for her, but it was a day she decided to not show up. The guy came back the next three days looking for her but she had disappeared. I called some friends at the police station and had them talk to the guy. Then, one night when David was locking up after a party, the guy came and tried to beat it out of David where his wife was. David truly didn't know where she was but the guy gave him a good beating anyway. He was in the hospital for nine days with a broken jaw, broken wrist, three broken ribs, and a collapsed lung. So, if I sound overprotective, that's why."

She stared at Michael, speechless. What could she say? She admired him for wanting to protect David. The lost puppy comment made sense now, and so did the fact that Michael seemed to keep his distance from her.

"Michael, I had no idea," said Sarah.

"I know you didn't. David doesn't talk about it. Actually, he really doesn't seem to see the enormity of both the situations. I love him because he's so carefree, but at the same time..."

Sarah completely understood. "I would never, ever hurt either of you. I promise."

"Can you say the same about your husband?"

"He doesn't know where I am."

"And why is that exactly?"

"Because there wasn't any other way for me," she said, deciding not to tell Michael about the photographs that Joe had of his bruises from their fights. She wondered if he'd shared those with the boys, or her father. Or Jen.

"Someone once said, you can run away from your problems but that only increases the distance from the solution," Michael said.

"There are things I'm not ready to face." Sarah choked on the last words.

Michael walked over to her and leaned his forearms on the table. He looked into her eyes. "Did your husband hurt you?" he asked.

Sarah stared at the floor. She didn't want to lie to him. Not now that he was being so open with her.

"Define hurt," she said, finally.

"I mean physically. Did he hit you?"

Sarah sighed as she nodded. "But, I hit him too. We were

both young and stupid. And, I—"

"Don't do that. Don't make excuses," he said, holding his hand up to stop her.

"But he took photos of his bruises. He said if I left him, he would ruin my life and show those pictures to everyone. I can't go back there now. Everyone has probably seen the pictures! I'll never get my job back. People will talk about me behind my back. I just can't go back," she sobbed.

Michael put a hand on her shoulder to comfort her.

David opened the back door. "Good Morning!" he shouted.

Sarah and Michael both said hello.

"Sheesh, what's going on in here?" David asked standing between them.

Michael went back to peeling potatoes, leaving Sarah to answer.

"Just talking about life," she said.

"Oh…he's asking you to leave isn't he? He thinks you're going to hurt us like the others," David said angrily.

Michael shook his head but didn't answer.

"No, he didn't ask me to leave. But he did voice his concerns. It's OK."

"It's not OK," said David.

"No, really, it's fine," Sarah said, wiping her nose.

"Are you going to quit now?" asked David.

She wanted to tell David more about her conversation with Michael, but Michael turned and spoke.

"No. She's staying." Michael called out from the stove, shocking both of them.

David lit up and clapped his hands quietly. Sarah excused herself and went to the bathroom.

She couldn't stop thinking about David and all that he'd been through. She wondered why he hadn't told her any of that before. She understood now Michael was so apprehensive about Sarah before. She didn't blame him.

She went back to the kitchen where they got busy getting ready for the breakfast crowd, wrapping utensils in napkins and filling syrup and ketchup bottles. Telling David about Will now seemed insignificant.

They went about the day in their comfortable rhythm, but there was no joking or being silly. During a break in the morning rush, David pulled her aside. "We need to talk."

Sarah nervously followed him out to the garden where two tables full of people were lingering from breakfast and enjoying the warm sun. David chose a table tucked away in the corner near the front door, just in case someone came in.

"Look, Michael filled me in about this morning."

Sarah burst into tears. "I would never hurt you or Michael!"

David got up and pulled her in for a hug. "Shhh. We know. Michael told me about the pictures."

"Oh, that," Sarah said, embarrassed. Michael and David were the only two people besides her and Joe who knew about that.

"Look, I know you said you hit him too, but that doesn't make it OK. Not to mention he's blackmailing you!" David said.

"It's all so complicated, David. My father…the boys….ugh…," she said, wiping the tears on her face. She noticed Michael in the front taking orders and then bringing out food. He wasn't asking them for help. As she told David about her life, she barely recognized the person she described a scared, lonely, hollow shell of a person afraid to do anything.

"I completely understand why you left. You've never been able to live your life," David said.

Sarah cried.

He put a hand on her shoulder. "I'm so proud of you," he said.

"For running away?"

"Well, that, and for sticking it out in that life for as long as you did without going completely insane."

Sarah laughed. "It wasn't easy…"

"No, I bet it wasn't. But you left and now you know what

you're capable of," he said. "I'm going to help you figure all of this out."

Sarah hugged him. "I'll be forever grateful to who—or what—brought me to you. I don't know what I'd do if it wasn't for you."

"I have that effect on people," David said grinning.

Then, she told David about her night with Will.

"Ohmygod! Why didn't you tell me *that* earlier?"

"I wanted to tell you. It's why I came in early today. "

"Well, I think that's great! Will is such a good catch," he said, winking.

"But, I'm still married," Sarah said.

"That one is tricky, but I think you should just allow things to happen. You're trying so hard to worry about what everyone else is thinking or doing back home you aren't allowing yourself to be happy. Stop thinking that you're so terrible for leaving and instead think about how happy you are—how much you've grown."

Sarah sighed. "I'm so confused. I don't know what's what anymore."

"Look, we don't get medals in heaven for sticking with people who don't appreciate us. It's not your destiny to be a doormat, Sarah. God put you here to be loved. You deserve to be happy," said David.

The front door rang and a large group of people walked in. Michael called out for help. David and Sarah stood up.

"We'll talk more later. OK?" David said, hugging her.

As she worked, she couldn't help but think about what David said about being happy. She had let everyone walk all over her for years, but she didn't know any better. Now everyone wanted the best for her. People cared about her happiness.

At the end of the day, Sarah left work and drove to the beach where she sat on the sand thinking about her life. Everything was getting so complicated. She wasn't comfortable with complicated. She liked things to be in order; she hated drama, and especially didn't like that she was the cause of anyone's pain.

She hoped the boys were doing all right and, surprisingly, she worried about her father. She couldn't care less about Joe. Her aunt and Jim had tried to tell her for years that she deserved to be happy. Sarah now understood what they meant. She was happy in Laguna. The thought of leaving made her sad. She felt at home here. This is where she belonged. However, she knew her time in Laguna was borrowed and that she'd have to go home eventually. She was going to have to find a way to break the ties at home if she wanted to continue her life in Laguna.

The thought of going home made her stomach tight. Getting Joe to agree to a divorce would be the biggest hurdle. Not to mention finding a place for her father to live. Maybe he'd come to California…she laughed at the idea.

It was time to make some tough decisions—go home for good or stay in Laguna.

24

She left the beach after an hour. She couldn't wait to get home to take a long shower and an even longer nap. It had been a rollercoaster of a day emotionally, and she was spent.

As she pulled into the garage, her cell phone rang. She didn't recognize the number. *What if it's Joe?* She took a deep breath and answered.

"Sarah, this is John Curran. I'm in charge of the Art Festival in Laguna. Have you heard about that?"

Sarah sat up straight and, for whatever reason, checked her reflection in the mirror as if he could see her.

"Yes, I have. Leslie told me about it," she said, trying not to sound nervous.

"Right, Leslie. She gave me your number. I hope that's OK."

"Oh, yes that's fine. What can I do for you Mr. Curran?" Sarah asked nervously.

"I saw some of your work while I was at Leslie's shop the other day. She had a couple of your photographs hanging in the back drying. I was captivated by your work."

Sarah's heart pounded. *Holy crap, is this happening right now?*

"Thank you. It's a hobby," she said, instantly regretting it.

"Well, I think it's time to make it more than a hobby. That photo of the two women walking on the beach is breathtaking. You really captured quite the moment between them. I can feel the love in that photo."

It was Sarah's favorite photo too. After she'd taken the picture—the day she left the hotel to come to Will's—she developed it the following weekend. As soon as she saw the photo, she knew she couldn't keep it—it belonged to them. She approached them on the beach one day and tried to give it to them. They both giggled like twelve-year-old girls when she tried to hand it to them. They couldn't believe that anyone would want to take their photograph. Sarah explained how she wanted them to have the picture but they told her to keep it.

"We don't need a photo to remind us of our love for each other," one of them said.

Sarah couldn't help but ask what their story was.

Eleanor and Helen had been best friends for over seventy years. They grew up on the same street as young girls, had been through marriages, children, grandchildren, losses of important people in their lives including two children— Helen's infant daughter and Eleanor's son who died in Afghanistan. They were so happy just to be alive and to have each other to go through life with.

"My husband's been gone for fifteen years," Helen said. "It's lonely sometimes, but there's no way I'm taking on another husband! What would I want one of those for? I have Eleanor!"

"My husband died five years ago. I couldn't have got through that without Helen. We laugh, go to dinner, go on vacation together, and walk the beach. What else do you need in life other than someone who gets you, I mean *really* gets you?" Eleanor asked rhetorically.

Sarah nodded as if she understood, but it was what she longed for.

"Oh, that's Helen and Eleanor—they're such great friends. I had a really great conversation with them," Sarah said to

John.

"Here's the thing, Sarah. That photo could make you some really good money. I know someone who might be willing to buy it. Would you be interested in that?"

Buy it? Who would want to by my work?

"Um...I guess. I mean, yes. Someone would buy my photo?" she asked naively.

John laughed. "Indeed. For a lot of money too. They'd purchase the photo and then the rights to the photo so they can manipulate it and add their product to it. I'll put you in touch with my friend from the ad agency. Her name is Maura."

"Wow. Thank you," Sarah said, taking it all in.

"No need to thank me. One more thing—I'd like to invite you to participate in the art festival this year. If you're interested, I'll squeeze you in. I really think your work will attract a lot of buyers. Then I can let Maura know you'll be at the show and she can see your photo there."

"I don't know what to say."

"Say yes," he laughed.

"Oh, yes! Of course! Thank you so much for believing in me and giving me this opportunity."

"My pleasure. My assistant will be in touch next week with your booth number and some other details."

After the call ended, she got out of the car and went inside. She couldn't believe that anyone would pay money for one of her photos. She immediately called Leslie.

"I'm so thrilled for you!" Leslie yelled into the phone. "He came in to pick up some supplies and saw your photos hanging to dry. He insisted on seeing more. I showed him a few things we have in the shop. I had no idea he wanted your number to ask you to participate the festival. Applications were due weeks ago. This is a really big deal!"

"I was more shocked that he said someone would want to buy my photo."

"You don't understand. He's setting it up for a bidding war. If you show the work at the festival then more agencies will see it and you could possibly get multiple offers. Then, he'll collect a finder's fee."

"This is all new to me," Sarah said, feeling out of her league.

"This is the break you've been waiting for! John Curran has connections all over the world. It's not something you can pass up Sarah."

The two-day festival displayed all mediums of art: jewelry, clothing, blown glass, ceramics, woodwork, forged metals, painting, sculpture, and photography. Sarah would have her own booth. It would be seen not only by the people who attended the event, but also by her peers. Sarah was most nervous about that part.

"Do I have to pay him or anything?" Sarah asked.

"You have to pay to participate in the festival, but Nathan and I will take care of that for you."

"What? No."

"We insist. Don't give it another thought. Now, go figure out what photos you're going to show. Come to the shop tomorrow and I'll help you choose. We have a lot of work to do in a short time, but we can do it. I'm so happy for you!"

Leslie also said she'd make her business cards to hand out at the festival. Sarah cried. Part of her wished she could show everyone back home how far she'd come, how capable she was, and how much she'd changed. She pinched her arm to see if this was all a dream, but she wasn't sleeping. This was really happening.

***

Sarah was at her patio table, looking at photos for the festival and sipping a glass of wine. She had laid out four pictures and stood up to get a better look at them. Out of the corner of her eye, she spotted Will coming out of the house. Rocky and Adrian trailed behind him. She grabbed the hair clip that was on the table and quickly fixed her hair. It was finally long enough to pull back again. As he approached, he smiled.

"Hi there! How are you?" she asked.

Will pulled out the chair and asked if he could sit down.

"Sure," she said.

"So, what are you doing?" he asked.

"I've been invited to participate in the art festival this year."

"That's impressive. Were you invited by John Curran?"

Sarah nodded; loving the fact that Will not only knew who John Curran was but that she had to be invited to participate in the show.

"Good for you. He's very well connected," he said.

Sarah blushed. "I'm still in shock."

Will smiled. "Wow, I have someone famous living in my guest house."

"I'm not famous," Sarah laughed.

"Well, you will be. You take professional quality photos."

"Thank you."

"When is the festival? I'd like to come."

Sarah's entire body smiled. "I'd really like it if you came! It's in a couple of weeks."

"Then I will be there," he said.

Sarah stared at him. He looked as though he had something else to say.

"So, why did you come by?" she asked.

"I came over to ask you a favor," he said.

Sarah wondered if he needed her to watch the dogs again. That had become a pretty regular thing, which was all right with her. She missed her dogs, so she didn't mind occasionally having to watch his.

"Ask me," Sarah chuckled, as she watched him look around nervously and squirm a little in his seat. He called Rocky over to his side and made him sit. She could tell he was stalling.

"Well, I have a, um…ah, I have. I mean, I need. God, this is *way* harder than I thought it would be."

"Is everything OK? Do you need something? Do you need me to move out?" Sarah asked. She wished he would just spit it out—the suspense was killing her.

He laughed. "No, I do *not* want you to move out. I'm just an idiot trying to ask you to accompany me to a charity event this evening. There. It's out."

They both laughed nervously.

"Wow, a charity event? Sounds fun. Where is it?" Sarah asked. She'd never been to a charity event before.

"Newport Winery. A friend of mine is insisting I bring someone to the event. She said there's an empty seat at the table, which I guess would be bad for whatever reason. Anyway, I tried to back out of the event but she wouldn't let me. I was going to bring my daughter but she got a better offer, apparently."

"Ah, yes. The better offer." Sarah smiled at him. She noticed that he had beads of sweat on his forehead. His nervousness made her giggle to herself. "Well, I was just going to order take-out and watch a movie tonight, so why not?" she said.

Will smiled and told her it started at eight o'clock and that he'd pick her up at seven-thirty.

After he left, she texted David to tell him about the date. He immediately called her and screamed with joy into the phone, teasing her that she and Will were a couple.

"We aren't *together*. We're two friends going to a charity event."

"Yes, you keep telling yourself that. If you didn't think it was a big deal you wouldn't have texted me. What are you going to wear?"

Panic overcame her, she only had a few hours before they needed to leave and she didn't have a dress to wear.

"Don't panic. Just wear the black dress you got last week for the festival," David suggested.

"Then I'll have to get another dress for the festival," she said.

"You don't have a choice. We'll find you another dress. It will be fine."

"It will?"

"Yes. Text me when you get home tonight to let me know

how it went."

"Wait, what if he wants to kiss me again?" she asked.

David laughed. "Will you just let things happen organically?"

Sarah sighed. He was right. She needed to relax and simply enjoy a night out with a friend.

25

She was dressed and waiting for Will at seven-thirty. Sarah wasn't sure if he was going to come to the door or if she should meet him outside. She was a bundle of nervous energy—her palms were sweating. She had tried meditating earlier in an effort to calm her nerves but it only worked in the moment. When she was in the shower, the fact that she was going on a date—*a date!*—settled in. Back when she and Joe were first together, dates consisted of a movie and a trip to Wendy's, then home to have sex.

Oh god, sex!

What the hell was she doing? She texted David and told him she was freaking out.

He texted back quickly.

Relax. It will be fine. Have fun!

That wasn't at all helpful. She spotted Will coming up the walkway and her breath quickened. She tried an old breathing trick from running. Whenever she would get a stitch in her side, she'd breathe out forcefully until there was no more air in her lungs. Usually that would make the stitch go away. She tried it now, hoping to make her heart stop pounding.

It didn't work.

He rang the bell. She jumped. Sarah steadied her breath and wiped the sweat off her top lip before she opened the door.

"Wow, you look fabulous," Will said.

"Thank you, so do you," she said. He had on a dark gray suit with a light blue shirt underneath. *No tie, very sexy*, she thought. His cologne filled her nose and went down into her soul. He had the same nervous look as earlier, which made her relax a little. Knowing that he was nervous too made her feel better.

"Can I just say that I'm a nervous wreck?" Will said.

"Ohmygod! So am I," Sarah said.

"I've never really dated," Will said.

"Me either!"

They both laughed.

"It's not like we've never met," Will said.

"I know!" Sarah laughed.

He winked at her and suddenly she wished he'd say forget about the wine dinner and take her to bed. Instead, he reached out his hand.

"Ready?" he said.

She put her hand in his and walked with him to the car. He opened her door and waited for her to settle in before shutting it, and then he walked to the other side.

"So, this is the car you've been working on since I arrived two months ago. Is this its first day out?" Sarah asked, as Will got in the car.

"I've taken her for a spin here and there, but you're the first passenger since I finished her."

"Does *she* have a name?"

"Marilyn."

"As in *Monroe*?"

"Yes, actually. No laughing!"

Sarah couldn't help but laugh, though she had to admit, the car did look like a "Marilyn." It was a pretty, golden color.

She seemed to remember seeing a picture of Marilyn Monroe in a gold sequined dress before.

"What kind of car is *Marilyn*?"

"She's a 1962 MGB Roadster. She's a rare beauty because she has a third seat in the back."

Sarah craned her neck to look for the third seat.

"I've never heard of an MGB, but the car does look familiar," she said.

"You've probably see one in the movies," Will said.

Sarah agreed and then wondered how expensive the car was if it was so rare. She couldn't stop smiling as he eased the car out of the driveway

"So, did you finally make your selections for the festival?"

"I think so," Sarah said. "I just need to get them mounted tomorrow. The problem is that I love them all. It's like trying to pick your favorite child. How do you do that?"

"I liked the ones you showed me earlier when I came over. Especially the surfer one. I love how you got the row of surfers at various stages of their ascent, as if we're watching a frame-by-frame video of it. It's so metaphorical—how we can be on the same path but arrive at our destination at different moments. I just love that," said Will.

Sarah nodded. Joe would never have put that much thought into one her photos. A few minutes passed before he spoke again.

"I say go with the ones you like and don't think about it too much."

"Yeah, that's what everyone else says too," Sarah said. She was slowly learning how not to overthink things. Rather, she was learning that what she wanted mattered.

They arrived at the vineyard just before eight o'clock. Tiny white lights lined the driveway, twinkling like fireflies. Even though it was dark, Sarah could still see the sculptures at the entrance of the vineyard and a pasture with horses grazing along the driveway.

"Wow, this is so nice!" Sarah said looking around.

Will told her the vineyard had over twelve-hundred vines

of Bordeaux style grapes. He said that during harvest time in September the public could help pick the grapes.

"I would love to do that someday," Sarah said.

"We'll come back then," Will said.

Sarah didn't tell him she would probably be back home by then. Why ruin a good night?

They were attending a charity event to benefit local hospice group. Will explained that when his grandmother was sick, she asked him to make sure that she didn't die in a hospital because she hated them, and doctors. When she became too sick to take care of herself, Will arranged for nurses to be at her house around the clock. When her illness got worse, hospice came in to help with the transition. He'd been so impressed with their professionalism and compassion that he knew, after his grandmother was gone, he needed to give back, and that money would not be enough. He became involved by donating money and time whenever he could. Three years ago, he became a board member. Tonight's event was their annual fundraising event. Sarah was touched by his compassion and his obvious love for his grandmother.

"What was her name, your grandmother?"

"Rosalie. She was the best. She took care of my sisters and me when we were younger. She was so much fun. She loved practical jokes and to dance. We always played cards with her. If you're ever in the mood, I play a mean game of pitch."

Will was unlike any man she'd ever met. He was endearing and compassionate.

"I like watching your layers peel away, Will Donovan," Sarah said.

Will smiled at her, as the valet opened Sarah's door. She stepped out and waited for Will who came to her side and took her arm.

"Well, I just hope I can watch your layers peel away soon," Will said.

Sarah blushed as his eyes locked with hers. Why did he rattle her so much, she wondered.

They walked up the gravel trail to where everyone was

mingling. His hand brushed the small of her back as they walked. As soon as people saw Will, they swarmed him to say hello. He spoke briefly with each person, but didn't introduce Sarah. She wasn't sure if she should assert herself or remain in the background. Then, Will gently grabbed her and put his arm around her, sending a shiver up her spine. He introduced her to Sheila Grant, President of the Visiting Nurses Association. Sheila was in her sixties and very attractive in an elegant sort of way.

"Very nice to meet you, Sarah. Will, I'm impressed...," Sheila said.

"Stop," Will said, playfully.

"I don't mean to put you on the spot, Sarah, but he's never brought a woman to any of our events," Sheila said, smirking.

"It's OK. We're just friends," Sarah said. She looked at Will who shrugged. Then she wondered if that sounded too casual, as if she wasn't interested in him.

Then, Barbara Woodbury joined them. She was very interested in who Sarah was, and not at all subtle about it.

"Who's this?" Barbara asked, giving Sarah the once over with her eyes.

"This is Sarah Rossi. She's renting my cottage; she just moved here from New Hampshire," Will said.

Sarah's face reddened. She wished she was a turtle so she could retreat into a shell for protection. She wondered who Barbara was, and if Will had more of a connection to her. She was loud and her voice drew everyone's attention. Even with heels on, she was shorter than Sarah and she had big Texas style hair. She wore too much make-up for someone as young as she was which Sarah estimated to be forty-five.

"So...this is the mysterious renter," Barbara said.

"I don't know about mysterious," Sarah said.

"Well, Will hasn't told anyone who was renting his cottage. And he didn't tell any of us he was bringing a date tonight either!"

Sarah pursed her lips. She wouldn't have told this Barbara

anything either. Will told Barbara she was making something out of nothing and tried to make light of it.

Barbara leaned into Sarah, hiding her mouth from Will's sight but said loud enough for him to hear: "If you want to know anything about Will Donovan, come see me. I've known him since we were kids," she said.

There was something about Barbara that Sarah didn't like. She reminded her of Jen: bossy, nosy, and a little too self-assured. Sarah could tell she was the type who loved to spread gossip.

"We're going to check things out," Will said, taking Sarah's hand and leading them away from Barbara.

"I'm sorry about Barbara. Yes, I've known her since we were kids, but I can't stand her. She seems to think we're best friends," Will said.

Sarah let out a breath. "Thank God, because I didn't get a good vibe from her at all. She reminds me of someone I don't like back home."

"Don't give her another thought. I'll protect you," he said, leaning into Sarah.

Warm air emanated from tall heat lamps that were along the path leading to a tunnel lined with oak planks. People sipped wine and had small plates of food. Some stood by high tables while others sat along the stone wall. A guy with a guitar was sitting on a small stool playing music on the far end of the path. He was singing Sarah's favorite Jack Johnson song. If Sarah closed her eyes, she would have sworn it was Jack himself singing. Will took two glasses of red wine from a waitress and handed one to Sarah.

"I really hate these things," Will said leaning into Sarah so only she could hear him.

"It's OK, we'll get through it," she said, winking at him.

They laughed and continued walking into the oak tunnel, where a silent auction was set up. Sarah checked out all of the items and couldn't help but notice some of the bids were ten thousand dollars and higher.

"See anything you'd like to bid on?" Will asked.

"I could probably find something, but I don't have that kind of money. Remember, I'm a starving artist slash waitress."

"I'd be happy to bid on something for you. I don't want anything, but I'll need to make a donation, so even if you don't bid I'll still have to pay. Feel free," Will said, and handed her a pen.

"Oh, I couldn't do that!"

"Why not? Have fun. I won't hold it against you. Bid on something, go on," he insisted.

She stared at him not sure what to do.

"Go. I insist," Will said. "If you don't, I will and give it to you anyway."

"OK, fine."

There were gift certificates for restaurants that she didn't know, so she passed by those. Then an item for a night on someone's boat complete with dinner for two caught her eye. She put a five hundred dollar bid on that. She continued by a row of autographed sports memorabilia; that wasn't her thing. She bid on some pieces of artwork, a gift basket filled with wine, and a balloon ride for four. Then, something special caught her eye—a private concert given by Jack Johnson, in your home, for up to twenty-five people. Her eyes went wide.

"I love Jack Johnson!"

"Bid on it."

She thought about it. "Oh, well if I win I'd have to have it at your house, and that would be too much to ask."

"I won't mind. Go for it. But if you want to meet him, I can arrange that," Will said, gesturing toward the guy playing guitar.

"Wait. That isn't Jack out there playing right now, is it?"

"It is. He's a friend of mine, actually. We did some surfing together when we were younger. He went to college where I grew up, in Santa Barbara. We met out on the water."

Sarah's jaw dropped. She quickly tried to do the math in her head to figure out how old Jack was. She knew that he was few years younger than she was, so now she wondered how old Will was. Maybe he was younger than she thought.

"Shut. Up."

Will laughed. "You like him?"

"Love him. Well, his music," she said.

"Bid on it, and if you don't win, I'm sure I can arrange for Jack to come by anytime you want."

"I wouldn't even know what to bid."

Will took the pen from her and wrote $10,000 on the bidding slip. Sarah's mouth dropped. Will smiled and pulled her along.

A group of people came by to say hello to Will, while Sarah continued walking and looking at the other items to bid on. She took a piece of spanakopita from a waitress. As she savored it, she turned to find Will. She went over to him and stood by waiting for him to notice her, but he didn't. He was talking to a guy that she assumed was a good friend, because they were laughing and smacking each other's shoulders as old friends do. The other people in the group didn't acknowledge her either. Some of the woman gave her sideways glances, but continued talking to each other. It became so awkward that she decided to go out and listen to Jack play.

As she got closer to the music, she searched for somewhere to stand when, as if planned, a group of people abandoned one of the tables nearby. She walked over and stood there. Jack was singing *Wasting Time*, another one of her favorite songs. She checked to see if Will was coming but he wasn't. She stood alone for fifteen minutes before he finally joined her.

"I lost you," Will said.

"I stood next to you for ten minutes but you didn't see me."

"I'm sorry. You should've grabbed me. Those were some very old friends and I would've loved to introduce you."

"I tried to get your attention, but the women were staring at me like I had ten heads."

"I feel like a total ass," Will said. "I really didn't mean to make you feel uncomfortable. I told you I'm new to this dating thing. I'm sorry."

She knew he didn't ignore her on purpose; she decided to shake it off.

"It's OK. This is all new to me too. I just felt like an awkward teenager back there, trying to sit at the cool table while everyone ignored me."

Will apologized again.

"OK, let's just have a good night," she said.

"Let's get out of here," Will said.

"We just got here! Besides, Jack Johnson is sitting in front of me singing. I need to soak that in for a little bit."

"OK, but we don't need to stay. I made my appearance and if you're uncomfortable I can bring you home."

"I didn't get all dressed up for an hour! It's Saturday night, and I say we have some fun."

"I like your style," he said. "OK, but when we leave here I want to take you out for a drink at a great spot on the harbor."

"Sounds perfect."

As people came by to say hello to Will he made sure to introduce Sarah and involve her in the conversation. Sarah loved that he was so attentive. He had his arm around her waist as he talked. She realized how much she liked having his arm around her.

Jack ended the song and said that he was going to take a quick break. Then he walked towards Will. Sarah shrieked like a true groupie. Jack and Will hugged and Will introduced Sarah, who jumped up and hugged Jack excitedly.

"Nice to meet you," Jack said.

"I just love your music! I've never met anyone famous before!" Sarah squealed.

"Are you having fun?" Jack asked, graciously.

"Yes! And, I love listening to you play. I love your music." Sarah's face flushed with embarrassment, realizing how ridiculous she sounded.

"Thanks. Looks like you got a good one here, Will.

Anyone who likes my music must be a keeper."

Sarah beamed.

"She is a good one," Will said, looking into Sarah's eyes.

Sarah held his gaze. Her heart was pounding from the excitement of meeting Jack but also because of her feelings for Will. Impulsively, she grabbed Will's face and kissed him on the lips. When she pulled away, Jack and Will were both staring at her. Her face reddened.

"Well, I have to use the bathroom and I need a beer. You think I can get one here?" Jack laughed.

"Not unless you brought your own." Will said, jokingly.

"Please. You think I travel without my beer?" Jack asked, figuratively.

Jack patted Will's shoulder and left them. Sarah couldn't stop smiling. Will teased her about how smitten she was with Jack.

"He's the first famous person I've ever met!"

"Ever?"

"Yes, ever. There aren't too many famous people in New Hampshire."

"Well then, you did pretty well. You weren't *too* crazy. Just a little," he said, holding his thumb and forefinger close together.

Sarah laughed and gave him a playful shove. He grabbed her hand again and led her to the friends that he hadn't introduced her to earlier. They were nice and tormented Will for not introducing her before.

Every now and then Will leaned into her, begging her to leave, but she insisted that they stay until the auction was over.

"We should stay since you're the organizer of the event, shouldn't we?"

Will rolled his eyes. "You're probably right, but I always sneak out early."

"That's because you come alone. We're staying, and then you can take me for that drink."

They left the vineyard after the auction ended. They didn't

win any of the auction items but a little over one hundred fifty thousand dollars was raised.

They drove to a restaurant at the marina in Newport that had a great bar overlooking the ocean. It was packed with people at just after eleven o'clock. People said hello to Will when they walked in, but he just waved at them. He held her hand and pulled her to a corner of the bar that was less crowded.

"What can I get you to drink?" Will asked.

"A whiskey and ginger ale," Sarah said.

"Wow. I would've figured you for a Cosmo or Appletini."

She laughed. "I like those too, but at the end of the night I don't like anything too sweet."

"Whiskey and ginger ale it is," Will said, as he signaled to the young bartender who came over as soon as she saw him. Sarah watched as they spoke briefly before the bartender went off to make the drinks.

"You're a celebrity around here, aren't you?" Sarah teased when Will.

"That's my daughter Lauren's best friend, Lainie. I've known her her whole life."

So sweet, she thought.

They took their drinks to a table in the corner by the windows. Sarah took a sip of her drink and smiled at Will.

"I had fun tonight. Thank you for asking me to come with you," said Sarah.

"You're just happy you met Jack."

She laughed. "That too, but I did have a great time."

"Well, we aren't finished yet," he said, holding his glass up to cheers.

The small votive candle on the table reflected in his eyes. Will reached for her hand. She let him hold it as she looked at him. He smiled at her, which melted her heart and made her feel uncomfortable all at once. She was beginning to have real feelings for Will, and that scared her to death.

"Do you worry about them?"

"Who?" Sarah asked.

"Your family back home."

"My boys, yes. Everyone else, not really," she said.

"I bet they miss you."

"I don't know…," she said. They probably did miss her, but she wondered if it was for the right reasons. Not just because she wasn't there to cook and clean for them.

"My kids missed Tiffany, and she didn't do anything for them. Mariella raised them. I'm sure your boys miss you like crazy."

"Your kids were more worried about you than Tiffany," she said, and as soon as she did, she regretted her words.

Will let go of her hand and looked at her with his eyebrows raised.

"Really? And, why do you think *that?*"

She sighed. The old Sarah would have made up a story about why she thought that. She would have tried to sweep it under the rug and pretend it never happened. She'd heard so many things about Will; it seemed unfair that she knew what she did.

"Brandon told me. I saw him a couple weeks ago after your weekly pizza night. I was sitting outside when they left and he came over to talk."

Will looked confused. "Why would he just blurt that out?"

He hadn't blurted it out. Brandon had come over to ask Sarah how she had settled in, seeing as he was partially responsible for the arrangement. He told her that he was happy that his Dad wasn't alone, and how Sarah's presence seemed to be bringing their father out of his funk. He went on to say that he and his siblings had been trying to stay close to home so that they could keep an eye on their Dad because they were worried about him. Sarah told Will all of this.

"I'm blown away," said Will, leaning back in his chair.

"I think they felt protective of you. When you went into hiding they had to deflect the questions and it was hard on them," she said.

Will folded his arms across his chest and furrowed his brow. He looked angry, Sarah thought.

"I went into *hiding?* Who told you that?" Will asked.

Sarah swallowed hard. The alcohol was making her feel dizzy. She reached for her water and took a sip before answering.

"David told me. But Brandon mentioned it too. He said how hard it was because everyone talked about it," she said.

Will shook his head. "I wasn't *hiding.* I was trying to make my kids life as normal as possible. Brandon was off at Berkley, Anthony was a senior, and Lauren was a sophomore in high school. How could I work my usual eighty-hour weeks and be a single dad? So, I scaled back my workload. I tried to do the right thing."

He was being defensive and Sarah felt awful for making him mad.

"I shouldn't have said anything," she said. She reached for her water again.

"No. You shouldn't have," Will said.

They sat in silence sipping their drinks, avoiding each other's eyes. After a while, Sarah suggested maybe they should go home and to her surprise, Will quickly agreed. They walked out to the car in awkward silence. She wasn't sure if she should apologize again. They drove home with the radio on and didn't say a word to each other.

Suddenly, Will stopped the car on the side of the road not far from home. He got out, walked to her side, and opened the door.

"Come on," he said.

Sarah's eyes widened. "What?"

"Come on. I'm not going to hurt you," Will said, as he smiled and reached out his hand.

His smile made her relax. She put her hand in his and he pulled her close. Their foreheads touched. She could feel the warmth of his breath and his heart beating against her chest.

"I'm sorry I ruined the night," Sarah said.

"I'm not upset with you, Sarah. I'm confused about what my kids think of me, not to mention the rest of this town. You're the only real thing in my life. Thank you for sharing what Brandon said to you."

"You're not mad?"

"Hurt, not mad. As parents, we think we know our kids and then suddenly, you realize that maybe you only saw what you wanted to see. My kids are my life and I love them so much. I'm sorry for my reaction. I tend to shut down when it comes to talking about my divorce. I guess I see it as a failure and I hate failure. I'm working on that with my therapist," he said.

She understood more than he knew. In part, she'd stayed with Joe all those years for the same reason. Because she didn't want to admit that she'd made a mistake marrying him. Not only that, but Will had tried to keep his kids out of the drama just like she had with the boys. Sarah told Will all this.

"I'm sorry for overreacting," Will said. "It's just that no one has ever told me any of that before, including my kids."

"I'm sorry…," Sarah said.

Will sighed. "Let's dance," he said.

"There's no music," Sarah said.

Will reached in the car and turned up the radio. They swayed in each other's arms to beat of the music. He put his arm around her waist, leaned into her neck, and began kissing it. Sarah melted into his arms as he brushed her neck with his warm breath and soft kisses. Sarah grabbed his face and kissed him passionately.

After several minutes, he rested his forehead on hers. Sarah breathed deeply, rubbing his back.

"We are getting into trouble aren't we?" he said.

"Yup."

"It feels so good."

"Yup," Sarah said, kissing his neck.

"We should stop," he said.

"I know…it's all happening so fast," she said.

"You have things to work out at home first," Will said.

She knew he was right.

They drove the rest of the way home holding hands, listening to music.

"I don't want this night to end," she said, as they pulled into the garage.

He leaned in to kiss her briefly. Then he got out of the car, walked to her side, and opened the door. He reached for her face cupping it in his hands.

"I *really* like you," he said.

"I *really* like you too," Sarah said, smiling. His lips landed on hers. He held her there, sealing his words with his kiss.

They stood kissing until she was shivering from the cold. Will walked to her door.

"Go get some sleep. We can talk tomorrow," Will said.

"OK," Sarah said, reluctantly. She knew that asking him in would get them into trouble.

"Good night, Sarah."

"Good night, Will."

She went inside and fell onto her couch. She'd never been happier in her entire life.

26

Sarah met Jillian at yoga class at Heisler Park next morning. After, they went to Jillian's house. Sarah was planning to spend the day with her and some of her friends at a party in San Clemente. Sarah filled Jillian in about everything that had happened between her and Will over the last few days. Jillian was not nearly as excited as David had been when she texted him the night before; in fact, she was the polar opposite.

"How can you even think about being with another man when you haven't even finished your marriage? How are you any different from Joe? He cheated, and now you're doing the same thing," Jillian said.

Sarah stiffened. "I haven't done anything, Jill. I've had two fun nights."

"You kissed him," Jillian said.

Sarah got hot with anger.

"I'm sorry," Jillian said. "But I know what it's like to be on the other end. You do too. I just don't know how you can do this."

"Yeah, well. I found my husband having sex with my friend. This is different."

"No, not really," Jillian said.

"Joe not only cheated once, but multiple times during our marriage! I'm not the bad guy in all of this! My boys, who you've been so concerned about, have not returned one single solitary phone call or text from me in weeks. How do you think I feel about that?"

Jillian hung her head. Sarah got up and gathered her things.

"Don't go, Sarah," Jillian pleaded.

"I won't sit here and listen to you tell me what a horrible person I am. I've had enough of that in my life," Sarah said.

"I'm sorry but you abandoned your entire family and seem to be just living life as if they never existed. I don't understand how someone can do that. How a mother can do that? I just don't get it."

Sarah left Jillian sitting at the table and walked out the door. She drove to Newport and parked her car at the marina where she walked around for a while, lost in her own thoughts. She was so angry at Jillian but she couldn't deny she had a point. The comment that hurt the most was the one about abandoning her family. She didn't abandon them—she'd found herself. If only they could see her now. She'd love for the boys to be here with her to see how different life could be. She took out her cell phone and called Meg. Someone who knew the old her and could help her sort all this out.

"I thought you'd fallen off the face of the earth," Meg said.

Sarah sensed anger in her voice. "Sorry, but I've been busy," said Sarah.

"Busy? Seriously? You told me you were going to check in once a week," Meg said.

"And you told me that you didn't want to know anything about what I was doing. You had my number. Is something wrong?"

"Wrong? Hmm, well…you completely abandoned your family and left everyone else to pick up the mess," Meg said bitterly. "I knew you needed to get out of here for a little bit, but I had no idea that you'd be gone this long. It's been almost three months. Where the hell have you been?"

"I'm in California," Sarah said.

"Doing what?" asked Meg.

Sarah thought about how to answer. "I'm just living life," Sarah said finally.

"Have you called the boys?"

"Meg is there something wrong with the boys, because if there is I don't understand why you didn't call me. I gave you my number for that reason."

Meg interrupted her. "Their mother's been gone for three months without a trace."

"Whoa, Meg. I have called them! I've sent text messages, emails—I've tried every way possible to get in touch with them, but they haven't returned one attempt."

"Yeah, well...," Meg said.

"Meg, why didn't you call me? I thought I told you to call me." Sarah grew more angry. She wasn't sure if it was with herself or Meg for not picking up the phone to tell her that the boys were having a hard time.

"You're mad at *me*? Unbelievable," Meg said.

Sarah shook her head in confusion. Meg seemed to be talking in circles; she wasn't making any sense.

"Meg, I'm sorry, but I thought we had an understanding that you were going to keep an eye on the boys and call me if there was a problem. Just tell me why you're so upset."

Meg let out a forceful breath, then went on to tell her about how Joe had found Sarah's note the morning after she left and went crazy. He called all of Sarah's friends trying to get answers out of them. He even Meg who had told him the truth—that Sarah had called her early on and that she didn't tell her where she was going. She said that Joe and Jen were parading around town as a couple and not even trying to hide their relationship. Jen was telling everyone that Sarah had mental illness like her mother. Why else would she up and leave her family like that? Meg said she started telling people it was Jen who was crazy and how Sarah had found Jen and

Joe having sex in the back of Joe's truck on New Year's.

"I still can't get the image of Joe and Jen having sex out of my head," Sarah said.

"Zach and Cam are in the middle of all this craziness. Cam can't decide whether to be mad at you for leaving, or to be mad at Joe for having the affair that drove you away," Meg said.

Sarah began to cry.

Meg told Sarah that Zach had an incident with the police when he threw a beer bottle at a police car. He was now living with his girlfriend, whose parents had bailed him out of jail because Joe wouldn't.

Sarah listened in awe. She'd known that leaving would cause problems, but to hear that Zach was in trouble tore her apart.

Meg continued. "Then it got around that you had taken a leave of absence from work indefinitely and Joe really lost it because he knows you aren't coming back. Holly and Nicole are on your side and secretly have their bags packed in their closet, ready to make their move. Heather and Kristen are definitely *not* on your side. They've been trashing you since day one. You should hear them. I can't believe how high and mighty they've been. As if they live the most perfect life on the planet. HA! We all know *that's* not true!"

"I should come home," Sarah said with a long breath.

"NO!" Meg shouted.

"OK, now you're really confusing me. A minute ago you were pissed off and making me feel like shit."

"I know. Listen, your father is doing well. Joe and Jen are practically living together at Jen's. If you come back now it will only make things more complicated."

Sarah stared out at the ocean, watching the waves roll in and out. It had been a such a crazy morning and now she was more confused than ever before.

Meg continued. "I'm just saying to give it some more time. Keep trying to get a hold of the boys. I'll try to talk to them and see if I can get them to call you back. Ease into this because it's not going to be easy."

"Why were you so mad at me a few minutes ago?"

"You caught me off guard. It's been so hard. When I didn't hear from you, I resented that I had to keep defending you. I don't know why I didn't call you. I just didn't want to have the pressure of knowing where you were and then feeling like I needed to let everyone else know. When I heard your voice just now, I lost it. It was easier just to be mad at you, I suppose."

Sarah tried to put herself in Meg's shoes and knew that she had put Meg in a terrible spot, which is why she hadn't called her before now.

"I'm sorry I put you in this position. I wish you could be here with me. You'd love it. I'm standing in a marina in Newport Beach right now. It's so beautiful here," Sarah said.

"What have you been doing out there?" Meg asked.

Sarah told her about the café and some of the people she'd met, including Leslie. She told Meg all about the art festival, leaving out the part about Will and her apartment. It wasn't worth getting into all that just yet.

"Wow, it all sounds so great. I'm happy for you, Sarah. I really am."

"Thanks. I know I have to come home soon and figure everything out with the boys. And Joe. And my dad," Sarah said sighing.

"Give me a few days to get in touch with Zach and Cam. I'll call you once I talk to them," Meg said.

"OK. I'll look into flights and I'll come home after the festival."

"Hang in there," Meg said.

Sarah hoped Will wasn't home when she pulled into the driveway. Her mind was spinning after talking to Jillian and Meg; she needed some time to think things through. But Will's car was in the garage.

She hurried to her house with her head down.

"Hey."

She turned as she unlocked her door. Will was standing

there with his hands stuffed in his jean pockets.

"Oh, hi! You startled me," she said.

"You must've been deep in thought. We were all waving at you as you pulled in."

"We?"

"My kids and I were standing over there," he said pointing towards his back door. The three kids waved.

"I'm so sorry," Sarah said, as she waved awkwardly to his kids.

"Ah, don't worry about it. I—*we*, were wondering if you'd like to join us for dinner. We're making pancakes. It's the kid's favorite."

"Oh, I wouldn't want to impose," she said, hoping he wouldn't press the issue. She needed some time alone to think about everything that'd happened with Jill and Meg.

"It wouldn't be imposing if I invited you. Would it?"

Sarah really wasn't in the mood to hang out with Will and his kids at this moment, but with the kids standing there waiting for her answer how could she say no?

"OK, can I shower first? I've been out all day. Just give me twenty minutes," Sarah said.

"That's all the time you need to get ready? Wow, I'm impressed," Will said, grinning.

"I'm not a complicated girl," Sarah teased.

A half an hour later, she knocked on Will's back door. She'd put on a simple cotton dress with a sweater, and was holding a bottle of wine. She wasn't sure if Merlot went with pancakes but she brought it anyway. Will's daughter, Lauren, opened the door.

"Thank you for letting me crash your party." Sarah said to her.

Lauren was tall and had bright blue eyes and thick, straight dark brown hair that draped down her back. Her smile lit up her face, just like her father's.

"We've been trying to get Dad to have you over for a while."

Sarah wondered why Will hadn't mentioned it before. She

followed Lauren to the kitchen. The boys sat at the kitchen island, both were looking at their phones. She said hello to Will and gave him the bottle of wine.

"I wasn't sure if wine went with pancakes, but I didn't want to come empty handed," she said.

Will laughed. "Well, let's find out. I'll open it."

He left her alone with the kids while he went to retrieve the bottle opener in the dining room.

"So, did you have a good day today?" Lauren asked, breaking the silence. She seemed very mature for her age.

"Well, not really. I had an argument with a friend today. Two friends actually."

Will stopped what he was doing and looked at her inquisitively, which made Sarah regret saying anything.

"It's OK. Nothing major," she said, lying.

Will handed her a glass of wine.

"OK, so should we get going on the pancakes?" Will asked, clapping his hands.

"I want banana!" Lauren said.

"No, chocolate chip," said Anthony, looking up from his phone. Anthony was the middle child of the three Donovan kids. He didn't look like his siblings at all. In fact, he didn't look like Will either. He was six-two and lanky. His skin and hair were both light and his voice was deep. Sarah got the impression that he was a very serious kind of guy.

"Hell, give me banana chocolate chip," Brandon added. He was the oldest and Sarah could tell that he was the life of any party and yet, he was mature. Sarah could tell that he would be successful someday.

Sarah laughed. "Now that sounds delicious!"

Will told Sarah to sit down and relax while he cooked. Sarah had never had a man cook for her before, even if it was just pancakes. Sure, Joe would "man" the grill if steak or burgers were on the menu but this was different. Sarah watched Will interact with his kids. He joked around with them and they teased him. She could tell they were close.

Will poured batter onto the griddle while Lauren took out

orange juice and a container of strawberries from the refrigerator. She washed the berries and got out a cutting board. Sarah went over to her and asked to help. Lauren handed her the knife then she went back to the refrigerator for a fresh pineapple. They stood next to each other cutting fruit.

Will asked the boys what they did the night before. They had gone to a party in Newport on a yacht. Some famous rapper had come to sing but Sarah didn't know whom they were talking about. Lauren had gone to the movies with a group of friends and then to a beach party.

She had never been able to get Zach or Cam to talk to her this candidly. She was envious of the bond that Will had with his kids.

Will piled an enormous amount of pancakes onto a platter and told the boys to get the syrup and the paper plates. Will had made some banana pancakes, some with chocolate chips, and a combo of both to appease everyone. Sarah helped Lauren bring the fruit and drinks into the dining room, and took a seat next to Will who sat at the head of the table. Lauren sat across from Sarah and the boys sat across from each other.

The kids grabbed pancakes and began eating. Will apologized for the paper plates, which made Sarah laugh.

"Please don't apologize for that. It's pancakes for crying out loud. I don't expect you to break out the china," Sarah said.

Will filled her glass with more wine. Sarah helped herself to a banana chocolate chip pancake and some fruit. She sipped her wine and concluded that wine most certainly did not pair well with pancake syrup, but the pancakes were delicious.

"Great pancakes!" Sarah said.

"Yeah Dad, they're great," Anthony said.

Lauren leaned into her dad and kissed him on the cheek.

"Yeah, thanks," Brandon said, as if he didn't want to be left out.

"Do you have kids?" Anthony asked candidly, but the question made her stomach drop.

She hesitated before she answered. "Yes, two boys. Twins actually."

They all stared at her. She smiled at them and took a sip of her wine feeling their eyes on her.

"How old?" Lauren said.

Sarah cleared her throat and held her breath briefly before she answered. "They'll be eighteen next month."

She avoided looking at Will but she could see him in her peripheral. He'd leaned back in his chair.

"So, they're still in high school?" Lauren asked.

"They graduate in May."

"You left them?" Brandon asked.

Sarah put her fork down. She wasn't in the mood to go through this again.

"Guys. What's with the third degree? We invited her over for pancakes, not an interrogation. Give the lady a break," Will said.

Sarah loved that he came to her rescue.

"Will, it's OK," Sarah said, trying to keep the peace.

"No, it's not. Topic change. Brandon what's going on with Talia?" Will asked.

Brandon shot a look at his father that Sarah had seen many times from her boys whenever she asked them personal questions.

Lauren spoke for him. "Talia broke up with him last night."

"That's tough," Sarah empathized, but Brandon didn't look at her.

Then, his face softened a little. "Screw her," Brandon said. "What are your kids' names?" he asked, deflecting the conversation away from his love life.

She smiled as she thought of them. "Zach and Cam."

"Wait, you left your kids and came to California?" Anthony said as though he hadn't been in the room the entire time.

"Guys, can we please *not* grill her," Will said. He shook his head in disapproval of his children's rudeness and told Sarah she didn't need to tell them anything.

Sarah wanted to divert the attention away from Brandon, who clearly didn't want to talk about Talia, so she gave them a brief account of her life back home with her husband, two kids, father, and the two dogs.

"Are you here for good?" Lauren asked.

"I...well....I will have to go back, eventually," Sarah said, avoiding Will's eyes.

She collected herself and asked where the bathroom was. Lauren pointed toward a door in the hallway. In the bathroom, she pulled out her phone and texted David. She told him she was at Will's having pancakes with his kids. David texted back instantly.

David: What? R u kidding? Everything OK?
Sarah: No. Told them about my boys.
David: Oh...and?
Sarah: Idk, kids seem upset. Will's trying to keep the peace
David: R u in broom?
Sarah: Broom?
David: Bathroom?
Sarah: Lol...yes. Wish I could run.
David: Relax. Kids are just sensitive.
Sarah: Maybe. I have to get back out there.
David: Good luck. CML
Sarah: K

In the dining room, the kids were stoic, which made her wonder what Will had said to them.

"Maybe I should go," she said to no one in particular.

Will stood up. "No. Please don't."

"I've ruined pancake night."

"No, you didn't," Lauren said. She was like her father trying to keep the peace.

"I did. I'm just going to go," Sarah said, fighting back tears. She'd had such a wonderful night with Will the night before and now she felt as if none of that mattered. She wanted to go home and crawl in bed.

"Please don't go. We just got off on the wrong foot. Stay and hang out with us," Will pleaded.

"I think I should go. Dinner was nice, and again, I'm sorry for ruining the night," she said. She turned to go before anyone could convince her to stay.

Will followed her to the door and asked her stay again, but Sarah just wanted to run back to her little cottage and hide. She was relieved when Will shut the door rather than follow her out. She crossed the driveway quickly.

The entire day had been a disaster. She put her pajamas on and climbed into bed. She knew that David was probably waiting for her to call him, but she wasn't ready yet, so she shut off her phone, turned on the TV, and fell asleep with it on.

27

The next morning as she was getting ready for work, the doorbell rang. She opened the door. Will smiled at her. Seeing him made all of the anxiety she was feeling fade away.

"Can I come in?"

"Sure," she said, as she stood aside.

He hugged her, making her heart beat a little faster. He let her go and touched her face.

"I want to talk about what happened with my kids."

Sarah shook her head. "It's OK."

"No. I feel terrible. I never even thought they would care why you were here or what your story was. I underestimated them."

She just stood in the middle of the room with her arms folded. He asked her to sit with him on the couch.

"My kids are stronger than I ever was at their age. They have unbelievable insight. Anthony said the he thinks my guardian angel sent you to me. Can you believe that?"

"I don't know about that," Sarah said.

"I haven't been this happy in years. That's because of you. You make me happy, Sarah."

He told her how the kids opened up to him and said that

ever since their mom had left they felt protective of him. They never wanted to hurt his feelings by spending time with their mom, so they would sneak up to Beverly Hills to see her. Will said he was shocked, and hurt, to hear this but he understood it. They never really talked about the divorce before because he was trying to shelter them as much a possible from the drama of it all. He didn't want the kids to feel like they had to choose sides but by not talking to them had created unnecessary tension. His kids also told him it was time to move on, that they were all fine with the divorce and that it was all right for him to happy.

Sarah thought about her boys and wondered if they would ever feel the same way. She wondered if they wanted to talk to her but were afraid of what Joe would say.

"I don't care why you left New Hampshire. But I'm glad you did, because I wouldn't have met you. That's all that matters to me now."

Sarah's voice caught in her throat. She smiled, trying hard not to let his eyes penetrate her. He leaned in and kissed her; she melted.

"I've never been this happy either," she said. "I know I left my kids behind and that seems like a really shitty thing to do, but whatever brought me here—to you—was something bigger than me."

Will hugged her. Being in his arms felt so safe.

"Would you like to spend the day together? We can take a drive up the coast, grab some lunch and talk. What do you say?" Will asked, as he touched her hair.

Sarah smiled. "I have to work."

"Take the day off," Will said.

"I can't lie to David, he'll see right through me," Sarah said.

"Then don't lie. Tell him you need the day off."

She thought about it for a minute. She knew David would tell her to go with Will, but she didn't want to do that to Michael.

"Don't you need to work too?"

"I'm the boss. I can do whatever I want," he said smiling.

"I have Wednesday off. Can we do it then?"

"OK, sure. You're right, you can't call in sick; that wouldn't be fair to Michael and David," he said. He leaned in to kiss her. "It's a date then."

"It's a date," she said.

***

On Wednesday, they drove up the Pacific Coast highway in Will's Mercedes. It was seventy-five degrees and the sky was a deep shade of blue—there wasn't a cloud in it. They talked about everything from their childhoods to present day during the two-hour drive. They arrived in Santa Monica at eleven o'clock.

"Do you like waffles?" Will asked.

"Yes," she replied tentatively.

"There's a great waffle place with awesome food. You up for it?"

"Sure!" Sarah smiled.

Jake's Waffle Joint was small place tucked in between a liquor store and a convenience store in a small shopping plaza.

"I know it doesn't look like much, but trust me, the food is amazing," Will said, sensing her trepidation as they walked up to the restaurant.

"I trust you," she said.

Inside, the place was full of people. The décor was old and nothing to write home about but everyone seemed to be enjoying themselves. They found two stools at the counter and ordered coffee.

"I used to come here all the time years ago," Will said. "I don't think they've changed a thing since the last time I was here, oh, maybe six, seven years ago."

Will's excitement for the place was infectious. The restaurant reminded Sarah of all the mom and pop diners back home. Places that were passed down from generation to generation and where everyone knew everyone.

She ordered a waffled topped with peanut butter, banana, and bacon. Will ordered the banana stuffed French toast waffle.

"You need to try this!" he said with a mouth full of food.

She reached over and took a bite. The cinnamon bread with bananas and pecans mixed with the cream cheese frosting was to die for.

When they finished eating, Will took her to the Third Street Promenade—a posh outdoor shopping center not too far from the waffle place. They went in and out of shops, laughing and talking. They stopped to watch a woman on the promenade who had a guitar and a microphone. She was belting out some song with all her heart.

"Is she famous?" Sarah asked.

"Not yet, but she will be. She's really great isn't she?"

Sarah nodded.

When the woman finished singing, they clapped and Will put a twenty-dollar bill in her empty guitar case.

"Come on," he said. "I want to show you the pier."

They walked to the famous Santa Monica pier with the iconic Ferris wheel, which they rode. She loved being high above the pier looking out over the ocean. When the Ferris wheel stopped and rocked back and forth, Will put his arm around her. She settled into him as they waited for the passengers down below to board.

"It's so beautiful up here!" she said, looking out at the ocean.

"You're beautiful."

Sarah turned to look at him. He smiled at her then leaned in to kiss her. She melted into him, returning his kiss. His tongue grazed hers. His lips were soft and warm. The wheel jerked forward and began to move slowly.

"Oh!" she said.

Will held her tighter. "I got you."

She felt so safe in his arms. As the wheel spun around two more times, they stole kisses from one another. She never wanted the day to end.

After, they played some of the carnival games like ring toss, balloon bust, and the water race. She saw how competitive Will was, but it was all in good fun. He won her a stuffed monkey that she held onto for the rest of the day.

"We need to get a corn dog," he said.

"Corn dog? I don't know…"

"Don't tell me you've never had one!"

Sarah shook her head. "Nope."

"Oh, come on. We're getting you one, for sure."

He held her hand as he led her to the corn dog station. While they waited in line, Will put his arm around her waist. Everything with him felt so perfect.

He handed her the corn dog and she took a bite. The cornbread had a nice crispiness to it. She bit into the hot dog and the two flavors merged in her mouth.

Will waited in anticipation. "So?"

"It's good," she said.

"Aw. Just good? I love these things," he said, as he took a big bite of his. He smiled—his mouth full of corndog. She couldn't help but laugh.

"I meant it's great!" she said, hoping he'd believe her. Then she kissed him.

When they were done with their corndogs, they walked along the beach for an hour talking.

"So, I know you don't want to hear this, but Jill's right. You have a lot to figure out back home," Will said.

She sighed. "Yeah, I know."

"But, I'm here for you," he said, pulling her close to him. They touched foreheads. "And I'm falling for you, hard."

She sighed. "I'm falling for you too."

Her body began to tremble.

"Are you cold?" Will asked, as he held her tighter.

"No. I don't know why I'm shaking. I'm just happy," she said.

Will looked at her smiling. "I'm falling in love with you, Sarah."

Even though she felt it too, she didn't say a word. She let

his words settle in. She felt like she was falling in love with him, but she wasn't ready to say it yet. It didn't feel right saying that to him when she still had so much unfinished business back home. She kissed him hard on the lips.

"I'm just not ready—" Sarah said.

Will touched her cheek, and looked deeply into her eyes.

"It's okay...," he said, then he kissed her and all the other noise around them faded away. After a while, a teenager called out "Get a room!" They both giggled and walked away, laughing that a teenager was the one to yell that.

"This has been the best day," she said, kissing his cheek.

"It's not over yet!" Will said, smiling at her.

"Does it ever have to end?"

"No. No it doesn't," Will said. They kissed again.

A little while later, they walked back to the car. "Should we get a bite to eat?"

"I feel like we've eaten all day!" Sarah said.

"Touché. We could go to the movies or go get a drink somewhere in Newport?"

"Drinks sound nice."

Will took her to a piano bar in Newport. They found a table near the window. Will excused himself and went to the bathroom. Tears filled her eyes as she thought about going home and facing the twins, and her father. She thought about telling them about her new life, about Will. She knew that wouldn't go over well.

"Whatchya thinking about?" Will said, as he kissed her neck, startling her.

"Home."

"You miss it?" he asked, as he sat down.

"No. Not at all. That's the funny thing. I'm a completely different person here. Back home, I was angry and bitter. I took medication just to get through the day. I drank myself to sleep at night because I couldn't deal with the loneliness."

"I'm sorry," Will said.

"Don't be sorry. It was my life. My choices."

"You said you're different, stronger now. You just need to

believe that you deserve to be happy," Will said.

Sarah wiped the tears that fell on her cheeks and sniffled.

"My aunt and Jim tried to tell me that twenty years ago. I didn't believe them. But, now being here, *with you*, and feeling happy for the first time in my entire life, I understand what that means."

He reached across the table and took her hands in his.

"I'll help you figure this out."

Somehow, she knew that at as long as she had him by her side that everything would be all right.

"I think I need to go home," she said.

She tried to pull her hands away from his but he held on tightly.

"For good?" Will asked.

"No. I need to finish things there. I need to make arrangements for my dad. I need to see the boys," Sarah said. Then she told him about Meg and what she'd said about Zach getting into trouble.

Will nodded his head. "I understand," he said.

"I don't know when I'll be back," she said.

"I'll wait," he said.

Sarah cried. Will was different from any man she'd ever met. Being around him made her want to be a better person. She could truly be herself with him and felt that he understood her like no other. She wanted nothing more than to be with him forever.

28

Sarah spent every day of the last week with Will going for walks, watching movies, kissing on the couch. It was *the* best week of Sarah's entire life. Will was warm, sensitive, romantic, and understanding. He made her feel as if anything she wanted was possible. He was supportive of her decision to go back to New Hampshire, which she planned to do the week after the festival, even though she was unsure when she'd be able to return to California.

On the opening day of the festival, Sarah woke up early. She was going to walk on the beach before spending the day with Jillian at the spa. The night before, she set up her booth with Leslie and Anita. Sarah had a few prints framed and hung for sale, and Leslie prepared a flipbook filled with more prints that people could order. When they were finished, Sarah stood back to take it all in. Her eyes welled with tears as she thought of Jim. He would be so proud of her. She hadn't contacted him since she left the conference in Vegas. She felt terrible that she hadn't called to check on him. She wished he could see all that she had accomplished since she left New Hampshire. He would be so proud.

Will ran up the driveway returning from his morning run

as Sarah walked to her car. She went to him to say good morning. He was sweaty but that didn't stop her from kissing him hard on the lips. She couldn't get enough of him.

"Where are you heading so early? No work today for you, right?" he asked, breathing hard from his run.

"Beach. I need to calm my nerves," she said.

"Want some company?"

She smiled. "Sure. Can you go like that or do you want to shower first?"

"If you can take my smelly self, I'll go like this."

Rocky and Adrian were barking inside the house. They could hear Sarah and Will.

Sarah gestured toward the house. "Wanna get them?"

"Really? Wet, sandy dog in your car later? Hey, it's up to you…"

"Why not? It'll be fun. I love watching them chase the pelicans on the beach. Go get them. You can vacuum my car later," she teased.

They drove to the state beach in Corona Del Mar. It was cloudy, so they practically had the beach to themselves. In California, even the slightest bit of clouds or rain would send the locals inside to cozy up by the fire and cook comfort meals, much like people back east did with the snowstorms.

At the beach, they let the dogs out of the car and watched them run at lightning speed toward a pelican that took off in flight. Sarah laughed as Will ran after them.

The feelings she had for Will were intense. Their relationship was growing stronger every day and it was getting harder and harder not to make love to him, but they had agreed to wait until she went home and sorted things out there.

Sarah didn't even notice her apprehension about the festival anymore as they walked along the beach, holding hands, the dogs following them. It was just what she needed to calm her nerves.

They left the beach just before nine, a little later than she had hoped. Will drove home so they could get there faster.

Sarah took a quick shower, gathered her things for the show, and then left for Jillian's. Will was out by her car.

"Good luck today," he said, kissing her slowly.

"Thanks," she said. "I had a good time this morning."

"Me too. Thanks for letting me join you," he said.

They kissed again. Sarah just wanted to stay in his arms all day.

"Sarah…," Will said, as he pulled away but kept his forehead pressed on hers. "I love you."

Sarah's heart skipped. She felt ready to say it too. "I love you, too," she said, then kissed him again. Her heart felt so full.

"You really are my angel."

"I'm just a girl from New Hampshire. I'm no angel."

He lifted her chin. "You are," he said. Then, he kissed her.

She began to cry but she didn't pull away from him. Soon, Will was crying too.

"We're such babies!" Sarah cried, as she wiped the tears from Will's face.

"What the hell is up with that?" Will laughed.

"I don't know, but damn, this is intense. I don't even want to go to Jillian's now. Can I just stay here with you all day?"

Her cell phone rang so they stopped kissing. Jillian was wondering where she was.

"I'll be there soon," Sarah said, and hung up. "I have to go."

Will kissed her again and said, "I don't know if I'll be able to keep my hands off you later," he said.

"I hope you won't," Sarah winked.

***

She arrived at Jillian's almost an hour late, but Jillian was so easy going she didn't even mention it.

"Are you ready for your day?" Jillian said, as she met Sarah in the driveway.

"I am!"

"Great. I have massage appointments for us at twelve-thirty. Then David is going to meet us for manis and pedis later. He's going to bring snacks too."

"Sounds perfect!" Sarah said. They brought her clothes in the house for later. Jillian had champagne waiting for them.

"We need to celebrate your first real show!" Jillian said as she popped the cork on the champagne. She poured two glasses and added some orange juice and a strawberry to each glass. "Let's go sit on the deck," she said.

Sarah followed her outside. The ocean air hit her face and Sarah breathed it in.

"I'm so jealous you get to wake up to this view very day," said Sarah.

"Well, I told you to come live with me but you refused," Jillian teased.

"I'm just really comfortable at Will's."

"Uh-huh…'comfortable'…that's it," Jillian said.

Sarah and Jill had come to an understanding once Sarah told Jill she was going to New Hampshire to figure things out. Sarah smiled at Jillian who took a sip of her champagne, as if she were waiting to Sarah to continue. Sarah's smile grew.

"Oh for crying out loud Sarah, you have a shit-eating grin on your face. Spill it!" Jillian said.

"Spill what?" Sarah blushed.

"What happened with you two this week?"

Sarah smiled. "We had *the* best week. We hung out every day after work talking, going to dinner, watching movies, going to the beach. He's just so amazing," Sarah said.

Jillian laughed and raised her glass and banged it to Sarah's.

"I really am happy for you," Jillian said. "Is he willing to wait for you?"

"He is," Sarah replied.

"So have you….you know?" asked Jill.

Surprised by the question, Sarah choked on her drink. "No, he says we should wait until I figure things out back home first."

"Sounds like Will all right. And I agree with him. You don't want to give your ex, well soon to be ex, anything to hold against you in the divorce. If Joe finds out you have a boyfriend out here, he can make your life miserable in divorce court. First, he'll claim you abandoned him and the boys, and that you did it because you were having an affair. Why haven't you served Joe with papers, anyway?"

Sarah shrugged and took another sip of her champagne. "I don't know."

"Well, you have to if you're ever going to be truly free."

Sarah sighed. "I know."

"OK, today isn't about the past. Today is about the present! We'll focus on experiencing the joy of today, and then tomorrow we'll call Selena and get those documents together to send them to Joe."

Selena was Jillian's friend, and a divorce lawyer. She'd offered to help Sarah with her divorce when she was ready.

They finished their champagne and left for the salon. After their hair was done, they waited in the locker room lounge to get their nails done. David came bounding in hollering.

"Man in the room! But I'm a gay man and I don't care about your lady parts!"

Sarah and Jillian laughed. They were the only women in the lounge at the time, which made it even funnier. David came in holding bags of food from the café.

"Michael went all out girls. He's been working on this all day. OK, well, not *all* day, but he put a lot of love in these dishes. He's so happy and excited for you, Sarah."

Sarah smiled as she thought about her new and incredibly supportive friends, and how far she'd come with Michael. Ever since their talk at the café that morning, he really seemed to soften and let Sarah in. Once he knew she wasn't going to hurt David, or steal from him, it was as if a completely different person emerged. Michael was a big teddy bear inside and had the most generous heart. Sarah understood why David loved him so much.

"I'll give him a big kiss later," Sarah said.

Michael prepared seafood salad with chunks of lobster, scallops, shrimp, avocado slices, and apple slices. The fish was so fresh, and the dressing he'd prepared from scratch was a nice complement. There was also a Greek spinach pie that was to die for. It had lots of layers of buttery phyllo dough, spinach, and feta cheese. It melted in her mouth. He also sent along two bottles of Prosecco that David opened as soon as he arrived. The three of them ate and talked about who they thought they'd see tonight at the festival. Jillian was working for her gallery and helping to support some artists that were going to be there.

Then the conversation turned to Sarah. Sarah blurted, "I'm in love with Will!"

"Oh, honey, paahleease. We know that," David said.

Sarah laughed. "Do you realize that I've *never* been in love before? I loved the guy I sorta dated in college—more like just slept with, not dated. And, I did love Joe at one point. But, this? This is something completely different! This is the 'swept off my feet' kind of love that I didn't think was real. I can't *believe* how intense my feelings are for Will after such a short time. And, we have so much in common, it's crazy," Sarah said.

"I know I've given you a hard time about you and Will, but I really am happy for you," Jillian said. "You guys really do make the cutest couple."

"Thanks, Jill, that means a lot to me," Sarah said. "And, I think you need to give Trevor a second chance. You guys are perfect for each other."

David nodded his head in agreement. Trevor still called Jillian on occasion but she wouldn't accept his dinner invitations. She'd meet him for a walk on the beach or a hike at the park, but beyond that, she kept her distance. Jillian was adamant that she wouldn't consider a relationship with him until he wasn't living with his ex-wife.

They had just finished their lunch when they were called in for their manicures and pedicures. They sat in side-by-side the pedicure chairs talking and laughing. The afternoon flew by, and before long it was time to drive back to Jillian's to get dressed. David came with them too.

Sarah came out in her new off the shoulder red dress that she had found the day before at a discount store. David gushed over how pretty she was. Jillian came down in a black sequined dress that Sarah thought made her look like a movie star about to walk the red carpet. David looked handsome in his suit and bowtie. They all admired how each other looked until the doorbell interrupted them. Michael came in looking debonair in a black suit. Sarah went over to him, hugged him tight, and thanked him for lunch.

"I'm glad you enjoyed it. Are you nervous?" Michael asked.

"Just a little. I've never done anything like this before in my life, so yeah I'm a *tad* nervous."

"There's nothing to be nervous about. Your photos speak for themselves. All you need to do tonight is mingle with people, answer questions, and drink champagne. It will be fun," Jillian said.

"You really think my photos are good?"

"Really. I would never lie to you about that. I've seen a lot of crappy art in my time, trust me. You, my friend, have a tremendous gift."

Sarah blushed. "What if no one buys anything?"

"Stop worrying!" David said.

Sarah tried to relax but her nerves were getting the best of her.

They arrived at the festival a little before four o'clock. They walked up to her booth and Sarah stopped to take it all in. Her photographs were mounted and hanging on the wall of her booth in front of her. It was as if she was looking at someone else's pictures but they weren't, they were hers. One picture that she had taken at Limestone Canyon was one of her favorites and she secretly hoped it didn't sell. She and Allana had stayed until sunset that day and Sarah was able to get a great shot of the red rocks coated with the fading sunlight. The shadows were just right, the contrast was just right, and she just loved it.

A hand on her shoulder startled her. "That one's my favorite."

Sarah turned to see Jim standing in front of her, and she instantly burst into tears.

"What are you doing here?" she shouted as she threw her arms around his neck.

"Leslie flew me out."

Sarah was stunned. She had told Leslie about Jim. However, Leslie never mentioned that she had called him.

"I don't know what to say!"

"Your work is breathtaking, as usual," Jim said, squeezing her hand.

"Thank you. But, I can't believe you're here. Your heart? How did you fly?"

"Leslie sent a plane and a doctor to fly with me. Don't worry though. I got the 'all clear' from my doctor back home."

Sarah was speechless. Leslie had done so much for her. Everyone had done so much for her. How would she ever repay the people from Laguna?

Will came up behind her, which made her feel relaxed and nervous all at once.

She introduced Jim to Will.

"He's a friend," she said.

Jim laughed as if he already knew the truth. Her head was spinning. It was all so much to take in. She smiled and turned back to her exhibit. She was suddenly overwhelmed thinking about her boys. She wished that they were here to see it all.

She turned to Jim. "There's a piece of me that wants to call my father right now. Not because I miss him, but to tell him I told you so. I want to tell him that my ridiculous hobby isn't so ridiculous. I just wish he could see how happy I am. How good of a photographer I've become."

Jim put his arm around her shoulder and squeezed her. "You've always been a good photographer, kid. I'm very proud of you."

"No cryin'! You'll ruin your makeup," David said, causing Sarah to laugh.

David handed her a glass of champagne. She raised her glass.

"I'd like to make a toast," Sarah said, and the others raised their glasses. "I'd like to dedicate this night to all of you, my amazing supporters, and best of friends. I feel so incredibly blessed to have met all of you. My soul has never felt so lifted, and for that, I will be forever grateful. To all of you!"

They cheered and hugged. Leslie and Nathan joined the group. Sarah went to her.

"I can't believe you brought Jim here! How can I ever thank you everything you've done for me?" Sarah asked.

"You just did," Leslie said, smiling.

John Curran came by with a local reporter to take some pictures with Sarah in front of her exhibit. The reporter asked her questions and a photographer took Sarah's photo in front of her booth. It all felt so surreal.

The night flew as she talked to everyone who came by her booth. She was excited to see Allana, who wasn't going to be able to make it but did after all. Sarah sold a lot of her work too. Maura, from the ad agency, offered Sarah a million dollars for her photo of the two women on the beach. "I have a company interested in using the photo for an ad campaign."

Sarah heard *million* and practically fainted. "They will pay a *million dollars* for my photo?" Sarah said, shocked. She wasn't sure she wanted to part with the photo, but that was a lot of money.

"They might even pay more."

"OK, wow! I mean, yes!" Sarah said excitedly.

Maura told her she would be in touch.

Jim stayed for a couple of hours mingling and looking around. Then he left early because he was tired.

"Thank you for coming," Sarah said.

"My pleasure, kid," Jim said.

She hugged him tight and said goodbye. Sarah told him she would meet him in the morning for breakfast and to catch up.

At the end of the night, Will called for a car to bring them home. Sarah wasn't drunk but she was definitely feeling the effects of the alcohol. As they rode home, they talked about the night.

"I can't believe the turnout," Sarah remarked. "And people actually *bought* my photos! I'm still in shock!"

"I'm not. You're a brilliant artist."

I'm an artist! She rolled down her window and screamed. "I'm an artist!"

Will laughed and pulled her away from the window. Sarah reached over and kissed him on the neck. He turned and kissed her. She wanted nothing more than to make love him tonight and she told him so.

"I don't think I can wait anymore either," he replied.

They stood in the driveway kissing for a while before he led her to his house. In the kitchen, he put his arm around her waist, leaned into her neck, and kissed it. Every nerve in her body fired off as he brushed her neck with his lips. Will teased her as he whispered in her ear, "I want you so bad."

Sarah grabbed his face and kissed him.

He reached behind her back and found the zipper at the top of her dress. He slowly pulled the zipper down her back, sending shivers up her spine. His hands were warm on her bare back. He eased the dress off her shoulders and let it fall to the floor. He kissed her collarbone, and then he cupped her breast and kissed there too. He reached behind her back to unhook her bra, exposing her nipples and set to work licking each one, making them harden.

Her hands fumbled as she unbuttoned his shirt. She slid her hands inside and ran her hands along his chest before undoing his pants. They let them fall to the floor. They were both in their underwear, kissing and moving their hands all over each other.

Will lifted her and wrapped her legs around his waist. His

fingers grazed between her legs.

"Let's go upstairs," he said breathlessly, as he kissed her.

He put her down and they both ran up the stairs, giggling as he grabbed at her. They fell onto his bed.

He kissed her breasts and made his way down her stomach, slipping her panties off while he kissed her body. He reached her stomach and made his way back to her breasts. Her nipples were hard and sensitive, her body covered with goose bumps. He kissed her collarbone, her neck, and finally he reached her mouth again. She took her turn kissing and touching him until he couldn't take it anymore. He pulled her to him and wrapped his arms around her, kissing her deeply. Her body arched and she wrapped her legs around his hips. Tears streamed down her face. Without a word, he wiped the tears from her cheeks as they made love. When she looked into his eyes, she saw that he was crying too. They held each other tighter. Their bodies were truly one. She'd never felt such love for someone in her life.

After, they lied next to each other, panting. Sarah's body was charged with electricity.

Suddenly, Will started to laugh which made Sarah laugh too.

"I love you!" Will said, kissing her all over her face.

Sarah laughed and returned his kisses.

"I love you too! That was mind-blowing. Can we do that again?" Sarah asked eagerly.

Will laughed. "Give me a few minutes."

Sarah snuggled up to him and put her head on his chest. Will's arm was over his eyes, and in a minute, he was snoring gently. She was wide-awake and feeling more alive than ever before. Sleep was not going to happen. She went to the bathroom and took a shower. While she was letting the warm water rush over her body, the door to the shower opened, startling her. Will entered the shower and they began to kiss.

"I was worried when I woke up and you weren't there," he said.

He kissed her hard as the water ran over them. Sarah's

body instantly reacted to his touch. She was still sensitive from the last time. They made love again with the steamy water spilling over them.

"That was fucking amazing, Will Donovan."

"*You* are amazing, Sarah Rossi. You really are," Will said, as he handed her a towel.

Sarah toweled off and then went out to get dressed but she realized her dress was down in his kitchen. Will gave her a pair of his shorts and a shirt to wear. She had to roll the shorts over a few times so they wouldn't fall down, but being in his clothes, surrounded by his scent, made her feel happy and safe.

"You hungry?" Will asked, as he threw on a t-shirt and pair of shorts.

"Totally. Got any chips and salsa?"

Will laughed. "Of course. Let's go downstairs and I'll make you something."

They made love a couple more times throughout the night, falling asleep just as the sun was beginning to rise.

PART III

GOING HOME

29

Somewhere in the distance, Sarah heard a buzzing noise. It stopped suddenly and then began again. Her mind was foggy from sleep as the sound began to register. She opened her eyes and looked around. Will slept soundly next to her. The buzzing stopped and Sarah closed her eyes. Then it started again. Sarah got out of bed and followed the sound to the floor by the bed. Her eyes stung as they adjusted to the bright light on her cell phone display. She focused on the caller's number.

Shit.

Her voice cracked as she said, "Hello."

"I know it's early. I'm sorry..."

Sarah looked at the clock. It was five-thirty in the morning. She and Will had just fallen asleep an hour ago.

"Meg, what is it?" asked Sarah.

"You need to come home," Meg said. There was an urgency in her voice that made Sarah's stomach drop.

"Why? What happened?"

"It's Joe. It doesn't look good. They flew him to Mass General in Boston in a Life Flight helicopter because he took a turn for the worse. Manchester Hospital can't handle burn victims."

"Burn victim? What the hell? Are the boys OK? Oh my god, the house!"

Will stirred and rolled over. Sarah put her hand on him to steady herself.

"Zach and Cam are fine. It was a car accident. Joe hit a tanker truck carrying gas."

"Shit."

Will sat up and mouthed, "What's wrong?"

Sarah shook her head back and forth.

"You need to come home," Meg said.

"Of course. I'll get on the next possible flight. What the fuck, Meg?"

"It's not good. The doctor said he might not even make it through the flight to the hospital. You are next of kin. It will be up to you to make the decisions."

"Meg, please tell me this isn't happening!" Sarah yelled.

"It is. Call me when you get home. You can stay here if you need to," Meg said.

Sarah threw her phone on the bed and held her head repeating, "Oh my god," over and over. Will put his arm around her.

Sarah tried to wrap her head around the news. All she could think about was the boys. Where were they? How were they taking the news? Was anyone with them? She hated herself for not being there with them.

She told Will what was going on. He listened and shook his head.

"God, I'm so sorry. What can I do?" Will asked.

Sarah shrugged and shook her head.

"I'll make coffee. You should call Leslie. Her pilot can get you home quickly," he said as he pulled on shorts.

"I'm scared," Sarah said, crying.

"It's gonna be OK," he said, rubbing her back.

She shook her head. Everything was about to change. She desperately wanted to call David, but she knew her friend all too well, he probably just went to sleep a few hours ago. She called Michael knowing he would be either at the café or up having coffee.

"Uh-oh this can't be good," Michael said after answering on the first ring.

Sarah told him what was going on.

"I'm sorry about your husband. How long do you think you'll be gone?"

"That's the million dollar question. I just don't know. The boys will need me now."

"I'm waking David. He needs to go with you."

"Michael, no. You can't afford to have both of us gone! Who will help you to run the café?"

"I'll be fine. I'll call Jess. Not another word. David will go with you. You don't want to walk into the lion's den alone. The last thing I want right now is for you to worry about me." He told her he would wake David and have him call her back.

Sarah called home next. She got the machine. She left a message and told them to call her right away. She tried the boys cell phones but neither answered. She left them both messages. She called Leslie and explained the situation. Leslie said she'd call her pilot and call her right back.

She found Will in the kitchen. He was waiting for the coffee to finish brewing.

"You OK?" he asked putting his arm around her.

Sarah leaned her head on his shoulder. "I'm so freaked out right now. I tried to call my house and the boys but no one's answering," she said.

Her phone began to ring. She jumped and answered it quickly.

"I'm on my way, honey! Book us a flight. I'm in the car and should be at your place in thirty minutes."

Sarah burst into tears at the sound of her best friend's voice. For a guy who hates the morning, he sounded as cheery as ever.

"Now don't do that," David said. "There is nothing to cry about."

This only made Sarah cry harder.

David kept talking, "OK, now stop. If you cry, I'll cry and you don't want a gay man to cry, especially at six in the morning, while I'm going ninety-five down Canyon Road."

Sarah couldn't help but laugh.

"I can't help it. I'm scared to death right now. I can't stop shaking. I'm so far away from home," Sarah said.

"I know but there's nothing we can do about that. Take some deep breaths."

Sarah did what he said. "Ok, I'll see you when you get here."

Will handed her a cup of coffee. She took a sip.

"Maybe you should call Linda," Will said.

Sarah nodded. "I'll call her once we hear back from Leslie and I have my flight info," she said. "I'm gonna go to my place to shower and pack."

Will hugged her. "It's gonna be OK," he said.

"I'm not so sure…"

Even if Joe survived, his life would be changed forever. She thought about what Meg had said about Sarah being the next of kin. Sarah would have to make all of his medical decisions. She would have to care for him now. So, no, it wasn't going to be OK. She thought of Joe's mother, Judy, and what a wreck she must be. He was her only son, her pride and joy—even though he never amounted to anything. It didn't matter to Judy; she loved him anyway. She thought about her boys and how scared they must be. She was so far away and wouldn't be home until much later. So much could happen between now and then.

Sarah had just gotten out of the shower when she heard David coming in the house.

"What time is our flight?" David called out as he came in.

"Leslie's plane can be ready by nine," she replied from the bathroom. "I'm getting dressed. I'll be out in a minute."

"I'll make coffee!"

Sarah dressed and packed a suitcase. She wasn't even sure what she was putting in. She looked around and wondered if she would ever be back. She had just had the most unbelievable night of her entire life. She was totally in love with the most incredible man. Her career was taking off. And now she was leaving Laguna, probably for good. She sighed. When she finished packing, she went to the kitchen.

David rubbed her back as she poured a cup of coffee. She was surrounded by the most incredibly caring men in Laguna—such a stark contrast to her life in New Hampshire.

She tried the boys again and to her surprise, Cam answered after the fifth ring.

"Cam?"

"Mom?"

"How are you, honey? I heard what happened to Dad."

"Where are you?"

"California."

"How did you find out about Dad?"

She told him that Meg had called.

"What do you want?" Cam asked.

"Well, I wanted to see how you and Zach were handling this and to tell you that I'll be home later tonight."

"We're fine. We've been fine. You don't need to come here."

There it was—the anger she was expecting but hoping desperately wouldn't be there. Her chest tightened.

"Well, I am. Cam, listen, I know this has been hard."

"Mom, I gotta go."

"Cam, wait! Where is Zach?"

"He's at Maddie's."

"Who's Maddie?"

"His girlfriend, Mom. If you'd been home for the past few months you'd know that."

Sarah stared at her phone. He had hung up on her.

Will knocked on the door as he let himself in. Sarah was on the couch still stunned from the conversation with her son. Will sat down beside her and put his arm around her. Sarah curled into him burying her head into his chest while powerfully sobbing. He held her tight and said nothing. He just let her cry.

David called out from the kitchen that the eggs were ready. Sarah didn't feel like eating. Her stomach flipped and she held her mouth for fear that she might spontaneously throw up.

"I can't eat."

"You have to eat. We have a six-hour flight ahead of us. If you don't eat you'll puke on the plane, and I'm not dealing with puking. That's where I draw the line. Now eat."

She tried to take some bites but they lodged in her throat even after taking a swig of coffee to wash it down. She pushed her plate away.

"I don't know how I'm going to do this," Sarah said.

"I know," Will said, as he rubbed her back.

"What if Joe dies? What am I going to do?" Sarah asked looking back and forth between David and Will desperately hoping they had an answer.

David put a plate of food in front of Will, a heaping portion of eggs with toast and jam.

"He's not going to die," David said, as he sat down next to her. "You need to be strong and walk in there without all the baggage of the past, but with the new, strong you. Baby steps, girlfriend. Baby steps."

Sarah leaned on his shoulder. Maybe David was right. Take things one day at a time and focus on the twins.

Will drove them to the airport. They said a tearful goodbye.

"After the night we just had we should be laying in each other's arms all day," Sarah said.

"We'll have our time together soon. Stop thinking about me and focus on the boys. I love you, Sarah."

"I love you too."

"That's all I need to hear."

Sarah kissed him hard on the lips. Tears spilled out of her eyes. He was the best thing that had ever happened to her and now she was leaving him and she had no idea when, if ever, she'd return.

30

I t was a gray day in New Hampshire—typical for this time of year. The trees were still bare. Snow piles still lined the streets, dirty from sand and exhaust from cars. It was depressing. She drove holding the wheel tight with both hands as she thought about facing everyone.

David rested his head against the window with his eyes shut. He twitched like a dog dreaming. They'd talked a lot during the flight about what to say to the boys, to her father, to Joe. Sarah wondered if Jen would be around.

Sarah pulled into her driveway and shut the engine off. Everything looked exactly as she'd left it. The Christmas wreaths she'd hung months ago were still hanging on the windows. The mechanical reindeer were still on the front lawn. She sighed.

David put his hand on her shoulder. "You can do this," he said.

"I'm not so sure," she said, holding back tears.

"Well, there's no turning back. Come on girl, we'll do it together."

At the front door, Sarah froze unsure whether to ring the doorbell or to walk right in. David reached in front of her and knocked hard on the door. The dogs began barking like crazy. She saw Cam stop short as he reached the door and saw his mother. Sarah stiffened.

Cam opened the door slowly. They all stared at each other. Cam stood aside, waving her and David in. The dogs nearly bowled her over. She wondered who took them for walks while she was gone. *Probably no one*, she thought. She patted them until they calmed down.

She hugged Cam, but he didn't return the embrace. She could feel his pain and a wave of guilt rolled over her.

"Cam, this is my friend David."

David extended his hand. Sarah willed Cam to shake it but he didn't.

"Friend," Cam said. It wasn't a question.

"Cam," Sarah scolded. "Yes, he's a *friend*, a great friend who came for moral support."

"Whatever, Mom. We didn't ask you to come back."

It was clear that Cam had changed. He had an edge about him now, and she knew she was the cause of it.

"Well, I did. Where's Grandpa?"

Cam smirked. "Watching TV. Good luck with that one." Then he walked out of the house leaving her and David alone.

Her heart slammed against her chest as she took off her coat. Her shaky hands hung it over a chair in the kitchen. Even though she'd only been gone for a couple of months being in her kitchen felt like a weird déjà vu. Everything was exactly the way she left it. Dishes were piled in the kitchen sink and crumbs littered the counters. The dogs' water bowls had spilled over and water seeped across the floor. She picked up a towel left near the sink and threw it over the spill.

In the other room, the television was blaring an episode of *Jeopardy*. She stopped just before entering the room to settle her nerves. David followed behind her; his presence was comforting even though she knew it would raise questions. She reached for his hand; he squeezed her hand, encouraging her to go in. Sarah called out to her father but he didn't turn.

She called out again. The television was so loud she wondered if he could hear her at all.

"DAD!"

He turned slowly and focused his eyes on Sarah. She was struck at how much older he looked, and weaker. His eyes narrowed at the sight of Sarah.

"Where the hell did you come from?"

"California."

"Who the hell is that?" he asked, waving his hand toward David.

"My friend. David. David Luciano."

David moved toward her father and extended his hand. Sarah feared her father would refuse to shake it like Cam, but her father surprised her and reached out to shake David's hand. She let out a sigh of relief.

"Friend, huh? So is he the reason you abandoned us all?"

"Dad, no. He's a friend, nothing more," she said.

"Mr. Kush, I'm a friend of Sarah's. I'm just here to support her."

"Support *her*? So, did she tell you she snuck out of this house, like a coward, and hasn't called any of us since?"

David hung his head avoiding her father's eye contact.

"Dad, I know you're upset—"

"Upset doesn't even begin to describe how I feel about you. Disgust is how I feel. Disgrace is how I feel. You're not my daughter anymore."

The words hit her like a fireball, burning inside of her and rising up like a volcano. The reason she left was because her father and Joe had pushed her down for so long. She wasn't going to let him talk to her like that anymore.

"Don't talk to me like that."

He waved his dismissive hand at her, which fueled her fury.

"I mean it. Don't talk to me like that anymore."

"You don't belong here!" her father. His face was red and a vein in his temple bulged.

"This is my house," Sarah said, but even as she said the

words, she knew it wasn't true anymore.

David grabbed her arm in an effort to calm her down, but Sarah moved away.

"Get the hell out!" her father demanded.

"I'm not going anywhere, whether you like it or not. I'm staying, so get used to it."

"Joe pays for this house, not you. You don't exist here anymore," her father said, raising his voice.

"Joe hasn't had a job in months! I pay for this house!" Sarah said. Her body shook with anger. She stormed out of the living room. David followed behind her. She walked out the front door and onto the lawn where she let out a scream.

"I don't know why I thought *that* would have gone any differently!"

"Honey, calm down," David said, as Sarah paced around him.

"I can't, David. I can't do this. I just can't." Her body shook. It was as if something had exploded inside of her.

David grabbed her shoulders, squaring her off to face him.

"You will get through this. You've always known this day will come. Focus on why you really came back here—to help the boys."

Sarah rolled her eyes. "Yes, and did you see how Cam treated me? I expected that reaction from Zach, not Cam. I can't even imagine how Zach will be towards me."

David hugged her and Sarah felt her body relax.

"Thank God you came with me," she said.

"Thank Michael. He's the one who insisted I come."

Sarah thought about that. The fact that he insisted David come with her, not knowing how long he'd be gone, it meant the world to her.

"So, what do I do now?" she asked.

"Good question," said David.

"I wish I knew where Cam went."

"He's right there," David said, pointing down the road.

Cam walked towards them with his hands stuffed in his front pockets, his head hung low. Her heart leapt. He looked so sad, so lonely. Sarah left David and walked towards her son. He stopped when she got close and waited for his mother to speak.

"Cam, I'm so sorry...," she said, trailing off.

"It's fine, Mom."

"No, it's not. We need to talk about it."

Cam rolled his eyes.

"Let's go somewhere to talk. Somewhere away from here," she said.

"Will he be coming?" Cam asked.

She looked behind her at David who was kicking the ground with his feet.

"Well, I can't leave him here with Grandpa. He'll eat him alive," she said.

Cam laughed, and Sarah saw a glimpse of the son she'd always known.

"Did you eat dinner yet?" Sarah asked.

"No."

"Where's Zach?

"He went to the hospital with Aunt Monica and Uncle Rich," said Cam.

"Why didn't you go?" Sarah asked.

"I don't want to see Dad like that."

They all went to the tavern in town and ordered drinks and food. Cam explained how their grandfather was constantly saying terrible things about Sarah. He told her how Zach moved out two months ago because he couldn't handle being around their grandfather.

"He couldn't take the abuse, so he left to go live with Maddie and her parents."

"Wait, abuse?"

"No, Ma he didn't hit me, or Zach. I meant verbal abuse. Dad was hardly ever home after you left, so it's been me and good old Grandpa Kush."

"No wonder why you're so pissed at me."

Cam nodded his head and laughed.

"I called you almost every day. Why didn't you answer my

calls?" asked Sarah.

Cam shrugged. "Dad hounded us every day if we heard from you. I guess it was just easier to ignore you so we didn't have to lie," said Cam.

Sarah understood that.

There was an awkward silence at the table. She watched Cam fidget in his seat and look around as if he was nervous about something. Sarah sensed Cam had something to say.

"Everything OK?" Sarah asked.

Cam cracked his knuckles and ran his hand through his hair. Sarah could feel his leg shaking under the table.

"You can tell me anything. No more secrets," Sarah said.

Cam sighed. "Me and Zach knew about Jen before you left," Cam said.

Sarah's mouth hung open.

"How did you know?" Sarah asked.

Cam shrugged. "We just did," he said.

Sarah had so many questions and began firing them at Cam.

"Ma! I don't want to talk about it. It doesn't matter now," he said. Then he got up and went to the bathroom.

Sarah's head was spinning.

"They knew about the affair?" she asked David.

He shook his head. "He's right though. None of that matters now."

"What do I do now?" she asked.

"Just be supportive," David said.

She wasn't sure what to say now or how to act anymore. So much had changed since she left—including her.

Cam came back to the table and sat down, avoiding eye contact. "So, are you here for good?" he asked.

"Well...," Sarah said, taking a deep breath. "For a while anyway."

Cam's cell phone rang. It was Zach. They talked for a few minutes while Sarah and David listened. Cam ended the call and smiled. Sarah wondered if maybe it was good news about Joe.

"So?" she asked impatiently.

"Zach said the doctors are hopeful Dad will make it."

"Oh, Cam. That's good news!"

"He's shocked that you're back. He's changed a lot since living with Maddie's family. Her parents told him the only way he could stay was if he got good grades. He might even make honors this semester."

Sarah's eyes widened. "Honors? Wow."

"Now see, there's the positive side to you leaving," David said.

Cam and Sarah laughed. Maybe he was right, Sarah thought.

Cam looked at her nervously. "I decided I wanna be a writer," he said.

"A writer? That's great!" Sarah said, feeling proud. He was creative, like her.

"Yeah, I have like a hundred short stories written, and I started a novel but I think it sucks. I dunno," he said.

"I'd love to read your stories," David said. "I have my BA in English. I wanted to be a writer once too."

Sarah looked at her friend. "How come you never told me that before?"

David shrugged. "I guess it never came up," he said, smiling.

"I've never showed anyone my stuff before," Cam said.

Sarah understood that feeling all too well.

"Sometimes you have to take a risk," she said. She'd always thought Cam would be a doctor or a veterinarian, but he was a writer and she couldn't be more proud. And, she could never have predicted Zach making honors. She had always thought he would end up like Joe with no real career, scraping his way through life because he knew how to work the system. Had her leaving really been a good thing after all?

***

They dropped Cam off at the house, and then went to Meg's. She wasn't ready to stay at the house, with her father, just yet.

"Why didn't you tell me Cam was gay?" David asked on the way to Meg's.

Sarah looked at him, confused by the question. "He's not," she said.

"Oh, he is honey. And if you don't know, then maybe he he's not ready to face it yet."

"What are you talking about? How would you know that from just a few hours of meeting him?"

"I just know. Listen, if he hasn't come out yet, you shouldn't say anything to him."

"David, you can't just tell me my son is gay without telling why you think that."

David sighed. "Being gay isn't like a rash that you can physically point to and say, 'Oh yes, he's gay.' I can just tell. Sometimes people suppress those feelings for a lifetime, others know from a young age and can't hide it and others, like me, wait until we have the confidence to face it. It's not that big of a deal, I just figured you knew."

"But he had a girlfriend."

"And I was married. What's your point?"

Sarah looked out the window deep in thought.

"So, I'm supposed to take that information and do nothing with it?"

"Um, no. You need to tell him you love him no matter what. He'll get it. And now that I'm here, he'll see that you're open to it."

"You got all that from meeting him today?"

"Yup. It's a gift."

Sarah stared out the window. She didn't care if Cam was gay, or not, but the fact that he'd been hiding it all this time made her sad. How could she have not known? Then again, she didn't know he was a writer either. What else didn't she know?

Meg sat on the front porch, drinking a glass of wine as they pulled in the driveway. Sarah waved to her.

"Ohmygod you look incredible!" Meg exclaimed, as she

hugged Sarah.

"You look mighty fine yourself."

"Oh, thanks. Weight Watchers. I lost forty-five pounds," Meg said, as she spun around.

"Congratulations. And I like the hair. It's so much longer. And you got rid of the gray!" Sarah said.

"Yes, I did. You inspired me to make some changes," Meg said.

"Me?"

"All this running away business got me thinking about myself and how I put myself last on the list all the time and how unhappy I was. I always put the kids and Mike first. And, somehow, I thought that meant I was doing my job right. When you took off, I really thought about it. And, you know what? I often daydreamed about running away too, especially when the kids were little. Sometimes they'd be yelling at each other and I'd think, 'I can get in the car and drive away'. Of course, I never did it."

"Well, as I've learned, running away is great but the problems don't go away, eventually you have to face them," Sarah said, thinking of her conversation with Michael.

"True. Honestly though, when you left I really started looking at how much I do for them and how little I did for *me*. So, I started making changes. The kids help around the house now. Mike grocery shops. And, we got this calendar app that helps us organize everything. I started losing weight and exercising. And now, I'm starting a new job in a couple of weeks. I'm like a whole new person!"

"Wow! That's great! I'm so happy for you," Sarah said. "You'll have to tell me about the job later."

Sarah introduced David, who hit it off with Meg right away. They went inside and Meg showed them to her daughters' room.

"Where are the girls going to sleep? I don't want to put anyone out of their room, especially on a school night."

"Are you kidding? They're down in the basement right now, setting up camp. They're teenagers…they don't care.

Besides, it's a half-day tomorrow so I'm not worried about it."

David asked if he could shower and so Meg showed him to the bathroom. Sarah told Meg all about her day and her meeting with Cam, her confrontation with her dad.

"What are you going to do about Joe?"

"Wait it out, I suppose. If the hospital needs me to make decisions I will, but for now, I think I'll just stay away from there."

"That's probably the best thing to do. What about Zach?"

"Cam spoke with him earlier and he thinks that Zach will want to see me."

They talked a while longer and then David came in. He sat down next to Sarah.

"I'm exhausted," he said.

"Me too," Sarah said.

"Well then, I'll let you two get some rest," Meg said, leaving them alone.

Sarah took a shower, and when she came back, David was fast asleep. She lay in bed, thinking about everything that'd happened in the last twenty-four hours. The festival and her night with Will felt like a distant dream. If David weren't asleep in the next bed, she would have believed all of that had been a dream.

31

Sarah waited anxiously on Meg's front porch for Zach to arrive. He'd called while she was having breakfast. As soon as she heard his voice, she burst into tears. He said he wanted to talk to her, in person. Sarah dressed and waited anxiously for him to arrive.

A small white car approached the house slowly. Sarah strained her eyes searching for Zach inside the vehicle, but she couldn't make out who was in it. Her stomach dropped as the car eased into the driveway. Sarah focused her eyes on the girl in the passenger seat wondering if that was Zach's girlfriend.

Zach got out of the car and Sarah drew in a sharp breath. He kept his head down as if he was trying to pretend he didn't see Sarah standing on the porch. She resisted the urge to call out to him. He walked around to the passenger side and waited for the girl to get out. He reached for the girl's hand and they walked up the driveway together.

Sarah could sense his nervousness as he walked toward her. *He looks older*, she thought. When she'd left, his hair had been a huge source of contention because it hung in his face in the most annoying way. Sarah was constantly nagging him to move it away from his eyes but even if he did, he still had to hold his head cocked to the side just right to see. Now, his hair was buzzed short. It made him look more mature.

Maddie smiled at Sarah first. The girl was tiny, probably just five feet. Her long brown hair had streaks of blonde highlights that framed her face. Her eyes, although heavily made up, were striking. They were the color of sea glass.

"Hi Zach," Sarah said, but Zach's eyes remained focused on the ground.

The girl nudged him.

"Mom," Zach said sheepishly.

Sarah introduced herself to Maddie, who smiled at her. Sarah sensed she had something to do with Zach agreeing to meet.

"Do you want to go inside to talk? Or we could go for a walk."

Zach looked up at the porch where Cam and David were quietly observing.

"Who's that?"

"That's my friend David."

"Friend?"

"Yes, he's a friend. A very good friend. My best friend actually. He's here to support me."

"Support you?" Zach scoffed.

"He came with me to support me, like I'm assuming Maddie is doing for you."

Maddie smiled and Sarah relaxed a little bit.

"Fine. We can go inside if you want."

Meg and her husband were at work and their kids were at school. They had the house to themselves. They all walked in silence as they went inside and sat in the large family room. Sarah offered everyone a drink, but no one wanted one. Sarah sat down next to David on a small couch. Her boys sat on the long sofa with Maddie huddled up next to Zach. The anguish on the boys' faces made her heart ache.

"Any more news on Dad?"

"He's stable, I guess. We were there yesterday and the

doctor's think he'll make it, but he looks like shit. Half his face is burned off," Zach said shuddering at the thought of it.

"How are you holding up?" Sarah asked.

Zach smirked and shook his head. "Fucking great, Mom." Maddie scolded him for swearing. Zach rolled his eyes at her. After a long pause, he spoke again.

"Mom, I can't sit here and pretend everything is fine. You haven't been here in months and now you're asking how I'm doing, how Dad is doing. It all seems a little…fake."

There it was. Sarah sighed. She knew this wasn't going to be easy.

"I'd like to try and explain everything," Sarah said.

"I know you left because of Jen and Dad. You don't have to explain."

"Oh, Zach," Sarah said, as she looked at both her boys. They looked so hurt and angry. She didn't blame them for that; it was deserved. She fought back tears. "I left because I was dead inside. I knew Dad was having an affair, but never in a million years would I have thought it was with Jen."

"So, why didn't you call him out on it? Why'd you let him get away with it?" Cam asked.

Sarah breathed in. "I did confront him about it, but he denied it. And as for letting him get away with it…I never looked at it that way. He knew I knew about his affairs. I guess the difference this time was that I saw it. I literally came face to face with it and I couldn't handle it. So, I left."

Both boys looked at their feet and Sarah wondered if they were really listening. She continued.

"Having the two of you was the single greatest thing I've ever done. Being your mom gave me purpose. It gave my life meaning. You both taught me so much about myself, and love, and I don't want you to think for a second that I left because I don't love you. It's just that I've lived my entire life taking care of other people. I never really got to find out who I was. I let Grandpa and your father dictate my life. I let them tell me what I could do, and wanted to do and not do.

"I got in the car that night thinking I'd go somewhere for

a night or two. I drove all night thinking about everything and before I knew it, I was in Ohio. Then I remembered about this photography conference that Jim had told me about at Christmas and I figured I'd go. I just kept driving until I ended up in Las Vegas, which took me a few days but I saw the Grand Canyon. Which was amazing.

"While I was in Vegas, it was as if I came alive. Like I'd been living life in black and white, and suddenly I saw color. I realized not only how much I love photography, but also how good I am at it. I remembered my dream of being a magazine photographer and traveling the world, and I knew that going home would make all of those feelings go away. I also knew that if I came home I'd never be able to get away again...so, I kept driving..."

"Where'd you go?" Cam asked.

Sarah smiled as she thought about it. "California. Laguna Beach."

"Why there?" Zach asked.

"It's just somewhere I always wanted to go," Sarah said.

"What did you do there? Why'd you stay so long?" Zach asked.

She knew she needed to answer his question carefully. She told the boys about meeting David and the café. She told them about Leslie and the art festival. She told them about the beauty of California and meeting Jack Johnson. She left out the part about Will.

"If Dad didn't get in the accident, would you have ever come back here?" Zach asked.

Sarah blinked and looked down at her feet. "Yes. I had my flight booked for next week actually. It's just...I feel like that's where I belong. If that makes sense. I hope to get back there someday..."

The boys nodded.

"I've talked a lot to Maddie and her Mom about everything, and they've really made me see your side," Zach said. "I never really did that before—thought about your side. I only ever heard Dad bitch and moan about how he didn't get to do the things he wanted in life because you got pregnant with us. He made it seem like it was all your fault that his life was so fucked up. I just never realized that maybe you were missing out on things too."

Sarah's eyes filled with tears. David put his arm around her supportively.

"Well, I'm sure you both know that in order to get pregnant it takes someone else. He was in it with me from the beginning. We both had chances to walk away. I still don't know why we didn't just end it once we knew we weren't meant for each other. But, life is complicated. My father made life even more complicated."

"Tell me about it," Cam sneered. "Grandpa's a total prick."

"Cam," Sarah instinctively scolded, even though she knew he was only being honest.

"Well, he is. The things he said about you after you left…," Cam said, shaking his head.

"Try growing up with it," she said, rolling her eyes.

Everyone laughed.

"Mom," Zach said.

"What?" she said, smiling.

"We have something to tell you," he said.

"Not now," Cam said.

The boys exchanged looks and whispered back and forth. Maddie leaned in and said something to them and then the three looked at Sarah. She straightened her back and took in a breath as she braced herself for what was coming.

"He took her on our hunting trips last fall," Zach said.

Sarah's eyes opened as wide as they could go. It was as if she'd punched in the stomach.

"What do you mean?" Sarah asked.

"They told us not to say anything. Dad said Jen liked to hunt but that you'd be mad so he told us not to say anything. He said it wasn't a big deal," Zach said.

Sarah stood up and paced the room. She looked at David and spoke to him as if no one else was there.

"How the fuck did she pull *that* off? How did I not connect the dots that on the weekends he was gone that Jen was too? How did I *not know?*" Sarah said hysterically.

David shook his head in answer to her questions. Sarah turned to the boys.

"I tried so hard to protect you from all of this bullshit. I lived with Grandpa all those years putting me down, telling me I had to mind my *place*, which was to cook and clean and make his life easier. I spent years being married to your father trying to be everything that I was *supposed* to be, and hating every damn minute of it. And you know what? I let it all happen. I sat back and let it happen because I was too afraid. I mean, who was I if I wasn't taking care of everyone? Who was I if I wasn't Joe's wife? Who was I?"

"Sarah...," David said, attempting to calm her down. He pleaded with his eyes for her to stop.

Sarah looked at the boys who stared at the floor. She went to the window. A flock of birds fluttered away as she reached the window, squawking furiously as if they could sense her anger. She thought about the stories Jen used to tell her about the men she'd meet at the bar and their sexual encounters. Sarah wondered now if Jen had been telling her about her own husband the whole time. Part of her wanted to know everything like when the affair started and what they did, but another part of her didn't. What did it matter? Especially now that Sarah's life was better than she could have ever imagined.

After several minutes, she went and sat down next to David. She couldn't look at the boys.

Zach finally broke the silence and told Sarah about being arrested for throwing a beer bottle at a cop car, how Joe refused to bail him out, and how Maddie parents did. They offered to take him in for a few days, and eventually they said he could stay as long as he needed. Sarah thanked Maddie for taking Zach in.

"He was a real mess, but he's changed a lot since."

Zach explained the reason he spent so much time away from home was because he couldn't take the tension, and he didn't know how to talk about it. Sarah had always thought that Joe and Zach were close, but she couldn't have been more wrong. Zach told her about how on the hunting trips Joe would drink until he passed out and, when he was awake all he did was complain about Sarah and how his life didn't end up the way he wanted.

"That's why I stopped going on those trips," Cam said. "I couldn't to listen to Dad bad mouth you."

Sarah regretted that she'd given up on mothering them when the going got tough. She should have been more in tune.

"Why didn't you come to me?" Sarah sobbed.

"We were afraid of Dad," Zach said.

Sarah didn't blame them.

"I should never have let your father make me feel so insignificant," Sarah said.

"That's what Maddie's mom made me realize," Zach said. "She's a psychologist. She really made me see everything different. She said that maybe you left because you needed some time away to figure everything out. And, she made me realize how wrong it was for Dad bring Jen on trips with us."

Sarah went over and hugged her boys. "I thought about you every day," she said. "I wish I knew you were having such a hard time."

They were all crying and wiping their noses, even David. Sarah got some tissues, and then sat back down next to the boys.

"Your Dad is going to be in the hospital for a while, so I I'm back indefinitely. We have time to talk this all out."

"Maybe we can come to California with you," Cam said.

"That's a great idea!" David said, looking alive for the first time.

Sarah turned to him wide-eyed, questioning what the heck he was doing.

"Well," David said. "What are you going to do here? Take care of Joe? The guy who abused you? Who cheated on you? A guy who you gave everything to and who never once appreciated you? Can't one of your brothers take your father? Then Jen takes care of Joe, and that leaves the boys to come to Laguna and hang out with you for the summer, or longer."

Cam and Zach nodded in agreement. Sarah's eyes went from David to Maddie, who nodded too.

"My head is spinning. I can't even think about that right now. They need to finish school first," she said.

"So, we can come to California after that?" Cam asked.

"We'll see," she said. She thought about Will and telling the boys about him. Would they be able to understand that she'd found love?

The boys agreed they'd finish out the school year and they they'd talk about it. That gave her time to figure out what to do with her father, and time to figure out what to say about Will.

When the boys pulled out of the driveway and were out of sight, Sarah hit David's shoulder.

"What were you thinking back there? Now I have to tell them about *Will.*"

David apologized. He hadn't thought of that.

"How am I going to have them live with me in that one-bedroom house? They are so mad at their father about Jen, what will they say when they find out their mother has a *boyfriend?*" Sarah screeched.

"It will all work out. Don't worry," said David.

"How can you be sure?"

"Because, it always does," David said.

David walked into the house leaving Sarah in the driveway. She thought about all of the information she had now. She missed Will and wished she could talk to him about everything. Inside, David was sitting in the kitchen with his laptop open and a cup of coffee in his hands. He smiled at her.

"I'm not mad at you," she said.

"Please. I know that," David said.

She sat down next to him.

"Coffee?" David offered.

He fixed her a cup and set it down in front of her just as her cell phone rang.

"Mom," Zach's voice quivered.

"What's the matter?"

"Dad wants to see you."

Sarah grabbed David's arm and held it tight. David's face contorted from the pain.

"I thought he was in a coma?"

"He was, but I guess it changed this morning. Aunt Monica called me."

Why would Joe be asking for her, after all these weeks of her being gone? What did he want?

"I guess I'll go to Boston then," Sarah said, feeling nervous.

She knew she'd have to face Joe someday, but now that day was here. It was no use dredging up the past just yet. He needed to get better first.

32

Sarah and Meg went to the hospital while David stayed back with Meg's husband Mike. They drove the hour to Boston contemplating why Joe could possibly want to see her. Maybe he wanted to apologize they speculated but Sarah couldn't imagine it. Joe never apologized.

"Well, maybe he had a come to Jesus moment while he was in the coma and realized that he loves you and wants you back," Meg said.

Sarah burst out laughing. "No way...," she said. Thinking about it for a while then dismissing it. Even if he wanted her back, she was in love with Will now.

Sarah entered the hospital and a wave of panic overcame her.

"Meg, I don't know if I can do this," she said.

Meg put her arm on her shoulder. "You have to."

Sarah began to shake uncontrollably. Meg led Sarah over to a group of chairs where they sat down. "Take a moment. Relax. It's going to be OK," Meg said.

Sarah took some deep steading breaths, trying to calm down, but her hands shook despite her efforts to stop them. She wiped her eyes.

"I'll be fine," Sarah lied.

Meg nodded and stood up. She led them to the information desk and asked for Joe's room number.

"Only immediate family is allowed in the ICU. Are you immediate family?" asked the elderly volunteer behind the desk.

"I'm his wife," Sarah replied, her voice shaking.

The volunteer told her how to get to the ICU and then called up to the floor to let the nurses know Sarah was coming. Meg told her she would go get a cup of coffee and wait for her in the cafeteria.

Sarah rode the elevator up to the fifth floor alone. When the door opened, her feet moved before her mind could tell them not to. She stepped out of the elevator. The nurse's desk was in front of her.

"You here to see Joe?" a nurse asked, peering over the counter.

Sarah nodded. She walked quickly to keep up with the nurse, who seemed to have turbo charged sneakers, as she led Sarah to Joe's room. Sarah froze outside his room, not ready to enter just yet. She listened to see if she could hear any other voices in the room. Joe's parents maybe, or his sisters, or worse, Jen. All she heard were machines beeping methodically.

"It's OK, you can come in. He's stable right now," the nurse said. "If he doesn't wake up right away, don't worry. We have him on some medication for the pain. It will be a shock for you when you first see him. He's burned very badly."

Sarah nodded. Her stomach turned; she felt nauseous.

"Can he talk?" Sarah asked.

"He can get some words out. He asked for you as soon as he woke up so that's good," the nurse said, smiling.

Sarah's heart raced as she walked into the room. The curtains were drawn and the room was dark except a small light above his bed that illuminated the machines that beeped loudly. She walked slowly towards the bed and then suddenly stopped. She gasped and put her hand over her mouth.

Joe was covered in gauze that was soaked with blood. The skin that wasn't covered in gauze was charred black and red and oozed. His chest rose and fell slowly.

Sarah resisted the urge to run out of the room with the overwhelming urge to throw up. She swallowed hard, taking in deep breaths to steady herself. After a few minutes, she called out his name. He didn't move or make a sound. The clocked ticked above her head and with each tick Sarah grew more and more uncomfortable. After five minutes, she took another step closer to Joe's bed and called out his name again.

He opened his eyes and focused on her. Then his lids fell slowly, closing again. Sarah began to sweat.

"Joe, it's me. Sarah."

Nothing. She waited a few more minutes then she put her coat and purse down on the chair next to her. What was she supposed to do now? How long was she supposed to wait?

Fifteen minutes passed before the nurse entered the room again. Sarah was relieved to see her.

"Anything yet?" the nurse asked, as she went over to the machines and began her work.

Sarah told her that he had opened his eyes briefly.

"That might be all you get today. If he saw you, he knows you're here. You can talk to him."

And say what? Sarah thought.

"The others should be back soon. They went to get something to eat."

Sarah's heart slammed against her chest. *Shit!* "The others?"

"Oh, that's right you were out of town, right? His parents and his sister have been here all day."

Sarah wondered who had told the nurse she was out of town. Did this nurse also know that she'd run away?

Sarah gathered her things. She needed to get out before Joe's parents came back. She definitely did not want to face them right now. The nurse made a noise. Sarah wasn't sure if it was a silent sneeze or if she was saying something to her.

Then, Sarah's eyes locked with Joe's. He stared at her expressionless.

"I think he's waking up," Sarah said nervously to the nurse. Her eyes never leaving Joe's.

The nurse turned around and began talking to Joe as if he was a longtime friend, as if there was nothing wrong with him. She asked him how he was doing. He grunted. She seemed pleased with that response. She asked him if he felt any pain. He grunted. She adjusted something on the machine beside his bed.

Sarah looked around the room nervously, avoiding Joe's eyes that were fixated on her.

"I'll leave you two alone," the nurse said. "Go ahead, Sarah. He can hear you. He won't bite."

If she only knew.

Sarah eased herself down onto the chair by the bed. She held her coat and purse on her lap. She smiled awkwardly at him as he continued to stare at her.

"Joe, I'm sorry this happened to you."

Joe grunted.

"They said you wanted to see me. Is there something you need to tell me?"

His eyes looked up at the ceiling. Then after a long pause, he whispered. Sarah leaned in.

"Divorce," he said, barely getting the word out.

She stared at him unsure if she'd heard him right.

"Wait, what?" she asked.

He closed his eyes and breathed deeply.

Is he going back to sleep?

"Joe?"

After a minute, his eyes opened again and turned to her.

"Divorce," he said.

"Are you serious? You asked me here, after you woke up from a coma, to tell me you want a divorce?" she asked, incredulously.

His eyes went to the ceiling again. She could tell that speaking was taking everything he had inside of him. She waited.

"You…get…nothing," he said, saying each word slowly.

He was practically dying in front of her and all he cared about was asking her for a divorce, and making sure she didn't get anything. Sarah stood up. "I'm gonna go."

"If…I…die…," he said as he grimaced in pain. "You…get…nothing," he said through gritted teeth.

She thought of their life together. How she'd believed all those years that she didn't deserve to be happy. How he'd convinced her that she would never survive on her own. How she'd stayed with him for all the wrong reasons. How he'd refused to ever consider getting a divorce.

"Really? You want to make sure that I don't get any of your money?"

Joe blinked at her.

She shook her head. What exactly was it that he was trying to make sure she didn't get? He didn't have any money.

"I'm leaving," she said.

Sarah turned before he could speak again and hurried to the elevator, pushing the down button. She thought about Joe's parents and the possibility of seeing them in the elevator. She decided to take the stairs. As she ran down the steps, her mind vacillated between anger and sadness. She was sad that Joe was hurt as badly as he was. No matter how she felt about him, he was the father of her kids. They had history. Even *he* didn't deserve to be in such bad shape. She was angry because he had betrayed her so many times and she always looked the other way—for the sake of the kids. And now he was demanding a divorce—as if he came out of the coma just to say that to her. The lump in her throat had a grip on her neck but the tears stayed inside the confines of her lids. She was too angry to cry.

She arrived at the lobby and stopped dead in her tracks. Through the crowd of people walking towards the elevators, Sarah spotted Joe's parents, and Jen. Not his sister like the nurse had said—Jen. They must have told them that she was his sister so she could go up to the ICU. Sarah put her head down to avoid eye contact, praying they wouldn't see her as she walked quickly towards the cafeteria and found Meg.

"Let's go," Sarah demanded.

"What happened?"

"Not here," Sarah said, walking fast in hopes that the Rossi's hadn't seen her. She could hear Meg hurrying behind her to keep up. Sarah waited until they were in the car before she told Meg what happened.

"I don't know what I expected! Maybe 'I'm sorry for cheating on you' or 'sorry that things got so bad in the end.' I really didn't know why he called me there, but that was just ridiculous. I would have thought he'd be a little remorseful for cheating on me."

"Isn't this what you want?" Meg asked. "You said you were going to serve him divorce papers anyway."

"Not now! Not when he's lying in a hospital burned all over like that."

"I guess I don't see the difference," Meg said, keeping her eyes on the road.

Sarah seethed as she watched the trees whiz by at seventy miles an hour.

"The difference is that when I wanted a divorce all those years he told me he was *Catholic* and *didn't get divorced.…*"

"I still don't know why you're so mad. You *want* a divorce," said Meg.

Sarah sighed. "Yeah. But I wanted to be the one to do it. I wanted him to be served the papers," she said.

"Ah, so you're pissed because he did it first?" asked Meg.

"No. I mean, yes. I mean, I don't know…" Sarah said trailing off. When Meg put it like that, it sounded silly.

It wasn't that Joe wanted the divorce. It was the way he said she'd get *nothing*. As if he'd been sitting there in the hospital thinking that Sarah would try to take everything away from him, when really, he had taken everything from her. He made a promise to her when they married to take care of her and the twins. They made a commitment to each other to make it work even though neither of them was ever really happy. Her entire life had been spent doing the right thing despite her needs and wants.

She took out her phone and texted David about what'd happened. She told him to pack up because they would be staying at the house with the boys. It was time to make a plan.

When they pulled into Meg's driveway, David was waiting on the steps with their luggage. Sarah said goodbye to Meg, thanking her for taking her to Boston.

"Call me if you need anything," Meg said.

Sarah hugged her while David put their luggage in the car.

"Do you want to talk about it?" David asked on the way to Sarah's house.

"No. Not really," Sarah said, turning up the radio.

Now, after being on her own for a while, she finally knew who she was—a strong, capable woman. She had felt alive and happy for the first time in her life, thanks in part to Will and everyone out in Laguna who believed in her and encouraged her. It was time to take charge of her life.

They arrived at her house. She turned to David.

"You should go back to California. I think I'm going to be here for a while, at least until the boys finish school."

"What happened in Boston?" David asked.

Sarah sighed and then told him.

"Meg seems to think I'm being ridiculous for being upset that he called me there to tell me he wants a divorce and he wants to make sure that I get *nothing*," Sarah said.

"Well...it is strange but honestly, why do you care? It's what you want anyway."

Sarah shook her head. "But, I mean come on. He literally came out of a coma hours before. Don't you think he could have waited?"

"Sure. But, once a douche always a douche," David said, smiling.

Sarah laughed and sighed heavily. "I guess you're right."

David put a hand on her shoulder. "I agree that his timing was off but if he wants a divorce just give it to him."

Sarah nodded. "Ugh! But that means he gets the last word!

Just like *always*."

"Well…," David said.

They sat in silence for a minute before she got out of the car and retrieved her suitcase from the trunk. David followed her into the house.

"Are you sure that you want to do this?" David said, at the front door.

"I have no choice."

Linda greeted her at the door. Sarah hugged her. "I'm going to stay here now," Sarah said.

Linda nodded. "How are you doing?"

Sarah thought about how to answer. "Well, I just saw Joe."

"And how is he doing? I heard he stabilized once they got him to Boston."

"Well, he asked for me because he wanted to tell me he wants a divorce, so I'd say he's doing all right," Sarah said sarcastically.

Linda shook her head. Then Sarah introduced David.

"You can go home, Linda. I'm going to clean the house today. I'll take care of my father," Sarah said.

"He's not going to like that but I'll leave you to it. Call me if you need me. I'll come back tomorrow morning," Linda said.

The TV was blaring and the house smelled musty. Sarah went around the house opening windows while her father continued watching television, not acknowledging her at all. David sat at the kitchen table texting while she got out cleaning supplies and began cleaning. In the kitchen, she put dishes in the dishwasher, cleaned the counter, and then scrubbed the sink. She pulled items out of the refrigerator and tossed mostly everything into the garbage. David helped hold the trash bag. They worked in silence as they cleaned the inside of the fridge together. He cleaned all of the shelves in the sink, while Sarah scrubbed the inside of caked on spills. As they were putting everything back in, they laughed at how empty the refrigerator was now.

"Thank you for helping me," Sarah said.

"Girl, I'm here to help. That's why I came."

"I know, but I feel like I need to do this all on my own. I created this mess and I need to clean it up on my own."

David hugged her. Sarah broke down into tears sobbing on his shoulder. He kept whispering that it was going to be all right. Something inside of her believed him. After a few minutes, Sarah pulled away.

"I can't thank you enough."

"Well, you may change your mind once the cavalry arrives."

"Cavalry?" Sarah asked, but as soon as she did, she understood what he meant. "Oh, please tell me you didn't."

"Leslie and Jillian are on their way. Michael sends his love. He told me to stay as long as it takes. He's got everything covered at the café for now."

"Please tell me Will isn't coming," Sarah said, as she fell into the chair behind her.

"Just the girls."

Sarah stared out the window, feeling a flood of emotions wash over her. The thought of having people here supporting her filled her up. She was relieved that Will wasn't coming. She wasn't ready for that yet.

"Thank you," she said, crying.

David hugged her. "Let's get back to work. I can't take that smell anymore. What is it anyway?"

Sarah laughed. "Boys."

David went to the bathroom and began cleaning while Sarah vacuumed. She went into the living room where her father sat under an afghan that was given to him and her mother for their wedding. Sarah cleaned up the tissues that were strewn on the floor, and then gathered all of the half-empty cups of water and tea on the table in front of him. She could feel him watching her.

"Dad, do you need anything?"

"Not from you."

"Well then from who?"

"I've managed just fine without you all these months. Go back where you came from. You're no longer my daughter."

"The funny thing is you can't change the fact that I'm your daughter. And I'm here for a while. Joe's probably not ever coming back, so you're stuck with me now. I'll go get you some tea."

She returned with the tea and set it down in front of her father. She adjusted the afghan on his lap and tucked a pillow behind his back.

"Anything else?" she asked.

Her father didn't respond. Sarah went back to vacuuming and when she was finished, she got out the mop and began cleaning the floors. David came down from upstairs.

"You really don't want to go up there," he said with his face contorted in a way that meant it was a disgusting mess up.

"Well, I've gotta tackle it at some point. If you want to mop, I'll go up and change the sheets. I bet that hasn't been done since I left."

"That bathroom was completely disgusting. I've never seen anything like it."

Sarah laughed. "Why didn't you just come get me? I would've done it."

David waved her off and took the mop from her hand. As Sarah climbed the stairs, the smell hit her midway. She immediately opened all of the windows and began stripping sheets off beds. She piled laundry into baskets and fought back the urge to vomit from the stench of dirty laundry. When she came downstairs, David was sitting next to her father on the couch. They were watching *Dr. Oz*.

"Everything all right here?" she asked them.

David gave her the thumbs up. Her father stared at the television. She left them to go down to the basement, where the washing machine was. She sorted the laundry and began the first of many large loads. She spent the rest of the afternoon organizing and cleaning. By dinnertime, Sarah was so exhausted she couldn't get up from the chair she had plopped herself on. They ordered pizza and had it delivered just before Zach and Cam arrived home.

"Smells clean in here," Cam said, smiling.

Zach nodded in agreement. Sarah told them how she and David had scoured the house from top to bottom all day.

"David and I will be staying here tonight. Well, for a while actually."

Just then the doorbell rang. David went to the door to pay for the pizzas. Sarah was grateful she didn't have to get up; her muscles ached. He brought the pizzas in and the boys jumped up to help him. Her father perked up at the smell of cheese and pepperoni that filled the room. Cam went to the fridge to get drinks and commented how clean it was in there.

"I saw Dad today," said Sarah.

Zach and Cam widened their eyes.

"And?" Cam asked.

"And he's angry," Sarah said. She didn't want to get into what Joe had asked for just yet. The boys were dealing with enough.

"Wait until you see your rooms," Sarah said, changing the subject.

"Thank god. My sheets stank like wet dog," Cam said, stuffing pepperoni pizza into his mouth.

Sarah bit into her pizza and closed her eyes savoring the bite. It'd been so long since she had good pizza. David commented on how greasy it was as he blotted his piece with several paper towels.

"The grease is what makes it so good!" Sarah laughed.

The boys agreed, and even her father chimed in to say that David was taking off the best part of the pizza. David looked as if they had just told him to eat dog poop. Everyone laughed.

Zach's cell phone rang, and everyone went silent while he answered it. The smile on his face slowly faded and he lowered his head so no one could see him.

Zach ended the call and threw the phone across the room. Cam choked back tears, while her father kept asking what was going on. Sarah knew instantly—Joe was gone. Zach stormed out of the room and out the front door, slamming it shut as he went. Cam shook as Sarah held him. Her father asked what was going on.

"Joe's gone, Dad. Joe's gone...," Sarah said.

Her father burst into tears. It was the second time Sarah had ever seen him cry. Her body was numb, but the tears weren't there.

33

Sarah didn't sleep all night thinking about everything she needed to do over the next few days: settling debts, dealing with insurance companies, meeting with the lawyer. Then, there would be the funeral and seeing old friends, facing Joe's parents, facing Jen. She cried after the boys had gone to bed. It broke her heart that her kids had to go through losing their dad just as she'd lost her mom at a young age. The doorbell rang while Sarah was making a cup of coffee. *Probably another neighbor with food*, she thought. She got to the door and looked out the window. Leslie and Jillian were standing on her doorstep.

"We're here to help!" Leslie said cheerily.

"You flew all night?" Sarah asked, her voice breaking.

"We did," Jillian said.

Sarah broke down. Having both of them here meant more than she could express.

"Now, now," Leslie said, pulling Sarah into a hug.

"This means the world to me," Sarah sputtered through her tears.

Sarah led them in and introduced them to her father, who was up and sitting in his chair watching the morning news.

Sarah woke David and they took Leslie and Jillian out to breakfast to fill them in on everything.

They arrived home to two cars in the driveway. One was Linda's and the other Sarah immediately recognized her father-in-law's black Mercedes.

"Whose car is that?" David asked.

"Joe's father," Sarah said.

Leslie put a hand on her shoulder. "It's OK. Deep breaths. Go in there strong, OK?"

Sarah nodded.

Mario was in the living room talking to her father. He stood up when he saw Sarah. Her adrenaline pulsed through her body.

"Hello, Sarah," Mario said, calmly.

Sarah braced herself. "Mario, nice to see you."

Mario reached out to hug her. He told her how sorry he was that his son had treated her so badly over the years and that she deserved much better. "I didn't understand why you left earlier this year and I was not happy about it. Then I found out about Joe and Jen. Trust me, I let him know how I felt about that. I thought I raised him better than to cheat on his wife. Judy is having a hard time with everything that's why she's not here," Mario said.

"It's all right, I understand," Sarah said. Although she couldn't help but wonder how they didn't know about Jen. She thought everyone knew. She also wondered why Jen was at the hospital. But…none one of that mattered now.

"I just can't believe he's gone. I feel so bad for the boys," Sarah said.

"I know," Mario replied as he held her hand and broke down in tears.

Sarah spent the rest of the day making phone calls. The boys sat with her at the kitchen table all day. They'd been quiet since they got the news about Joe and kept close.

Sarah called her brothers to tell them the news. Frank said, "That sucks." He didn't offer to fly home or ask her if she needed anything. He didn't ask about their father either. She called Billy next. They hadn't spoken in almost a year and even then their conversations were light, only ever scratching the surface. She told him what had happened to Joe.

"I'm so sorry," Billy said. "I know you guys had your problems, but this really sucks."

"Yeah. It's the boys I feel bad for," Sarah said.

Billy agreed. "I was about their age when Ma died," he said.

Sarah let out a breath as a flood of memories washed over her. How Frank took off for Colorado after their mother died and never returned. How Billy enlisted in the Army without telling anyone. How she had to take care of her father—because he couldn't do anything for himself—all while taking care of infants. She thought about how she raised the twins without being able to call her mom with questions or to get reassurance. How much she missed Billy when he left.

She told Billy how she hadn't been home for the past three months. She told him about her life in California, about her job, her friends, her new photography business, and then she told him about Will.

"I've never felt this way about anyone in my life, Billy. He makes me feel so loved."

"You deserve it," Billy said.

Sarah sobbed. "I can't stay here, Billy."

Billy knew right away what she was getting at. "I can take Dad in. I mean, I have to talk it over with Kerry, but we'll figure something out. After Courtney and Maggie were born, I began to realize how much pressure you must have been under as a kid—having to take care of Frank and me all the time. Courtney is almost nine, the same age you were when mom got really sick. I can't imagine putting that kind of responsibility on her," Billy said.

She wiped the tears from her eyes. He'd never said any of that to her before. He finally understood what a burden it was for Sarah all those years.

"Kerry said something to me recently that really got me thinking. She asked why I was able to move away from Dad

—and you—and never feel obligate to return. When I enlisted, I just wanted to get as far away from him as possible. I just couldn't be around him. He always made me feel like shit. Like Ma's depression was *my* fault."

Sarah sighed. No matter how many times she told him that wasn't true, Billy's couldn't shake that story he played in his head.

"Billy...you know you weren't the cause. I told you that depression ran in Ma's family."

"No, I know. I've worked it out with a therapist and talked a lot to Kerry about it. I know that I wasn't the cause, but it's still how he made me feel—the way he looked at me with disgust, or the way he talked to me like I was stupid."

"That's just Dad. He does that with everyone," Sarah scoffed.

"Yeah...I know. I just never thought about you and that you might need help. We didn't talk about things like that. Besides, you always seemed to have everything under control. I'm trying to say I'm sorry, Sarah. Sorry that you had to deal with him all alone all these years."

"It's okay," she said, and she meant it. There was no use going over things in the past now and wishing things had been done differently.

"I'll book a flight today and come home for the funeral. We can talk to Dad together, and I can help you with anything you need done up there," Billy said.

"Thank you. Thank you *so much*," Sarah cried.

"It's time someone took care of you," Billy said.

***

David went to the grocery store with Jillian. He cooked all afternoon and the house smelled like heaven. He made a big batch of homemade tomato sauce with meatballs and sausage, fresh bread, cookies, lasagna, salad, and so much more. Zach and Cam ate everything he put in front of them.

The day seemed endless as Sarah took phone call after phone call from friends and family who were shocked to hear the news about Joe. In a small town, news travels fast. Sarah kept each conversation short by explaining the details of the funeral, and then told whoever it was on the other end that she was waiting for a call and needed to get off the phone, which was a lie.

Leslie hit it off with Sarah's father, and she actually had him up and about a little bit. He still wouldn't look at Sarah, and only answered her in short sentences. That was fine with Sarah though. She no longer needed his approval. If he wanted to treat her that way, it was his problem, not hers.

Zach and Cam went with Sarah to the funeral home while everyone else stayed at the house. They met Joe's parents there. She was nervous about seeing Judy but as soon as they got out of the car, Judy began to cry and came to hug Sarah.

"I'm so sorry my Joseph was not a good man," Judy said.

"No need to be sorry now," Sarah said. Had his mother really thought that Joe was a good man? Did she not believe Sarah all those years?

They decided to keep the calling hours short, just two hours. Zach couldn't stand the thought of standing in the line for longer than that, which was fine with Sarah. She wasn't looking forward to it either.

When they got back to the house there were cars lining the street. Sarah recognized most of them. Inside the house, it was noisy. Sarah took in the scene. All of her friends from Laguna seemed like they belonged. David was serving food. Jillian was consoling Joe's aunt. Leslie was talking with Linda.

Sarah saw Meg and went to her. She hadn't talked to her since that day in the car when they'd gone to see Joe.

"I'm sorry I got so mad that day," Sarah said.

"Don't be," Meg said, hugging Sarah. "None of that matters now."

34

They arrived at the funeral home early. The boys were solemn as they walked toward the casket, closed due to Joe's injuries. Sarah hooked her arms with the boys and told them it would be all right. Zach was the first to breakdown. Cam reached out and hugged his brother. Sarah tried to be strong for the boys but inside she was a mess. Sarah held them tight.

When people began to arrive, Sarah guided the boys over to where the funeral director told them to stand. Joe's parents and sisters stood with them. His sisters had been pleasant, but Sarah felt as if they were keeping their distance.

During a lull in visitors, David came up behind her and handed her a bottle of water.

"How's it goin'?" he asked.

"It sucks," she said as she sat down. "I'm exhausted. The boys are doing good, I think. All of their friends just came through and they were happy to see them."

"I saw them in line. Rowdy bunch."

Sarah laughed. "Yes. Yes they are."

David rubbed her back caringly.

"I could never have done this without you. How am I ever going to repay you?" Sarah asked.

"Repay me? Are you crazy? This is what friends do," David said.

Sarah smiled, and then her body tightened as she saw Jen coming in the door. Sarah widened her eyes. David immediately looked to see what, or who, she was looking at.

"Is that Jen?" David whispered.

Sarah nodded.

Jen's mother and father had come with her. They held onto Jen as if she might fall down. Jen sobbed as she walked straight to the casket and knelt down and wailed. The entire room turned to see what was going on. Jen had on jeans, a black t-shirt, and a black leather jacket. Her black leather boots came up to her knees.

"She looks rough. You are way better looking," David whispered.

Sarah cackled. Her laugh turned heads, including Jen's. Sarah stood up as Jen approached. Her parents hung back looking somber.

"Hi," Jen said. She was shaking.

"Do you think you should be here?" Sarah said.

"I came because you guys are my friends."

"Friends don't sleep with their friend's husband!" Cam said.

The funeral home suddenly became quiet. Sarah grabbed Cam's arm. Billy stood by Sarah and put his arm around her giving her strength.

"You're the one that left!" Jen said.

"Because you were having sex with Joe in *my* truck!"

"Joe's truck," Jen corrected.

David suggested Jen should leave.

"Who the hell are you?"

David folded his arms across his chest and stared at her. Sarah thought about her life back in California—about her friends, her career, and Will. Suddenly, Jen didn't matter anymore.

"You know what Jen, I couldn't care less about you sleeping with Joe, because if you hadn't I would never have left this godforsaken town. I think I owe you a bit of thanks, actually."

Jen stared at her.

"But you don't belong here now. I don't care what you and Joe had. My kids don't need to see you here. Please leave," Sarah said, staring at Jen.

David patted her arm and if she didn't know any better, she thought heard him squeal.

The funeral director came over to ask if he could help. Sarah explained that she wanted Jen to leave. After a couple minutes of discussion, Jen agreed to go.

When Jen was gone, all of the anger Sarah had been carrying seemed to rise up into the air and disappear.

"Mom, are you OK?" Cam asked.

"I'm fine," she said. And for once, she wasn't lying.

"I can't believe she showed up here!" Zach said.

"Me either Zachary. Me either."

***

After ceremony at the cemetery, everyone went back to Sarah's house. David, Leslie, and Jillian skipped the cemetery and went straight to the house to set up. When Sarah arrived home with the boys they all were busy setting out trays of food.

Billy had been a tremendous help with their dad all day, pushing him in the wheelchair. He was attentive to Sarah too, making sure she was all right every now and then. They had stayed up late the night before talking about everything. His wife had stayed back with their kids, which gave her and Billy time to catch up and reconnect.

Sarah was exhausted from everything. She cried for the boys and the anguish that they were going through. She felt bad for Judy who couldn't seem to reconcile that her son wasn't perfect like she had believed. Joe's sister Monica had given the eulogy at the funeral. She talked about Joe's big personality and how he was always up for a good time. She reminisced about her little brother when they were growing up and how he always followed her and Cristina wherever they went. She talked about how much Joe loved the boys and that they were the one thing that Joe did right in his life. Monica didn't mention Sarah in the eulogy. It made Sarah sad that Monica couldn't seem to face the reality of who Joe · really was, but then again Monica was a lot like Judy. She saw only what she wanted to see.

The boys were handling everything as best they could. Zach had come to stay at the house with Sarah and Cam. Both boys were opening up more and more about things and the three of them were bonding in ways they never had before.

Sarah had sat down with Linda and explained what the plan was for her father. Sarah felt bad letting Linda go after so many years, but Linda was gracious.

"I'm happy for you, and your father. Billy should spend some time with your father to clear up those loose ends. It will be good for both of them," Linda had said.

Linda had made Sarah feel better about the decision to send her father to live with Billy. He and Kerry would be coming to get their father in a few weeks. They were busy creating a space for him and arranging nursing care.

They decided that the boys would finish out the school year and then Sarah would put the house on the market. Both boys planned to come out to California with Sarah for the summer. Cam said he might stay there with her. Zach planned to attend community college in the fall in New Hampshire. Sarah would introduce them to Will, when the time was right.

35

The next morning Sarah sat at the kitchen table thinking about the last few days, and how the boys had buried their father. She knew, from having lost her mother so young, that it got harder as the years passed by. Not having her mother to call for advice as she moved through adulthood was hard. Even though Joe wasn't perfect, she knew the boys would miss their father.

David, Jill and Leslie were going back to California. She was going to miss having them around. They'd been so helpful and gave her so much support. She couldn't have gotten through the last few days without them. Having them around, acting as a buffer between family and friends, was just what Sarah needed.

As she fixed another cup of coffee, her cell phone dinged. It was a text from Will. She looked at the clock. It was just after seven, which meant it was four a.m. in California.

Will: What are you doing?
Sarah: Having coffee. Why are you up so early?
Will: Look outside.

Sarah looked around her kitchen as if someone was playing a trick on her, and then she went to the window. She looked outside and saw Will leaning against a car. Her heart leapt and she ran outside.

"What are you doing here?" she asked as she ran towards him.

Will walked towards her with an enormous grin on his face. He scooped her up into a bear hug. Sarah buried her head into his neck and began to cry.

"I've been worried about you. I couldn't wait another minute to see you," Will said, kissing her.

"When did you get here? How?" Sarah asked.

"I came on Leslie's plane. Her pilot wanted to fly in last night so I hitched a ride. I'll fly back with them today. I just needed to see you. I stayed at the Inn last night."

"Why didn't you call me? I would have come to see you!" Sarah said.

"Leslie said you had a long couple of days and that you needed to get some rest last night."

Sarah had gone to bed very early the night before because she was mentally exhausted.

"Still, I would have come to see you. I've missed you so much," Sarah said, kissing him again. "Let's go get some coffee and talk," she said. Then she ran inside to change.

They went to the diner in town, and Sarah told Will about everything that had happened over the last few days. He listened intently as he held her hand across the table while she spoke. She finished by telling him she was going to put the house the market after the boys were done with school.

"Good, because I want you to move in with me," Will said.

She leaned back and stared at him. She wanted nothing more than to go back to California and start a life with this amazing, sexy man. Will was everything she ever wanted.

"I just don't know how long it will take me to get back there. The boys need to graduate, and I need to settle everything here—"

Will interrupted her. "Take as much time as you need. There is no rush to get back. Trust me, when you do get there we'll pick up right where we left off."

"But the boys…"

"The boys can live in the cottage," he said smiling.

"They don't know about us, and I'm not sure I'm ready to tell them either never mind have them live in your guest house."

"Well, we have time to figure all that out," he said. "Look, I know that you're just getting out there on your own and probably want some time alone, but I think you and I have something special. I don't want to make things more complicated for you. I just want to see where this thing goes. Who am I kidding? I want you in my life. For the rest of it. Just tell me you will come back to California and move in with me." Will smiled and squeezed her hands.

Sarah leaned across the table. She pulled him to her and kissed him hard on the lips. "Yes! I love you," she said as she held his face and looked into his eyes.

***

Later that day, as everyone from California was putting their luggage in Will's rental the car to head to the airport, Sarah stood with Will, hugging him.

"I don't want you to go," she said.

"We can call, text, Facetime…have phone sex," Will joked.

She held him tighter. "I gonna miss you so much," she said.

"I'll miss you too but, I'll come visit. We have a lifetime ahead of us, babe."

She cried into his chest. Then she heard a familiar whizzing sound of hummingbird wings. She picked her head up and didn't have to look too far. A hummingbird hovered between her and Will.

"What the…," Will said.

"Shhhh…," she said.

In a flash, the bird was gone. Sarah told Will about the hummingbird ornament that her aunt had given her all those years ago, and how the birds seemed to have guided her in her life.

"I think the bird came to let me know everything would be OK," Sarah said, thinking of her aunt.

"Smart bird," Will said, holding her close.

David cleared his throat. When Sarah looked up he and Jillian were standing nearby. Jillian hugged her tight and told Sarah how proud of her she was for her strength and dignity she'd shown over the past few days.

"Having you here for support meant the world to me," Sarah said.

"Anything for you, my friend," Jillian said.

David was next. Sarah hugged him.

"Take care of yourself. And call me. Often. Promise?" David asked.

She nodded. "I couldn't have done this without you," she said.

Leslie hugged her next. "Stay strong, my love."

"I will. Thank you for everything you've done for me. I am eternally grateful."

"No need to thank me. You just take care of yourself and get back to California soon. I've been waiting to tell you that all your pieces sold at the festival."

Sarah looked at Leslie in shock.

"You shouldn't be shocked! They were great. And, even more good news…Jim Curran wants to put your work in a couple of his galleries. You better hurry up and get back to California because you have a whole new career to attend to."

Jillian told her they could look for studio space to set up her business when she returned. Everyone congratulated her, but it all seemed like a dream that she couldn't wake up from.

"I feel like Dorothy in the Wizard of Oz," Sarah laughed. "I'm going to miss you all so much."

A few minutes later, they pulled away. Sarah wept as she waved goodbye.

***

Sarah was alone with her father for the first time since she had returned to New Hampshire.

She sat down on the couch close to him as he watched TV. She closed her eyes.

"You showed a lot of class these last few days," he said, startling her.

She opened her eyes and focused on her father. His eyes remained fixed on the TV.

"Thanks," Sarah said.

"I don't agree with what you did, but you had your reasons I suppose. I see how it's changed you."

She leaned forward.

"Thanks, Dad. That means a lot."

Her father reached out and patted her knee in a rare show of affection.

"I'm going back to California," Sarah said.

"I know."

"You do?"

"Leslie told me. I like her."

Sarah smiled. "She's a great woman," she said.

"Do what you have to do," said her father.

"I'm happy out there."

Her father nodded. Sarah wondered what else Leslie had said to her father.

"I'm sorry I left you," Sarah said.

He waved his hand. "Ah…"

They sat in silence while her father watched *Jeopardy*. Every now and then, he'd shout out an answer. Sarah couldn't help but wonder if he had changed too.

"You're a good woman, Sarah," her father said. "A good mother too."

Sarah reached out and held his hand.

"I love you, Dad."

"Yup," he said.

Sarah knew that was his way of saying he loved her too.

ABOUT THE AUTHOR

Kathy Sloan lives in Massachusetts with her husband, Tony, her daughters—Kassandra and Karissa—her son—Nathan—and a yellow lab named Duke. She works part-time at a local university and is a freelance writer. She loves to spend time with family and friends sitting by the fire drinking wine or at the beach relaxing. She enjoys yoga, meditating, and self-improvement through spiritual growth. Kathy reads as many books as time allows and loves to watch a good movie with her family. One day, she hopes to migrate to a warmer climate where she can read on the beach and watch the pelicans.

ACKNOWLEDGMENTS

If it weren't for Dave Harris sending me a message about National Novel Writing Month (NaNoWriMo) in 2011 this book wouldn't exist. I'd never heard of it before and decided to try it. Participating in NaNoWriMo helped kick-start not just this book, but reinvigorated my creative flow. *In Laguna* was a paragraph in a notebook before 2011 and probably would have stayed there forever. NaNoWriMo helped me to take that paragraph and turn it into a novel. So thank you, Dave! And, a big shout out to NaNoWriMo whose mission is to help inspire amateur writers.

I'd also like to thank my husband, Tony, for supporting me always and for coming with me on this journey. Thank you for your devoted love, humor, and cheerleading skills. I love you! To Kassandra, Karissa, and Nathan: you've cheered me on along the way and have been my constant supporters. Thank you for your love and encouragement! Let this be a lesson that you can turn your dreams into reality if you persevere. I love you all so much—and yes, I do think about running away sometimes, but you're stuck with me for a long, long time.

To all of my family and friends who've supported me along the way, thank you from the bottom of my heart. Your encouragement has meant so much! To my mom who gave me my love for books and reading: I Love you, Mom!

To Patty Inwood, who read the first twenty-five pages very early on and gave me the courage to keep going—you gave me my wings. Thank you for always being such an amazing friend and supporter.

To Karen Costa, my fellow writer, and friend—having you in my corner along the way has meant so much. No one understands a writer like a writer and I'm grateful for your camaraderie. Knowing you're there to share my ups and downs with helps make the process a little easier. Thanks for always being a text away.

To all of my beta readers: Sue Sachs, Lauren Mateychuk, Karen Hersum, and Jen McGugan—thank you! Your feedback helped this novel grow. I'm immensely grateful that you took the time to read *In Laguna*. You all gave me such thoughtful comments and suggestions that helped to make this book what it is today. I could not have done this without you. This book is for all of you!

I'd also like to thank my developmental editor Suzanne Lahna. Your feedback was amazing and it helped this novel be what it is today. Also, to my editor/proofreader Ed Londergan, thank you for taking on my project and helping to bring *In Laguna* to the finish line. I am forever grateful! I'd also to give a shout out to the Worcester Writer's Collaborative. I've made connections and received support and advice from members along the way. I'm grateful for such a wonderful group.

I also want to thank you—my readers—for buying my book, sharing it with friends, and telling others to check it out. Your support means the world to me! Big kisses!

I took a trip to Laguna Beach back in 2004 and a piece of my heart is still there. That trip planted the seed for this story. I hope to back to Laguna sometime soon.

Happy reading!

Made in the USA
Charleston, SC
17 July 2016